I0714667

dungeon crawl

Three Player Tag-Team Book 5

allyson lindt

acelette press

This book is a work of fiction.

While reference might be made to actual historical events or existing locations, the names, characters, places, and incidents are either the product of the author's imagination or are used fictitiously, and any resemblance to actual persons, living or dead, business establishments, events, or locales is entirely coincidental.

Copyright © 2022 by Allyson Lindt
All Rights Reserved
Cover Art by Romancepremades.com

No part of this publication may be reproduced, stored in a retrieval system, or transmitted in any form or by any means, electronic, mechanical, recording or otherwise, without the prior written permission of the author.

Manufactured in the United States of America
Acelette Press

For every person looking for yourself and that place where you belong.

introduction

Dungeon Crawl: A scenario in a role-playing game where the heroes navigate a maze of sorts—a dungeon—battling monsters, avoiding traps, solving puzzles, and sharing any loot they find along the way.

1 /
fallyn

My taste in men was just the worst. At forty, I was still shite for identifying red flags. A lifetime of bad dating decisions had helped me build up a blind spot when it came to detecting toxic guys.

As I walked through the Salt Lake International Airport, my tummy was a wreck of anticipation. I so very badly wanted this time, the men I was about to meet in person, to be different.

The relationship was better than any I'd had in the past, and I was just enough of an optimist to believe that it would continue to be. It wasn't unusual that I'd met both men online, and neither was the fact that it had been in a game. I'd been in video game testing for long enough, and an introvert even longer, so it made sense that I'd meet most people through a screen first.

What made this time different were the details. We hadn't exchanged real names, or photos. Individually identifying details were kept off the table. I was falling for their personalities, and they for mine.

Oh, yeah, there were two of them. And they both knew about each other and didn't have a problem with me *seeing* both of them. I was pretty sure they were together as well, but they insisted they were just co-workers with benefits.

Last time I'd tried a *with benefits* relationship with a guy I worked with, he got me fired when I tried to break up with him. And then stalked me for months anyway, insisting he could get me my job back if I'd just stop being a stupid cunt and go back to him.

Just. The. Worst.

It was easy to spot my bags when they came up on the luggage carrousel—I'd purchased the candy red Samsonite specifically for this trip. I wanted something that was distinctly me, and just as fresh and new as this opportunity.

Stalker-from-Quality-Assurance was the last *serious* relationship I'd been in, though oddly enough not the first, or last possessive, obsessive fuck.

Was it wrong that I just wanted a guy—or two—who would smack my ass, pull my hair, and call me a filthy whore in the bedroom, but treat me like a human being when we weren't fucking?

And on a completely unrelated note—I knew this was a small airport, all things considered, but I was about to drown in the sea of people. Why did I think flying out of my small, safe town, to a big city, to wander a convention center with tens of thousands of people, was a good idea?

Because RinCon was good for my career, and because my guys would be here. Puff69 and Archer —I didn't give them grief about their screen names because they'd never once teased me about calling myself D3m0nK1tt13–demon kittie.

I stepped outside the airport, and a shock of cold hit me. It wasn't quite so cold in Green Valley, the Northern California town I'd just left behind. And what we'd considered cold in the small London prefect I grew up in were almost tropical compared to this cold. The snow here wasn't as pretty as in California though. Gray slush built up along the curbs, and dirty mounds piled as tall as me near pillars around the roads and lots.

The guys didn't know what I did for a living, or any of the smaller details about my life, and I didn't know about theirs. They were programmers, or so they claimed. For all I knew, they worked help desk at some little call center.

Archer certainly had the voice for it. Sex line operator, maybe. I'd have paid to hear him say a number of things he'd said to me over the past several months, and he'd said them to me for free.

But they thought I was an Instagram influencer. Cosplayer.

A tiny misdirection on my part. Puff had assumed, and I let him. His suggestion to come out here and meet them and make the con part of my feed was appropriate to what I really did anyway.

I grabbed a waiting cab, let the driver load my bags in the trunk, and gave him Puff's address.

This was it. Last leg of my trip. I was finally meeting these guys in person. Seeing what they looked like. Learning their real names. Maybe fucking like bunnies, but more importantly, hopefully having a lot of fun both at RinCon and outside of it.

I should've grabbed one of the airsickness bags from the plane and brought it with me. It would be rude to puke inside this poor guy's taxi.

The smart thing for me to do on this drive would be to go over my work plans for the next week. While I wasn't an influencer in the sense Puff and Archer believed, I had an impact on opinions.

I broke video games. My online persona was an intentionally cold-hearted bitch. I loved her, because when I slipped into Online Fallyn, I was untouchable. People didn't sneer at me for the purple stripe in my long, dark hair. No one called me *shorty* and *cute stuff* while they patted me on the head.

And I could block anyone who thought they could control or deride me.

Besides, playing the games was fun, and finding the exploits was almost as entertaining.

Instead of making notes about work while I was in the cab, I couldn't stop thinking about intense, controlling Puff, and adorable, cuddly Archer, and this place they lived.

This city felt massive and small at the same time. I was used to being able to see mountains, but where were all the trees? And how come there were so many houses and apartment buildings, all jammed so close together?

The taxi navigated down one road after another, and when it turned onto a heavily tree-lined street, I would've let out a sigh of relief, if it weren't for the slushy roads. But I could do snow. I'd gotten used to light snow.

Not many of the houses were visible from the road here, and we had to slow down to find a lot of the numbers. Puff had told me his driveway was the one with the wrought iron visible from the road, and sent me a picture. The only picture I had from him.

As we crept down the road, a house number sign matching the photo on my phone appeared. "There. That's it." I pointed.

The driver slowed his already crawling car even more, and we headed down the driveway. As the trees parted, a large house came into view. It wasn't quite a mansion, but it was the closest I'd ever seen outside of historical buildings.

Puff probably wasn't some random help desk guy after all. Unless he was a trust fund baby.

We stopped at the head of the driveway, I paid, and I insisted I'd be fine if the driver left me here.

I wouldn't be. I was going to hurl. Taking a few deep breaths, I approached the house and rang the bell.

"What the fuck are you doing here?" The voice that came through the speaker next to what was probably a camera sounded a bit like Puff, but a lot angrier, and familiar for a reason I couldn't place.

This was a bad idea. Why had I done this?

Nope. This weekend was about embracing my online persona, and Online Fallyn would push ahead with no fear. "I'm Demon Kittie? I'm looking for Puff69."

"*Ha*." He let out a barking laugh. "No. Really. How the fuck did you get my address?"

I'd pictured dozens of scenarios about how this would go. He wouldn't like my hair. I wouldn't like that he lived in his parents' pool house. We wouldn't have anything to say to each other in person…

But this abrasive attitude wasn't on the list. "You gave it to me? Puff?"

The speaker went silent.

Now what?

I was debating turning away or trying again, when I heard noise coming from the other side of the door, and it swung open.

Oh.

Oh, fuck me.

I was staring at a very familiar face. He was the head developer for the game we'd met in. I'd seen him in livestreams, but he was gorgeous in person. Tall with dark, messy hair. A jawline that could slice glass, and a hard, slender frame hidden under a faded *Plaid Peanut Butter* T-shirt.

He was the kind of guy I'd stop and stare at on the street, while I fantasized about yielding without hesitation when he asked for my panties.

And I spent a lot of my show breaking his game.

If this was a movie, this was where I'd puke on his shoes, and the scene would cut to someone else. Instead, the best I could manage was, "It's you."

Elliot—Puff69?—rolled his eyes and let out a heavy sigh. "Go to hell, Fallyn." He let the door swing shut on me.

That was that.

What was I supposed to do now? Get a hotel, probably. Given that reception, things probably weren't going to work out with Puff69 and Archer.

Elliot and… one of his developers?

This was surreal. Sure, I played under an account that masked me, when I was playing for fun. It made sense they would do the same, because they wanted to watch people beta their game through an unobstructed lens. But what were the odds…?

It didn't matter. Would he call the cops on me if I hung out here long enough to figure out my next steps?

I called the one person I knew in the city besides

them, or at least knew well enough to have his number. *Please let him pick up.*

"Hello," Nigel answered.

"Hi. It's Fallyn." I usually only talked to him—anyone—over chat, but he'd given me his personal cell because the office tended to screen my messages.

He was their Quality Assurance Director. The only person at AcesPlayed who talked to me like I wasn't the scourge of the earth. "Hey. Are you okay? How was your flight?" He knew I was traveling here, but I hadn't given him any details beyond that I was meeting friends, and I was looking forward to meeting him at RinCon.

"I'm…" Not fine at all. "Can you recommend me a hotel that's not too far from the convention center? Or at least tell me what part of town I need to book in?"

"I thought you were staying with friends. What's up?"

It wasn't like I could say bad things about his colleagues, but I had to explain something. It was likely he'd hear about it anyway, and I'd rather he hear my version of the story too. "These friends I was going to meet… I only know them from the game. Like, I've never seen their faces and I only knew their screen names."

"Are you in trouble? I can track down owners of

IP addresses." No wonder Megan and Landon adored him.

Yup, we were close enough I knew the people he was dating—we all gamed together when I was playing as Fallyn—but I had to come out here for strangers. The one with the sexy voice, and the one with controlling streak. "I'm fine, I promise. Not in any danger." Unless the cops were on their way to evict me from this front porch. Was Elliot watching this on the doorbell cam? "Do you know who Puff69 and Archer are?"

Silence met me.

That wasn't a good sign.

"I'm not allowed to answer that," Nigel finally said.

Of course not. Because of privacy concerns and also because he worked with them.

I pinched the bridge of my nose. "I'm sitting on Elliot's front porch right now, and he just slammed the door in my face. I didn't know, hand to god. I had no idea I was…" Earhole fucking someone who possibly considered me his arch nemesis.

"I'll talk to him," Nigel said.

"No. No, no, no." I didn't want Nigel to get in trouble with his work. They'd already been mad enough when they found out I was going around them to bring bugs to him directly.

Which was a weird thing to get mad about, but people were touchy about me breaking their code.

You'd think I snapped their dicks off with my bare hands, the way they reacted sometimes.

"You're here to see him. He invited you." Nigel sounded sympathetic but insistent. "You're Demon Kittie? You didn't tell me. He's been swooning over meeting you for weeks."

I glanced over my shoulder at the doorbell cam. Swooning? Over me? "A girl's gotta have some secrets."

"I'll talk to him. Don't go anywhere." Nigel disconnected.

Like I said... My taste in men was just the worst.

What was I supposed to do about the woman sitting on my porch?

The woman wearing the face of my arch nemesis, for longer than I'd been part of AcesPlayed. The petite, spunky, gorgeous woman who apparently also possessed an incredible mind.

I mean, I knew Fallyn was smart. It took brains to make the online show that she did. Brains. Balls. And a lot of sadism. I should respect that. But…

And she was the same woman Link and I had been voiceterbating with for months. It was impossible to ignore that smooth, sultry voice tinged with a British accent, even if I wanted to. Except the woman online was much sweeter, far less crass, than the woman who spoke with a cockney twang in the videos that annoyed me when they were mild and infuriated me most of the time.

But Fallyn was Demon Kittie. The most

exquisite blend of bratty, submissive, and brilliant conversationalist…

Nope. This was a dream. Any minute now, I'd have to pee and wouldn't be able to find a bathroom. Or someone would come after me with a fire ax. Or my dick would shrivel up and fall off. Or worst of all, every redundancy we had in place for the game would fail, the entire thing would vanish, and nearly six years' worth of blood, sweat, and cum would be destroyed.

Worst nightmare, right there. Which must be why Fallyn was on my doorstep, claiming she was Demon Kittie.

And I couldn't stop watching her through my doorbell cam, like some sort of proper creeper. Was it better or worse that I chose to leave the sound off? I didn't want to hear who she was calling. I didn't want to admit that I was an idiot to not recognize that Demon Kittie and Fallyn had the same voice.

My phone rang, and Nigel's name appeared on the screen.

It was starting—things were breaking at work. The apocalypse mere days before our game's official debut. "Hey," I answered.

"Are you going to talk to her or sulk like a six-year-old?" Nigel asked.

Now I knew who Fallyn called. The office traitor. Was I being a little immature about this? Yes.

But I was going to allow myself the indulgence, because this was one of the most important weeks of our lives—of the lives of everyone I worked with. "Do I have a third option?"

"You have a lot of options, I assume. But if you're not going to let her stay with you, like you promised, I'll come pick her up."

"Does your girlfriend know you're getting some on the side?" Yup, that was me crossing a line. I knew it as soon as I said it. Nigel would be within his rights to deck me the next time he saw me.

Instead, he chuckled. "Megan loves Fallyn. They craft in game together. Hell, Landon adores her too."

My growl slipped out without my permission. "He's only been working for me for a few months, and you already have him hiding things from me?" Like playing the game however and with whomever he wanted.

"Do you want me to come pick her up? Save her from the troll who lives in the forest?"

I'm not the troll, she is. Nope. I would *not* say that out loud. I also hated the idea of someone else coming to Demon Kittie's rescue, even if she was wearing Fallyn's body.

I'd pulled strings with Chloe to get Demon Kittie a media pass. I'd spent nights hurrying to finish work so I could play with her and Link—both dungeon crawls and in-game sex hotels. And that entire time I'd cursed Fallyn's name every time she shared another broken bit of our beta with her audience.

"I've got it handled," I said to Nigel.

"K. See you at work Monday." He hung up.

I raked my fingers through my hair, steeled myself, and opened the front door again.

Fallyn scrambled to her feet from her spot on the porch, and whirled to face me. The conflicted feelings that surged inside me in response were suffocating. Did I want to fuck her or curse her name?

Both.

While we were both naked and I had her pinned to the wall, my cock buried inside her.

"Can we start again?" Her voice was timid. Sweet.

Arch nemesis.

I sucked my teeth. "No. We really can't. How do I know you're really Kittie?"

"How do I really know you're Puff69?" She countered.

"You're at the address I gave Kittie, and I answered the door. Because it's my house."

She winced. "I…" She sighed. "I know that the tattoos on the insides of your wrists cover a different kind of scar."

Old ones. Long healed ones. Mostly. Scars I'd never told anyone about except Link and the woman I'd stayed up too late one night sharing dark secrets with. "You can stay in the guesthouse. I'll get you a key."

"You have a guest house?" Her eyes grew wide, and her awe seemed genuine, which made her a lot cuter than I wanted her to be. Especially with the way her h's dropped off when she spoke. "Maybe it's a mansion after all."

The comment was soft, as if she was talking to herself.

It wasn't quite a mansion, but it was ridiculously big, especially for one person. I'd inherited it from my grandfather. It was the family homestead. "Yes, I have a guesthouse. I'll show you the way."

She grabbed her suitcase, and I resisted the impulse to carry it for her. It was wheeled, and she wasn't struggling, and—

"Let me get that for you."

"I'm okay, thanks." Fallyn held onto the handle tightly.

Right. To the guest house. We wandered through the living room to the dining room, and paused at the back patio door when I saw all the snow blocking the path from here to the house behind mine. I needed to shovel before we could walk that path. I didn't think this through very well because Kittie was supposed to stay in the spare room across the hall from me. Or even better, in my bed.

"Um…" Fallyn's soft voice interrupted my thoughts.

Kittie had told me she was shy in person. Part of her being here was to help her break out of her shell, at her request. This soft-spoken woman was a lot more like what I expected from Kittie than what I saw from Fallyn. Maybe they were actually sisters. The evil twin and the good twin.

"What's up?" I asked.

"We were supposed to meet Archer for dinner. Is that still on? Oh, crap. He works for you. He's going to hate me too."

Not likely. "I'm pretty sure Link has never hated anyone in the history of the universe. And yes, let's go get dinner. I'll shovel the path when we get back. You can leave your suitcase by the patio door."

Why was I taking her with me? Why was I doing anything with her besides giving her a hotel name and calling her a cab? Why didn't I let Nigel make good on his threat to come get her?

Because the longer she lingered, the harder it was to associate her with the streamer whose name I cursed on a regular basis.

So we trekked through the house, to the garage this time, climbed into my Bentley Bentayga, and headed to the restaurant where we were meeting Lincoln.

The drive was only about twenty minutes, but with me not trusting myself to say anything, and her fiddling with her fingers, her coat sleeves, her hair, and never uttering a word, it was possibly the most awkward twenty minutes of my year.

As we pulled into the parking lot, and I saw Link waiting for us near the front entrance, a new thought occurred to me. "Fuck."

"What's wrong?" She sounded so meek it was almost unreal.

"I probably should've warned him about who you are."

Kittie let out a strangled laugh. "Might be more fun this way. Actually watch his expression. See if he tells me to go to Hell, too."

"Might be." Might not be. I parked, and we headed toward Link.

When he saw us approaching, his eyes grew wide. When we were close enough for casual conversation he said, "Am I hallucinating?"

"And here I thought it was a bad dream." I scoffed. "Archer, meet Demon Kittie."

"'Allo." Kittie wiggled her fingers in a disturbingly adorable wave.

Link stared at her, mouth slightly agape. He gave a single shake of his head, and extended his hand. "It's Lincoln, actually. You can call me Link."

"Fallyn." She took his hand. "But you probably already know that."

He looked between us.

I shrugged. "It's really her. Whichever her you're wondering about."

"It's true. I'm both Fallyn and Demon Kittie. Nice to meet you," she said.

Link gestured toward the entrance. "This has got to be one hell of a story. I want appetizers while you tell it."

There really wasn't much story here at all, but I had a feeling there would be once word got out.

I was staring down the official release of a game that meant the world to me. It would be announced at one of the largest gaming conventions in the world.

And I was worrying about the fact that the woman I'd been *fucking* online was the same person who made our lives hell with her work. That was an added stress I didn't need.

It wasn't as though I expected anything more than the physical from Kittie—I wasn't interested in an emotional relationship. While she was here, she could be Kittie in the bedroom and Fallyn the rest of the time and it didn't impact me one way or the other.

**3 /
link**

People made a lot of assumptions. Based on what they saw, what they heard, prejudice, expectation, cultural norms…

Meeting Kittie—Fallyn—in person, I wasn't surprised. It almost made sense that the two of them were the same person, and I didn't have a problem with her videos—we did our job, and she did hers. It didn't seem that Elliot was too pleased about her being here though.

When I was younger, people looked at me and saw the fat kid. When I opened my mouth and random facts and observations spilled out, I became the fat, nerdy kid. Add to that the fact that I didn't date, but I liked looking at boys as much as girls, and I was the fat, nerdy, gay boy.

In my late teens, I decided I'd had enough, and I was going to change people's perceptions of me. I put on a lot of muscle, and kept my mouth shut and my gaze straight ahead, unless I really trusted the person I was talking to. All of which made me the big, scary, dumb kid.

That was fine with me. I preferred that people underestimate me.

Elliot didn't let anyone see the real him either, not even himself most of the time, but I knew that a soft gooey center hid behind a lot of walls. And I knew from talking to Fallyn in game that she was a lot the same.

"What's that?" Elliot asked as we headed inside.

I'd been too busy processing our situation to have any idea what he was talking about. "What's what?"

"That sound..." He veered toward the side of the restaurant.

I heard the faint whining at the same time Fallyn said, "Is that a dog?"

We followed the noise, and as we got closer, whining became growling and yipping.

Elliot dropped to his knees next to a thicket of shrubs and gingerly pushed his way through branches. "What are you... Oh, come here. It's okay, I won't hurt you." His voice was soft.

He emerged with bush bits stuck to his jacket, and a tiny black, brown, and white puppy cradled his arms.

Elliot and I had been fuck-buddies and co-workers for a long time, and there were times like this, when he had a tiny, shivering ball of fur in his arms like it was precious cargo, when I wondered if I felt more than that for him.

Not that I had any idea what *more* should feel like. Having a high IQ didn't give me any extra insight into emotions—mine or other peoples.

"He's so precious." Fallyn started to reach for the puppy, but her hand dropped away.

Elliot tucked the dog inside his jacket ever so gingerly.

"I'll go inside, see if he belongs to anyone." Was it wrong that I didn't know what I wanted the answer to be? A *yes* meant we couldn't take the little guy with us—not that I could care for a dog—but it also meant some asshole had left the poor thing alone out here.

It didn't matter. After about five minutes of asking around inside, no one claimed the dog. Though, one guy who radiated *white van with no windows* vibes offered to take it and *give it a good home*.

I assured him we had things covered. All I had to do was stand there and say the words, and he didn't argue.

I headed back outside to find Elliot still cradling the puppy, and Fallyn standing close, gently stroking the dog's tiny little head.

"No one claimed him," I said.

"We should see if he has a chip. If maybe someone lost him." Fallyn tweaked the puppy's ears.

Elliot's scowl was both cute and terrifying. "He won't stop shivering. We need to take him to the vet."

I had my phone out in an instant, looking for the closest clinic. "There's a twenty-four-hour place not too far from here."

"Let's go. You drive. I'll come back for my car later. Wait." Elliot handed me the tiny bundle of fur. "Hold him for just a minute."

The puppy was barely bigger than my hands, and I was both in awe of the tiny little bundle, and terrified I might hurt it.

Elliot shrugged out of his coat, folded it into a sort of portable nest, and held it out. I placed the dog in the middle, and it curled up soundly. The shivering had stopped, but it still looked so meek and tiny.

"*Now* you drive," Elliot said.

We headed toward my SUV, but Fallyn hung back. I jerked my thumb toward the vehicle, and opened both the front and back passenger doors. "Come on. Don't you want to know what happens next?"

Her grin was stunning and warm. Nothing like the smirks Fallyn wore in her videos. "Totally. I'm in."

I drove us to the address I'd found, and the staff buzzed us in. The dog didn't have a chip, but Elliot insisted we make sure it was okay.

There wasn't anyone else in the waiting room, but they had a lighter staff for overnight—which was any time after five according to them—and this wasn't an emergency, so we had to wait. The three of us settled into chairs, with me between Fallyn and Elliot.

The dog had woken up, and had energy. It wanted to climb up Elliot, crawl on me, and hide in Fallyn's hair. The group of us probably looked ridiculous to anyone else, three grown adults giggling while a yipping ball of fur used us as its own personal jungle gym, but people would assume what they wanted to.

"She needs a name." Fallyn extracted it from her hair and tried to hold it. "We can't just call her *Dog.*"

If we named it, there was some sort of rule about keeping it, wasn't there? I'd never owned a dog before. Or a cat. Or even a goldfish. Our work was too hectic for that.

"What's wrong with *Dog*?" Elliot grabbed it mid-air as it jumped from Fallyn's arms.

Fallyn's growl-sigh was as adorable as the puppy. "That's not how floofs get named."

"That's how Link names his characters."

I liked the idea of me being compared to a floof. It was fun.

"I thought the name was like the cartoon. Archer?" Fallyn looked between us.

The what? "Like a ranged fighter, in game." My character was a gunslinger, but the concept was the same. "An archer." The dog climbed onto my lap, and tried to claw its way up my shirt. I extracted him with care and held on as best I could.

"So… what are your other character names?" Fallyn asked.

Duh? "Monk, Mage, Gladiator, and Aragorn."

"Is Aragorn your Ranger?" The grin on Fallyn's face was perfect.

I nodded. "Of course."

"I love it." She took the puppy from me and cradled it.

The way Elliot watched her, I wasn't sure if he was upset or captivated. "If you don't want to call it *Dog* what would you call it?"

Holding it up, Fallyn studied its face. She scrunched up her nose and it *yipped*. "Queen Puppinald the First."

"First of all, you don't know that it's a *she* and second, once you shorten *Puppinald* it's *Puppy* and how is that better than *Dog*?" Elliot thought he had a point—he must've, or he wouldn't have said it.

But I saw Fallyn's logic. "It's cuter," I said,

The vet assistant saved us from having to decide. "Only one of you in the exam room," she said when we all stood.

"I'll go." Elliot was already following her before we could argue.

Which left Fallyn and me sitting alone in an empty waiting room… waiting.

I'd never been good at small talk. I hated discussing the weather or sports. Give me deep, philosophical conversation about the pros and cons of Java versus Python, and I was happy.

Fallyn fiddled with the zipper on her jacket, sliding it up a few inches before letting it drop.

This was nothing like in game, but there, we had Elliot to bridge the gap. Not always, though. There were times when she and I had talked long into the night. Late enough that it left me a zombie the next day at work.

"I never got to hear that story," I said. "Of what the infamous Fallyn is doing with my Director of Development."

Her smile was probably sad, but with her head turned down it was hard to tell. "Not much of a story. The woman you've been talking to online—Demon Kittie—is me. I didn't know I was talking to AcesPlayed programmers. I thought maybe you were just a couple of random basement dwellers." Her laugh was dry. "Sorry."

"Don't be. We all kept our details private for a reason."

"Elliot doesn't like me."

I shrugged. "Elliot doesn't like most people, including Online Fallyn. Elliot doesn't know you. I'd like to." Was I allowed to say that? Flirting wasn't my thing. Or talking to people in general. I always said too much or not enough.

"Me too." She finally looked up, and her smile reached her eyes. "Did you know he has a guest house? You probably knew that."

"I did. Elliot comes from money, but he's not a snobby rich guy or anything." Most of us had money now. Those of us who started with Cord, moved on to Rinslet, and then bought into AcesPlayed when it became its own company, had stock options and the kind of tenured salary that kept us comfortable.

But Elliot came from old money.

"What about you?" I wasn't sure what I was asking.

"I don't have a guest house."

I laughed. "I mean what about who you are? Where you're from?"

"Oh." With her sigh, she seemed to deflate. "Please don't be offended by this, but I have to be really careful talking about the real details of my life."

"Yeah. Of course." I always forgot things like that—personal details were personal. For some reason, her shrug off hurt more than normal.

The conversation died after that. When Elliot rejoined us, I swallowed back a *thank Loki*.

"Well?" I asked.

Elliot was still cradling the dog, but this time he

had a blanket. "*King* Puppinald is a boy dog. A mutt. And he's fine except for a little head cold. I need to stop by the pet store on the way home, get him some food, puppy pads, the basics, and then take him home."

"You're keeping him?" Fallyn sounded hopeful.

"Like I have a choice?"

Elliot had me hold King while he settled the bill, then we headed to the pet store, filled a cart with everything we could think of, and went back to his house.

There was very little discussion about it. For some reason we'd all assumed we were part of this excursion tonight, and I was here for it.

We set up a sort of pen in the corner of Elliot's bedroom, with bed, food, and all the essentials for King, and a dog crate went next to it all.

"What are you going to do with him while you're working?" I asked. "RinCon, long hours… Not the best time for a new dog."

"You think I didn't think of that, but I did. I called Mrs. Ria while I was in the exam room, and she's happy to watch him while I was working." Of course Elliot had a plan. He always did. Mrs. Ria was his housekeeper, and she'd been with the house most of Elliot's life. She was more of a mother to him than his own mom. That wasn't her full name, but it was what Elliot called her, and I was always terrified of butchering her Greek name, so I did the same.

"I hate to interrupt, because the puppy is *super* cute." Fallyn sounded hesitant, and snapped her jaw shut when we both looked at her. "I need to do a livestream. Check in. Tell my audience… something."

I remembered that. "You promised us a big surprise."

"You watch my show?" Pink spread across her cheeks.

I could almost hear Elliot behind me, rolling his eyes. But I didn't have a problem with it. "I do. It's… educational."

"Thank you for that." Her laugh was nervous. "And yeah, the surprise is RinCon."

"Don't let us stop you." Elliot waved a dismissive hand. Some of his good cheer had faded.

"Um…" The nervousness radiating from Fallyn was contagious. "Unless you want me to do this someplace that identifies you, I need a neutral back-ground. Neutral furniture. Things like that.

The reminder of who she was definitely put a damper on the evening.

Elliot picked up King further into the house. "Living room, probably. Come on."

Those were about the only words we said while we set up a space where Fallyn could stream from. She grabbed her suitcase from by the back door, and vanished into a downstairs bathroom to *make herself camera ready*.

When she emerged, my breath caught. She'd refreshed her makeup and pulled her hair into braids, which looked super adorable and tugable. The neckline of her top dipped low enough to show off generous cleavage, and the fabric should have been thin enough to show the outlines of a bra, but there wasn't such an outline.

My mouth was instantly dry. Yes, this was how Fallyn dressed on camera, but seeing her in person this way, knowing this person was attached to the mind I'd been talking to for months…

"Wow." My exclamation slipped out.

Pink dotted her cheeks, and she ducked her head.

Elliot rolled his eyes. "I'm not going to watch this. Keep King company." He handed me the puppy.

Watching someone stream in real time, being in the same room with them, was always odd. Fallyn wasn't talking to me, but with me here, she was focused on me. And she really was gorgeous in person. Possibly as uncomfortable with words as I was, but still cute.

While she talked, I absentmindedly entertained King. She ran through what people could expect from her trip, how excited she was to be here, and managed to leave out all the details about us, about her being here with us, or anything that indicated she was anything other than an internet persona who existed in a bubble with no one else touching her.

Was it disconcerting for her to portray that kind of front?

King yipped and jumped from my arms before I could stop him. Fallyn looked up, startled, as he ran up to her on camera, climbed up her leg, and jumped onto the table.

And now Elliot's new puppy was on Fallyn's livestream. Oops.

fallyn

I had a puppy climbing all over me. Running from one shoulder to the other. Hiding in my hair. I was laughing in spite of myself. I found my voice long enough to tell the camera that I'd have more from RinCon for them in the next few days and that my scheduled videos would go live before then, then I signed off.

Speaking of, I needed to update one of those videos to take out a reference or two to AcesPlayed, and I could clip this video at the end, before the puppy showed up, too. Normally I wouldn't edit my content for any reason, but if I was staying with Elliot… I should really trim some things out.

When I was sure the camera was off and the stream was over, I plucked King from my lap and held him in front of my face. "You're a little trouble-maker, aren't you?"

He stared back with the most unbelievable *who*

me in the history of *who mes*, and barked. He squirmed free of my grasp and bounded away toward Elliot.

"I think your dog is part cat," I teased.

Elliot scowled, but there was a smile underneath. "The mean lady didn't mean that. Don't listen to her." He scooped the dog up, and wrinkled his nose. "You kind of stink."

"You did find him in the dirt and bushes," Link said.

I couldn't believe this giant wall of muscle was the sweetheart I'd spent hours talking to online. Until he opened his mouth, anyway. He looked like he could pick me up and carry me on his shoulder, or cradle me in his arms, and never so much as disturb a hair on my head while doing it.

Sharp contrast to Elliot, who was examining King. "I think we need to give him a bath."

I'd had dogs growing up. It hurt too much to lose them, so I didn't anymore, but I had so many good memories of our doggos. The ones of bathing them were hit and miss. "Have you ever had a dog? Have you ever given a dog a bath?"

"That's what the groomers were for." Elliot frowned. "But how hard can it be? Hell, I bet there are hundreds of videos on it. And a lot of dogs like water."

"And just as many don't. Come on, boys. You too, King. We need a bathroom you don't care about getting dirty, towels you don't care about getting stained, and someone guarding the door while the other two of us hold the puppy down and wash him."

Elliot looked at me, brows raised. "Did you just give me orders in my house?"

"I did. You can get me back in the bedroom." I snapped my jaw shut. What in the what? I must've forgotten to put Online Fallyn away. I wouldn't apologize. I wouldn't apologize.

I ducked my head. "Sorry."

"Don't be." The way Elliot dragged his gaze over me was heat personified. "Follow me."

Somebody had flipped the switch on the asshole who closed his door in my face earlier. This man was more like the Puff I talked to online. Still in command, but with a layer of sticky caramel over his prickly pear attitude.

We gathered the supplies and Elliot led us to the same bathroom I'd changed in earlier. It was probably just a generic guest bathroom, based on its location, but was still bigger than any I'd ever had.

Link guarded the door, Elliot promised me he had a good grip on King, and turned on the water. I made sure it was a good temperature over the drain, taking care not to get any on the dog. He didn't seem to mind the noise, and was just happy to have Elliot giving him attention.

"All right, little guy. Let's do this." I got a little

bit of water in a cup, and poured it over King's back.

He yelped and wriggled free from Elliot's grasp.

"*Grab him*," I shouted.

King wasn't having any of that. He tore around the bathroom, leaving more water behind than stuck to his fur.

Link finally managed to scoop him up, and hand him back.

"Hold him tighter this time," I said.

Elliot looked me over, and an unexpected wave of desire flooded me. "Why am I the only one who's wet?" he asked.

"Maybe you're off your game." My teasing retort slipped out before I could filter it. Did that come out right? Did I even want to say that?

The corner of his mouth tugged up, and his smirk was both a threat and a promise. "Are you looking for a dirty response? Something filthy?"

Enough of my online persona was still near the surface that I grabbed a retort and swept hesitation aside. "A girl starts to have expectations…"

Elliot nodded.

What was he thinking? Dude had a scary poker face.

In a blink, he scooped up some water in his cupped hands, and splashed me with it.

I squealed in surprise, and looked down to see the water had made my top nearly see through, I'd left my bra off to tease the camera. "Oh, you asshole." I wasn't mad. Couldn't even muster a hint of it in my voice.

And the way he looked me over made desire pulse between my thighs.

"We have a puppy to wash," Elliot said.

Except as the *bath* went on, as much water got on both of us, and somehow on Link halfway across the room, as did on the dog and in the tub.

King seemed to be here for the fun, based on his yipping and jumping.

I didn't blame him.

Half an hour later, everyone—everything—in the room was half drenched. But King was clean, and Elliot had him wrapped in a towel, and cradled him. "I think the little bastard is falling asleep."

"I think he loves his Daddy." Link sounded adoring.

Too. Sweet. This was like what a Normal Rockwell painting *should* look like. Heartfelt, with an underlying hint of *someone's going to get laid tonight if they're lucky.*

Was it wrong that I wanted it to be me? After this roller coaster of a day, when I wasn't even sure how these men felt about me being here in person?

"We need to change," Elliot said.

I was about to push my luck a notch further. *Please let this pay off.* We were having fun, so it should be okay, right? "If I say *no*, then what?"

Elliot raised an eyebrow. Did he practice that in front of a mirror? "Then I'll make you."

"You'll *make* me change out of my wet clothes?"

"Do you really want to do this?" Elliot's question sounded sincere, rather than irritated.

"It's part of the reason I'm here."

Link made a noise that was half sigh, half quiet groan.

That was sexy, and it tied to so many memories of the things we'd talked about doing, when we chatted.

Elliot remained stoic. "If we do it, then there are rules."

"Like what?" There were rules in game—so many rules—around consent, reporting unwelcome advances, and with these two, talking through what we all wanted from an evening. I'd never had that face to face before, and it was reassuring.

"Like, this is only physical. No falling in love, or any of that bullshit," Elliot said. "And you can stop any time. Any of us can. But know that unless you do, I'm going to take, but I give just as good."

Holy shit, he was taking this seriously. *Hot.*

"And if you have any hard limits you know of that you haven't mentioned before, now's the time to mention them," Link added.

We'd discussed so much, I was pretty sure the important stuff was out there. Oh, except, "No water sports." That was the tactful way to put that, right?

Link cleared his throat and shot a pointed look at my soaking wet top.

I twisted my mouth in amusement and disbelief. "Don't spit or pee on me."

"Protection?" Elliot asked.

I was super turned on by the thought of either of them coming on me. Inside me. Or both of them. One after another. At the same time. But there was some reality to consider. "Are you clean?" We'd had this conversation, but I wanted to see their answers face to face.

"Yes," Elliot said.

Link nodded. "Yes."

"Me too. Condoms for penetration. Don't need them anywhere else." I'd like to avoid something like a pregnancy scare if my birth control chose today to stop working.

"Fair." Link was so compliant. But I know how their dynamic worked, and I figured he would be.

Elliot's sign-on was the big one. "Agreed. We all in?"

Link and I nodded.

"Good." Elliot pointed at me. "Grab her."

Link knelt next to me and took my hands. When he gently placed his shoulder near my gut and stood, I yelped in surprise. He was caveman-carrying me into the bedroom. *Fuck me* I liked this.

In Elliot's room, he set a mostly sleepy King in the corner, and joined us as Link put me on my feet.

"Out of the wet clothes." There was no room for argument in Elliot's tone.

I was going to do it anyway. "Make me."

"Did you really just…?"

I shrugged. "We just said *all in*."

With a nod, Elliot looked past me to Link. They didn't exchange words, but his expression threatened to turn the water on my clothes to steam. From behind me and without warning, Link grabbed my wrists and held them tightly.

The spike in my chest was fear mixed with desire. I didn't know these men. In fact, Nigel was probably the only person who really understood where I was.

But despite the rough start with Elliot when I arrived, I trusted that he and Link were the same people I'd been talking to online, and this was part of what we'd role played before. Technically, none of it was a new idea to us, but experiencing it in person was different… and delicious.

Elliot was rough when he shoved my shirt up, and the friction cranked my anticipation as much as having my bare breasts exposed so abruptly. Link only let go of me long enough to pull the top from my arms and toss it. The way Elliot looked me over when I was topless, Link's fingers digging into my wrists…

Fuck, I was turned on. My pulse hammered in my ears. Adrenaline sped through my veins. This felt incredible and we'd only started.

Elliot undid the button on my jeans with the flick of a wrist, and yanked the zipper open with a sharp tug. He shoved my bottoms to the ground, leaving me naked and trapped.

"I notice I'm the only one who had to take off my wet clothes." I was taunting him on purpose, but I kept my tone playful.

Elliot stepped closer, and I moved away instinctually. Except Link was behind me and I couldn't go far. Elliot planted his foot between mine, and pressed his thigh to my mound. Lightly at first, but increasing the pressure quickly.

Oh. Oh, *fuck*. That felt so good. Wrong, but good. The harder he pushed, the more I wanted to grind in response.

He moved one hand to knead my breast, and rolled a nipple roughly between his fingers. As he upped the intensity both on my chest and between my legs, I couldn't stop grinding against him.

I was desperate to get off, but this wasn't enough. Orgasm fluttered just out of my reach, but if I humped his thigh harder, if he twisted a little harder, maybe…

Elliot pulled away abruptly, and the slick trail I'd left on his pants was obvious. "You're right, I am wet. How about that?" He sounded nonchalant. "Kneel in the middle of the bed, and don't move."

"If I do move?" This was fun.

"I'll assume you want to stop, and the night is over," Elliot said.

Point taken. That was as effective as a threat could get. I did what I'd been commanded, and sat as still as possible, hands clasped in front of me.

When Elliot told Link to undress, and Link complied without question, that show was almost enough reward for my behaving.

Almost.

I'd never been with two men at once before, except the two of them online. I'd been in a few threesomes where there was another woman, but those were always awkward and tended to end with either a jealous boyfriend or him expecting both of us to get off solely on the idea of pleasing him.

Elliot and Link knew this. I'd told them the stories. So when a naked Elliot pulled a naked Link into a passionate kiss, like two men who were very much used to doing this with each other, my heart sank. The kiss didn't last long, though.

"Tonight our guest comes first." Elliot put some distance between him and Link, who nodded.

My skin was definitely on fire with need. Elliot pulled something from a dresser drawer, but I couldn't tell what it was until he slipped the blindfold over my eyes.

This required so much trust. Did I have that? My heart hammered against my ribs.

Elliot placed his palm on my bare chest, over my heart. "Would you tell me if you wanted to stop?"

I nodded.

"Say it."

"I'd tell you if I wanted to stop." Forming the words cemented them in my head. That he required them made me feel like he valued them.

"Good." The shift in Elliot's tone from cool and controlling to thick with need was as tasty as the rest of this. "Because I fucking love that *thump thump thump* against my skin."

I didn't try to hide my whimper.

And then he was gone. His touch. His presence.

"Lay on your back." Heat from his breath brushed the back of my neck.

I was past the point of arguing; this promised too much reward for me to be bratty now.

When he murmured, "Good girl," did I almost come?

Damn straight.

The headphones he slipped over my ears cut me off from the rest of the world in the most disconcerting way. I couldn't see. I couldn't hear.

Sensory deprivation was another of the things we'd talked about online, and the fact that he'd been paying attention was another reason to be so incredibly turned on.

Someone grabbed my wrists and pinned them above my head. I already recognized the feel of Link's hands on my skin, but cut off from two senses, I swore the feeling was amplified.

Nothing else happened. Time ticked away. Was this taking forever, or did it just feel like it?

No, they were definitely drawing the moment out. Would I hear them if there was discussion? Did they simply look at each other and know the best way to torture me in order to make me want this that much more?

A light brush on my lower legs made me jump, and the lightly teasing touch that slid higher up my skin didn't calm me. Elliot reached my thighs and added his other hand to the mix to push my legs apart. He brushed along the sensitive flesh until I couldn't help but gasp and squirm, both trying to get closer and pull away.

The weight of the bed shifted, and he was kneeling between my legs, but he continued to tease my thighs rather than move closer to the core of my need.

It was maddening not being able to see or hear. Even my own gasps were muffled.

The finger he drew along my pussy was a jolt racing through me, and I bucked my hips into his touch. This was almost more torture than if he'd gone for pain. He was brushing my skin. Finally parting my folds. Sliding along my slick slit, but not penetrating me. Not touching my clit.

I wanted to jerk closer to his touch, but would he pull away if I did?

The first penetration, when he slipped his fingers inside me, was like barely twisting the lid on a shaken bottle of soda. It made a difference, but it certainly didn't relieve the pressure.

Elliot's movements were deliberate and slow, and it didn't take long before I was rocking in time with the pace he set. As with his leg between my thighs, this wasn't going to get me off, but it felt really fucking good.

I only had so much patience, though. My *please* slipped out without my permission. I barely heard my own voice, and only inside my head, like I was trapped in a dream.

Elliot didn't pause or change pace.

It wasn't as though I'd hear him if he said anything.

"Please let me come?" I pushed the words out.

His hand fell away.

Was I wrong to ask? Did I need to beg?

I didn't have time to consider it further when Elliot moved his touch to my clit to circle and stroke. Tiny zaps of need zinged through me, one after another, firing so rapidly I couldn't register all of them. I was tumbling into the sensation because nothing else existed in this bubble.

When orgasm crashed over me, it was abrupt. Intense. All-consuming. And as I crested the peak of pleasure, Elliot thrust inside me.

His cock was a lot more satisfying than his fingers, and that first deep, fast penetration drew out my climax.

It seemed the time for restraint had passed on both our parts. He pushed my knees to my chest and fucked me hard and fast. There were no cues for me to tell how close he was, but the intensity had one orgasm blending into the next.

His hammering built to an intense crescendo and stuttered. Was it weird that I could tell he was about to come by the way he moved inside me?

No. It was perfect.

As he eased up my own climax slid off. He lowered my legs gently to the bed, and I was still riding the high of the entire experience. The pressure vanished from my wrists.

When the headphones were removed, the sound was jarring, despite the room being quiet.

Elliot's lips were on my ear again. "Still good?" he asked in a low voice that both threatened and promised.

I nodded and licked my dry lips. "Still incredible." My throat was raw. Had I been screaming?

"Good." The edge to his voice and the fact that he hadn't removed the blindfold had my pulse kicking up again. "Because I want to watch Link fuck you. I want you to feel both satisfied and used when the night is over. Our own personal fuck doll. Do you want that too?"

I couldn't hide my smirk. "Yes, sir."

The pressure on the bed changed again, and I assumed it was Link between my legs when they spread wider. When he slid inside me, he was more gentle. Moved more slowly. I knew his dick was thicker because I'd seen them both naked now, but all I felt was a cock buried inside me.

Link's slow hump built to a hard fuck, and Elliot was teasing my clit again. His touch was too much.

Way too much.

But I wouldn't ask him to stop. I wanted to see what was on the other side. When the wall of discomfort fell away, I was floating toward another orgasm.

This time I could hear the grunts. Link's drawn-out groans becoming punctuated. Desperate. He was spilling inside me, and for a blink I wished I'd let them do this without the condoms.

It didn't matter. The rush was incredible, and as he slowed to a stop, I was wrapped in the most amazing cloud of nothing-else-mattered.

Link slipped out of me, and rolled onto the bed next to me. He pulled me into him, his arms big and warm and safe, but he didn't remove the blindfold. Instead, he nipped my earlobe with his teeth. "When you're ready, you can take it off."

I wasn't ready. Not yet. If it came away, the illusion of this incredible moment in time would fade.

So I remained blind while Elliot cleaned me up, then joined us. At least, I thought he did, based on the way the mattress shifted.

"He's big spoon tonight," Link murmured.

That should seem weird, but it made too much sense. I could stay wrapped up like this forever. I barely knew these men and I already felt safe with them.

Odd, considering how the day started.

Not so odd considering my track record with men.

But I did know them. Both of them. The three of us had talked for hours. Had I gotten lucky? Were they actually who they presented themselves as online?

Not that the answers to any of those questions mattered in the long run.

No falling in love or whatever. Elliot's rule rang in my thoughts.

Not that I planned to. I was going home in a week. I'd have fun until then and make a clean break when we were done.

5 /
elliot

At some point during the night, King's pawing and whining was loud enough that I took him from his pen and let him sleep next to us in bed. I wouldn't let him get used to it, but this was his first night in a new place.

I didn't open my eyes again until morning. I was used to waking up to Link, and there was a familiarity and comfort in that. Technically, the two of us fucking was against work rules these days, but as long as we weren't blatant about it, no one brought it up.

Having a third person with us, though… It'd been a *long* time.

Why was my hip warm? And rapidly getting cold? Did Kittie whimper when she slept?

Because this was definitely Kittie, not Fallyn, because I was ignoring a lot of reality right now.

"What's wrong with King?" Link mumbled.

That was the puppy whining. And my hip was *really* cold.

Shit. Or piss. I jerked up with a start.

"Puppy needs to go out." Sleep lined Kittie's voice.

Eventually. "Not so much as he did a few minutes ago. Pretty sure he peed on the bed."

That had Fallyn and Link scrambling to their feet immediately.

"On me," I assured them. "The two of you are fine." Double fine now that I thought about it. They made an incredible view to wake up to with neither of them dressed. But not nearly as fun to enjoy as they could be, given my current situation.

I climbed from bed as well, and didn't miss the way Fallyn's gaze dropped to my dick. I scooped up King. "Let's see if you still need to go outside. Come on."

"Are you going to get dressed?" Fallyn asked.

"Would you rather I did?"

She twisted her mouth. "That feels like a trick question, but I'm not sure why. Your house, so I guess it's up to you."

"How about this—it's probably about twenty degrees outside," Link said.

"Pft. Fine." I exaggerated the concession in a playful tone, and yanked on some sweats and a hoodie. "Link knows where everything is, if either or both of you want to shower or anything. I'll be back in a few."

It had been years since I had a dog. I hadn't had one since I lost my childhood best friend and doggo, right after Dad tried to disown me for my *poor life decisions*—going into software development with a brand-new start-up, instead of to college.

When I saw King last night though, something clicked in my head and I knew I needed to bring him home. That this puppy needed me.

It was a weird compulsion, and it might be Fallyn's fault for messing with my head by being here.

No, that wasn't fair. I was happy to blame some things on her, but this was on me, and I had no regrets about the impromptu adoption.

I yanked on my shoes so I could shovel a small path in the backyard, and tried to introduce King to it, as I had many times last night. He was happy to jump in the snow, but didn't want anything to do with actually peeing. That was fine; I'd feed and water him and try again later.

I didn't think I was outside that long, but when I came back in, Link was already downstairs, showered and dressed. He and I spent enough time at each other's houses that we had clothes in both places. We weren't a couple, but we'd been FWB for years. I appreciated the way he tempered me, and not many people knew he had a darker side. It rarely came out, but I was his buffer when it did.

I put King in his corner with his food and water and kennel, and kept him in my sight as I joined Link.

"So... Fallyn is in your house. What will the world say?" His tone was conversational. He'd made himself comfortable on the couch.

I settled into my own chair. "I'm thinking they won't say anything, as in, let's keep it between us. Privacy seems pretty important to her."

"And you."

I smirked. "And you." I was the face of Aces-Played development. Aside from Dustin, our Director of Marketing, I got more face time than anyone in the company. Link tended to avoid the camera whenever possible.

He shrugged. "Fair point."

"Help me shovel a path out back to the guest house?" I asked.

"Are you really going to make Fallyn stay out there?"

"*Make*. It's not a bad place." Though, I was feeling a little guilty about it. Was I already getting soft about the situation? She hadn't even been here a day, and if she was just Kittie, I'd still offer her the room across from mine.

Link winced. "But last night…"

"Really fucking incredible. I'd fuck you both again in a heartbeat." It sounded cold, but I kept people out for a reason, and her…

"Why are you trying to pretend you don't care?"

No. I wasn't doing this today. Not even with him. I wasn't putting up with some sort of armchair psychology. "I *don't* care. I *do* want to pretend she's not Fallyn, and if she's streaming in my dining room, I can't do that."

King backed away from his bowls, yipped, and ran across the room. When he reached the door, he whirled and ran in a different direction.

Link shook his head. "Go get dressed. I'll take care of the shoveling."

"That's not what I was trying to do." I didn't shrug my work off on someone else.

"I know, and that's why I don't mind offering. Besides, I'm not going to get my arm reps in today if I don't do this."

I laughed. "Muscle-headed bear." I knew he was anything but, and he would know I was teasing.

"Twink," he countered.

I waved him off and pushed out of my seat. When I stepped on the bottom stair, King whined.

"Stay here with me, little guy." Link scooped him up and carried him toward the back door again.

I watched him grab the leash we'd bought last night, and slip that onto King.

Link had this under control, so I went to shower and dress. When I got back downstairs, Link was done, and Fallyn had joined him. They sat side-by-side on the couch, laughing, King settled between them on the floor.

Fallyn looked different than yesterday. Her damp hair hung around her shoulders, she wore a baggy sweatshirt over leggings, and her face was freshly scrubbed clean. She must've grabbed clothes from her suitcases by the back door, while I was outside with the dog. She was just as pretty, but in a different way.

And the brightness of her smile as she talked to Link...

Min—

That ping in my chest couldn't possibly be anything but discomfort. Neither of them was mine unless we were all three in the bedroom. "Who wants breakfast?" I'd bought extra food in anticipation of her visit, so I might as well cook.

"Delivery or are there dog friendly places nearby?" Fallyn asked.

"I thought we'd eat in," I said.

She raised her brows. "Is that a euphemism? Cuz I might want real food first."

Link shook his head. "It's a literal. Elliot makes killer French toast."

"No shit. Really?" Fallyn had the nerve to look surprised.

"My French toast has never killed anyone," I assured her with a straight face. "But if I'm cooking, you both have to help." Otherwise prep would take me half the morning.

"You don't want me cooking, I promise you." As Fallyn spoke, she fished her phone from the pocket on her top. "I'm the person who shares a picture of a burned-out stove top because I tried to boil water. In fact, I have a few. Do you want to see?"

Was it petty that I liked her more, knowing that she had at least one flaw? "We're good. Can you wash and slice strawberries?"

"Probably?"

"Great. In the kitchen, both of you." I pointed.

I told Fallyn what to grab from the fridge, and Link started the coffee. He and I had done this more times than I could count. After giving Fallyn some specific instructions on what I needed her to do, and making sure she was comfortable with it, I turned to the egg mixture and cooking the French toast.

While coffee dripped into the pot, Link gave his attention to whipping cream, and blending cream cheese and ricotta with marmalade.

"What's that for?" Fallyn nodded at the lightly orange mixture.

"Cream filling." I fixed her with the most strait-laced look I could muster.

Link's chuckle ruined my serious face.

Fallyn scoffed, but she was smiling. "It looks really good."

"Of course my cream filling looks delicious," I teased.

She slid fruit into a waiting bowl. "If you're trying to deter me…"

"Not at all." I grabbed one of the berries she'd removed a stem from but hadn't sliced, spooned a little mixture on it, and held it near her lips.

She wrapped her tongue around the strawberry and pulled it into her mouth in one of the single most erotic gestures I'd ever seen.

And I was coding an XXX video game.

Fortunately I had to move away, to give cooking my attention, and I kept myself from falling into that kind of teasing again during the rest of prep.

When the food was finished, we set the table, and sat down to eat.

"What does the *T* stand for?" Fallyn shoved a forkful of food into her mouth immediately after asking.

One of Online Fallyn's regular features was a cartoon version of me that was part alien, part me, wearing a monocle. She called him *ET Howard*. Her bits involving me tended to be less than flattering, and she liked to blame every decision Rinslet or AcesPlayed had ever made on me.

I could pretend I didn't know what she was talking about, but the question was a good reminder of who we actually were. No reason to ruin the light mood, as long as I took the nudge for what it was. "T is for Todd."

"Oh." Was she let down? By my middle name? Poor baby.

"Disappointed?" Link asked.

I should let him answer her questions, and enjoy my breakfast.

Fallyn shrugged. "I was expecting something exotic like Terrance or Tyrannus."

My snort slipped out. "Elliot Tyrannus Howard?" Though, *king bird* was a pretty cool middle name. I could change it…

"The Third, I assume," Fallyn said.

Thankfully not. "First of my name. My boring, basic name. Just like King."

"*King* is not a boring name." Link looked amused.

"It is when it's short for *Puppy*." Which I wasn't letting them call him too often if I could help it.

Fallyn shook her head, coffee cup halfway to her mouth. "That doesn't make any sense, and I'm here for it." She sipped her drink.

The question was, why else was she here?

There was the obvious—we met a woman

online, enjoyed her personality, and thought a week of sex and convention time would be fun.

But that was Kittie, this was Fallyn.

The line between the two was already getting blurrier than I was comfortable with, no matter how badly I wanted to embrace the denial.

**6 /
link**

This was too much fun. When I saw Fallyn yesterday, I hadn't been sure, but everything that unfolded since…

I was having a blast.

When we finished breakfast, Elliot took King outside, and Fallyn insisted on helping me with the dishes. Not that it took much to stick them in the dishwasher, but there was something sweetly domestic about the whole arrangement.

The three of us reconvened in the living room. "I've been wondering something," Fallyn said.

There was no telling where this conversation was going. We'd run the gamut so far. "What's that?"

"There's no Christmas tree in here. No ornaments." She looked at Elliot. "Do you decorate late, or are you just a Scrooge?" She sounded playful.

Christmas wasn't a favorite holiday of Elliot's. I

loved it, though, and someday I was going to get him to enjoy it just a little. Even if it was only for a minute or two. "He's just a Scrooge."

Elliot's expression said he didn't appreciate me taking her side. He'd used RinCon as an excuse to avoid the holiday for years, but there had been reasons before then, too. He also hadn't always felt this way. I remembered before…

I didn't need him to get over his past—I'd never ask that—but I would like to see him make new, better memories.

Expecting that from him was a lot easier than doing it for myself.

Elliot shrugged. "There you have it. I'm an asshole. I hate Christmas and by the way, Santa isn't real. Do you want to see where you're staying? Get situated?" Like that, he'd flipped into cool, friendly, and almost professional.

Which was also as fake as he ever got.

"I— Yeah, sure." Fallyn's tone fell to match.

Bullshit. "There's no reason to cut the morning short."

"We have work to do before go-live tomorrow," Elliot said. "And I'm sure Fallyn has her own work to get to. Videos to edit. Preparing to find what we missed." There was no malice in his voice. Or much of any emotion at all.

I could push back. Point out he was doing this to keep his distance from her. That wouldn't make the situation better. "He's right." I couldn't hide my wince on the words, and there was no hiding that I didn't believe them. "I need to get back to my computer." I stood and grasped her fingertips. "Fallyn, it was a lot of fun. I'll see you more this week?"

Her smile was shy. Nothing like on camera but just as alluring. "Count on it."

I said my farewells to Elliot, warned him quietly to be nice, and headed home.

We did work the rest of the day. It was amazing how many little things there were to do before a game went live, even though it had been open for early access for a few weeks.

Monday morning we were back in the office like the weekend had never happened. Except the pleasant memories still rang in my thoughts, and a giddy anticipation hummed under my skin that I'd see Fallyn again. I'd be lynched if nearly anyone in the office knew I was having thoughts like that.

I was in Elliot's office, talking through some next steps. A sign hung next to his whiteboard with a silhouette of Fallyn from her video thumbnails. The text across it said *Hours Since a Phallusies Attack*, and it had a counter on it. She called her channel Fallyn's Phallusies, and yes, we kept a countdown of how long it had last been since she roasted our game.

The sign hit me differently today than it had in the past, and I wasn't sure how I felt about it. Fallyn would probably laugh it off. I hoped she would, anyway.

Nigel walked in, waited the few seconds it took for us to look up in acknowledgement, and closed the door behind himself.

Odd.

"How's your houseguest?" Nigel asked.

I looked between him and Elliot. "He knows?"

"She called him when I wouldn't let her in," Elliot said.

"For hotel recommendations," Nigel added quickly. "She didn't sic me on anyone."

I knew there was more to that story.

"I assume you've already checked in with her." Elliot looked at Nigel.

"She told me she was safe and such. I was looking for your side of the story."

With a blank expression and a dismissive wave, Elliot turned back to his monitor. "She's fine."

Nigel looked at me.

Fortunately, the answer was easy. "She really is. Great last time I heard." She was so amazing. How was I smitten already?

"With that smile, no details, please." Nigel seemed to relax. "Are you telling anyone?"

In the office? That seemed like a really bad idea, though if we talked to her at all at RinCon it might be hard to hide that we knew her.

Elliot shook his head. "No. I'd appreciate it if you kept it under wraps too."

"For Link, but not for you." Nigel and Elliot could produce almost as much friction between them as Elliot and Fallyn.

"And also because we don't need that kind of tension in the office. Especially this week," I added.

Elliot and Nigel agreed on *that* at least.

This launch meant so much to everyone. It was one of the biggest milestones in my life. Other people had engagements and weddings and babies… This game meant that much to me, as had the last two I saw launched with fledgling companies.

We'd poured the last six years of our lives into making sure this was the best game we could produce, the last year watching select people play it, and today at ten in the morning, we were going to let the world have at it.

It was nerve-wracking and thrilling.

At about ten minutes before launch, Judith, the company owner, joined Elliot in his office. Which meant this was about to happen. For real. It was actually coming.

At five minutes to, every speaker phone in the office beeped, which equated to an off-kilter kind of tone echoing through every room.

Everyone in the dev room put their phones on speaker, and I assumed most of the rest of the crew did too. We hadn't talked about this as an office, but it seemed appropriate. We'd all sweated and bled together, we should count the game launch down together as well.

"I'm going to make this short." Judith's voice overlapped itself through the entire room, making her into her own backup announcer. "It doesn't matter if you've been here since the Cord days, if you've come on in the last year, or somewhere in between. If you're here today, be proud of yourself. Regardless of what happens next, we've already set records, broken barriers, and told the industry they're a bunch of stodgy old fucks and we know where the future is."

"Of course, what happens next is going to be even more incredible than what we've already seen." Elliot stepped in.

Was Judith smiling at that? She didn't do so often, mostly because she had a reputation to uphold, but I'd bet money she was in Elliot's office grinning. "Last call to tell us *no go*," she said. "Art?"

"Go." That was Phillip.

"Music?" she asked.

Brandon was in the office for this. It didn't matter that he was a consultant these days—he'd still earned this. "Go."

"Story?" At this point, Judith's going down the list was more symbolic than anything. No one was going to pull the plug.

"Go," Sonya said.

"QA?"

That was Nigel. "Go."

"Security?"

There was a pause.

"Luna? Danny?" Judith sounded concerned.

"Stop," Danny's whisper wasn't quiet when it was broadcast on every phone in the office.

Luna's giggle was infectious, and I'd fight anyone who said otherwise. "I'm kidding. We're a go."

"Thank you." Amusement tempered the edge in Judith's voice. "And last, but never least… Development?"

"Go." Elliot made the single word, two letters, one syllable, sound like the most potent invention in existence.

I swore a collective breath-holding rolled through the office. The seconds that ticked away on the clock were agonizing.

As the hand slipped closer to ten, Elliot spoke up again, "Ten. Nine. Eight. Seven. Six. Five. Four, Three."

This was really happening.

"Two."

Did it feel different from the other times?

"One."

Yes. It was so much better.

"*Go.*" Elliot would be pressing that last button he

needed to make our landing page live, as he spoke.

The phones stayed on, but everyone was focused on their computers. I didn't have to see to know that was true because I knew my colleagues.

"Server usage is pegged," Luna said.

"Bandwidth at max." That was Danny.

Status reports continued to flow in from everyone who was monitoring. There was extra pressure going live days before RinCon. Launching a few days early gave us time to make sure that the kinks were worked out before the show. That the queues had evened out.

But that everything was still maxed. That the buzz had shifted from *I can't log in* to *I don't want to log off*.

Of course, if the game crashed and burned, we'd hate the bad press. But we'd also spin it to our advantage. That was one of many things Dustin did exceptionally well. He'd learned from the best, and now he was the best. The student had become the master and all that.

Everyone hung up their phones. For the next several hours, half of us worked to optimize and correct and make sure the game didn't completely crash, and the other half tested any minor tweaks before they went live.

This was what happened when a game opened for the first time, if it had any good buzz at all. Everyone lined up to play, no one could get in right away unless they got really lucky, and servers and information pipelines got clogged until they were ready to burst.

But we kept it all online. The only reason anyone got up from their desks was to pee. Ivan, our office manager, made sure we had plenty of coffee, water, and whatever.

A little after two, Elliot emerged from his office. "Pizza in the break room. Go grab some, Team Beta, then Team Quail, and Team Starburst last. Everyone eats. No one spills on their keyboards."

A few of the team grumbled, and a couple more said *Okay, Dad.*

Yeah, it was tense in here, but it wasn't a bad kind of tension. I did love this place. By four in the afternoon, we'd balanced the load on the servers, and the game had stayed online, aside from a few individual channel crashes that we recovered from quickly.

A collective relief seeped into the air.

A murmur started on one side of the room, but I couldn't tell about what. Until my phone chimed with a new alert. Fallyn had posted a new video.

She wouldn't. Not today. It had nothing to do with us, I was sure of it.

Except the caption was *AcesSpayed? Why ET Howard's New Game is Totally Not Broken.*

A wave of protective fury sped through me.

She did. *Fuck.*

elliot

The adrenaline of an incredible game day launch spilled through me. I didn't need more Red Bull, but I was drinking another one anyway. It was going to be a long night, and excitement would only keep me wired for so long.

When Link walked into my office, I grinned. "What do you think?"

"We need to talk." His somber tone and expression were the opposite of what I expected.

"What's up?"

He closed the door.

I hated that. "Are you going to dump me?" I teased.

"No." Link almost cracked a smile. "But…"

"Don't do that. Whatever this is, get to the point." I could make up a billion scenarios in my head, but that was what we had Creatives for.

"Fallyn has a new video."

Oh. Fuck. Only a small portion of her videos were about our game, but there was no reason for Link to act this way if this wasn't related to us. I was already clicking through on my phone. "Let's see it, then."

AcesSpayed? Why ET Howard's New Game is Totally Not Broken.

Goodie. I was the topic of her video. Those were my favorite.

Totally not.

Her face appeared in the thumbnail, her hair in purple and black pigtails and a too-tight T-shirt with the neck cut into a V. Which made her look both sweet and seductive at the same time. Not a lie, and not that I gave a fuck.

"In case you hadn't heard, our old friend E.T. Howard has a new game out this week." Her video started with her doing an exaggerated, cockney version of her British accent, and bled into her real voice. "Is it today? It's today."

I might love that she tended to give me credit for the entire game, but the credit she gave me was never complimentary.

"And your favorite, most overpowered character, Jarlett Scohansson, is here for release day domination." Fallyn had a character she'd been building up since the start of beta. It didn't matter how many times we reset the servers, or that we'd threatened to just wipe her character, she always brought Jarlett back.

For the next half hour, Fallyn's video was a combination of insulting *ET*'s intelligence, pretending I demanded virgin sacrifices to make my evil games, and anime memes interspersed with Jarlett becoming so powerful she could explode and destroy everyone within a city by walking into it.

"I thought we fixed this." Obviously the video hadn't been made today, but she was releasing it now… The longer I watched, the higher my blood pressure rose. The more my fury skyrocketed.

My phone rang, and Kittie's number—Fallyn's number—popped up over the video. I ignored it.

I dialed Dustin on my desk phone while a chibi character made an obscene face over some in-game destruction. "I need you to send a takedown on a video," I said as soon as he answered.

"Fallyn?"

"Who else?"

He sighed. "I won't do it. She never breaks the rules, and we don't need her telling her audience we issued strikes against her. Not today." He clipped off the words. "Anything else?"

I snarled at the receiver, but his answer didn't surprise me. "No."

The line went dead.

"What now?" Link asked from where he was watching over my shoulder.

I didn't know. I couldn't think past the rage. I was used to this from her, but after this weekend—

The video stopped. I hit *Refresh* and the black screen told me *This content is currently unavailable.*

I stared at the screen, processing. Or rather, not wanting to. The anger that simmered inside wasn't productive right now, but I could bottle it for use later.

I am so sorry. The text was from Fallyn.

Fuck that. I deleted it without responding.

Link made a half-grunt, half-sigh and moved into view again.

"Do *not* defend her." I looked him in the eye. "I need you to have my back on this." It wasn't just the video. It was how cold it was. How many times she pulled my name into things. Had she done this before? Of course. Why did I think…?

Nothing had changed, and I never should have expected otherwise for a second.

"I'm with you on this." Link looked somber. Almost angry.

I wanted to look her in the eye when I talked to her, but I wasn't walking away from launch day for a petty fight. "I need to take a walk. Make a call. Come with me?" I said to Link.

He nodded.

We headed down to the street, and picked an empty spot in the currently unoccupied loading dock of the building next door. The sun had dipped behind the mountains already, and there was a bite in the air, but I didn't care.

I called Fallyn back on Facetime, and was a little surprised when she answered.

"I'm so sorry." The apology was clear in her eyes and her voice.

And I didn't buy it for a second. "Bullshit. If you were sorry, you wouldn't have posted it. Especially not today."

"I meant to cancel it. Or at least edit the scheduled video. It slipped my mind."

I glanced at Link. His expression was flat. That should have her more concerned than me being pissed off. "It's release day. What were you think—"

"There's no such thing as bad press," she talked over me. "It was meant to drive up game traffic."

I fucking hated that phrase. Scott spouted it from here until eternity, and even Dustin had made it a mantra, but that didn't mean I had to agree.

"So this was altruistic on your part?" Link asked.

Fallyn shook her head, making her twin braids bobble and jerk on the tiny screen. "No. It was completely a selfish business decision. It keeps the game I love online, and the hits I get from the keywords…"

"You humiliated us." I didn't mean to phrase things that way. Damn it. I needed to get myself under control.

Her brows were furrowed and her gaze downcast. "I reminded more people you exist. Scott McAllister knew—"

The comparison was a fantastic way to make me angrier. Not that I had any problems with Scott— I'd known him longer than almost anyone. Was a few years younger than him when we were in high school together. Even he'd be upset about something like this, he just wouldn't let the public see it.

But I wasn't Scott.

"We had so much fun this weekend," Link said.. "And now… this?" There was a sharp edge to his hurt, and if that was showing through, what he was hiding was far worse.

She'd pissed off the unflappable, always sunny Link. That took talent.

"I'm sorry. I really am." She repeated. "I meant to pull it…"

"But you scheduled it for today in the first place." This was part of the underlying problem. It wasn't as though making the video was a mistake. She didn't trip and fall and her tits hit the keyboard to create thirty minutes of *ET Howard* jokes set to anime memes, and then accidentally schedule it to go live exactly six hours after our game did.

Fallyn shrugged. "But now that I'm getting to know you…"

"What? Things have changed? Nothing's changed."

Her expression shifted. Or the connection out

here was bad. "No? Oh, right. Because *no emotions*. That was one of your rules, wasn't it?"

Of course she was going to bring the sex into this. But Link mentioned the personal things first. Still... "So if you hadn't met us this weekend, it would've been okay to post the video? You wouldn't be sorry now?" Stupid question. Of course it was okay because she'd done it.

Fallyn didn't answer.

I wanted to rip out my hair, or yell, or rage and throw things. If we were still in my office, I'd yank that *Days Since...* sign off my wall, and hurl it out a window. "Well?"

"Don't you dare demand I say anything." She was being belligerent? Now?

"I deserve an answer."

She scoffed. "I don't owe you that. I already told you what I was thinking, and me phrasing it a different way won't change anything. I also said I was sorry. Multiple times."

"But you're only sorry because the sex was good."

Fallyn stared at me through the screen. A second ticked away, and then two. "You're so fucking full of yourself."

"You were full of me too, and weren't complaining two nights ago." And now I was keeping it personal. This had all gone downhill. But I didn't see how any of that was my fault.

"I didn't come all the way out here to be your doll. I hopped on that plane to see if I clicked with the guys I'd met online, and maybe to face a few fears about crowds."

I was done with this conversation. Done with the circular argument and Fallyn's bullshit apology, and I wanted to hurt her. "The only thing that clicks about us is how much fun it is for us to fuck each other. You just do it differently than I do."

More silence, and she clenched her jaw. Was she going to hang up? "That's about what I'd expect coming from an emotionless void."

"Okay." There were far worse things she could've called me. Of course, going for the one thing I'd called myself during one of those late-night conversations of ours didn't seem super creative, but, "What you think doesn't matter."

"If that were true, you wouldn't care about my videos."

I hated that she was right. "What would your followers say if they knew who Kittie was in real life?" I was continuing to keep this personal, and couldn't find the desire to stop.

"I'm as much Fallyn as I am Kittie. You're the only one who seems to have a problem recognizing that. And I can embrace my inner bitch in real life if I need to. I can fake it till I make it. You, on the other hand, are a cold, uncaring fuck, and when love finally bites you in the ass, it will destroy you."

What? Where the fuck…? "I've chosen not to fall in love."

"That's not a thing. Either you love or you don't. It's not something you pick."

I had no idea why this was our tangent, but no backing down. I was single, I was detached, I had hold of my own heart, because I wanted to. "Bet me."

Link coughed. I glanced at him, but he had his jaw clenched tight.

"A bet comes with clear goals. There's an end game, or there are no winners or losers," Fallyn said.

I didn't lose. "The end game is whoever comes out on top at the end of your trip." On top of what? What was I doing?

Not backing down, because fuck her. I was right.

"*Fine.* Before I leave, I can make you fall in love, Mr. I-Choose-to-be-a-Calloused-Asshole."

My barking laugh slipped out. "Fall in love with *you*?"

"With me."

Yeah. No. "Fine. Because you can't. I will make you realize that Bitchy Fallyn—your online persona —is not a good end goal. You do *not* want to be her."

"Because you prefer submissive, docile Kittie, who only exists for you and purrs just because you offered your lap?" Her retort dripped with scorn.

"If that's what you think I want instead, you've already lost."

"Fine. It's a bet." An easy one on my part, because I already knew she didn't like embracing her online self in real life, she just thought she should for some reason. And I already knew I didn't like her.

"What are the stakes?"

"They're in the bet. If I fall, you get to break my heart. But when you realize you're running your show wrong, I get to see you choke on the truth when you admit it to your audience."

Fallyn shook her head. "Not gonna happen. Who's the judge in this pointless contest?"

I looked at Link.

"No," Fallyn said. "He's *your* friend."

"You'll never meet anyone more impartial." Though I hoped at the end of the day he'd side with me, one of the things I adored about Link was he was fair. And it didn't matter because I wouldn't lose.

"I'm in," Link agreed.

Fallyn pursed her lips and puffed out her cheeks and for a heartbeat, she looked adorably vulnerable.

Which I already knew didn't matter.

"Fine. Bet's on," she said.

**8 /
fallyn**

I didn't mean to tumble down that path with Elliot.

I didn't mean to drag up things he'd told me in confidence, or go for what I hoped would hurt him the most. When I said I was sorry, I meant it.

But years of dealing with internet trolls, of men telling me I was too loud or too obnoxious or would look better with their cocks in my mouth, or worse, and I had learned certain responses. One of them was *hurt them more than they hurt you.*

So, yeah. I fucked up not taking down the video before it went live, and I fucked up again getting sucked into that argument with Elliot, and now I was going to deal with the consequences. If I could talk this through with him in person, would it be better?

I was staying in the house in his backyard, it felt like I should at least have some sort of conversation with him. I tried to keep an eye and ear out for any sign of him coming home, but would he tonight? With the game being live, would he be in the office until late?

Would he simply find a way to avoid me, even if he came home?

I was trying not to stare out the window at Elliot's back porch, when his patio door slid open. My heart skipped and my stomach plummeted, and both relaxed in disappointment when an older woman stepped outside with King on a leash.

She was the same woman I'd seen do this multiple times today. Perhaps it was time I stop being a creepy lurker and go introduce myself.

I yanked on shoes and a coat, and tried to both hurry and look casual strolling outside. She looked up when I opened the cottage door, and I smiled and waved. "Mrs. Ria?"

She smiled warmly. "It's Elephtheria, you may call me Ria. Elliot told me about you. Fallyn?" Her accent was distinct, but her English was clean.

"That's me. Hi." I extended my hand.

She pulled me into a hug instead. "I'm so glad you're here. Elliot talked about you for days before you arrived."

He had? I doubted he'd be doing much more of that, but I'd take the compliment for what it was worth. "Do you know if he'll be back tonight?"

"Probably not, I'm sorry." Ria shook her head.

I crouched to give King some attention. "It's okay. Does that mean you'll stay the whole night?"

"I will. It's nothing to worry about, though. I have a good book and a brave guard dog."

King barked, as if he recognized her words, and tried to run circles around my leg.

"Careful, Puppy." I unwound myself from his leash, surprised I didn't trip.

"I'll tell Elliot you asked about him," Ria said.

I shook my head. "Please don't worry about it. I'll talk to him when he's not so busy. And I should let you get back into the warm house."

"You know where to find me if you need anything, dear." She squeezed my hand, and headed into the main house.

I headed back inside, and I was surprised to hear a knock a few hours later. Ria was back, offering me a plate of moussaka. I thanked her profusely, and enjoyed the dinner.

If things didn't get better with Elliot and Link, at least I'd made one friend while I was here. Two if I counted King.

Tuesday, I stayed in the guesthouse and worked on videos for games that didn't belong to ET Howard, as well as editing any reference to Elliot out of the video that had gone up yesterday, and reposting it with no fanfare.

If I were home, Tuesday nights would be when

I'd meet Puff and Archer in the game. We'd planned to play tonight in person, all of us in the same room, but I didn't suspect I was still welcome for that. Still, I had to log on and see if either of them would join me.

I waited for more than an hour before I decided that no, I wasn't going to be seeing their digital forms tonight.

Outside, the moon lit the snow and sent shadows spilling from trees. It would look gorgeous out there with just a few lights and decorations. Maybe I'd have some time to go see the local lights while I was here, but I'd probably be doing it alone. Maybe I could call Megan, see if she wanted to show me around town. Were we that kind of friends?

A weird popping sound echoed through the walls. What was that? I strained my ears, but didn't hear it again.

The light on the snow outside my window changed, drawing my attention. Elliot stepped out with King on a leash. Could I talk to him? See if it was possible to make this right, now that he'd had a chance to cool down? As with last night, I dressed quickly to run outside and catch him.

Unlike last night, with Ria, the instant he saw me, he turned and walked in the other direction.

"Elliot, wait. Please?"

He kept walking toward the front of the house.

Damn it.

I headed back to the guest cottage, my heart and limbs feeling heavy. When I stepped inside, the carpet squished under my feet.

What the...? I rested a hand on the wall to steady myself and see what was going on. Icy cold wetness met my palm. The carpet was soaked, and the walls were leaking.

Either Elliot's guest house was haunted, or a pipe had burst. Fuck.

I ran back up to the main home and hammered on the rear door as hard as I could without breaking the glass.

Seconds later, running footsteps sounded behind me, and I spun, startled to see Elliot sprinting toward me, with King hot on his heels. "What's wrong?" His question was breathless rather than angry.

"My house—your house—is leaking. I think a pipe broke." I gestured toward the guest house.

"Fuck. Water shut off is—" Elliot gave his head a quick shake. He pushed the back door open a few inches. "Easier for me to find. Tell Mrs. Ria. Get your stuff into the main house before it gets ruined." He didn't wait for me to respond; he was already running toward another part of the yard.

I found Ria inside, and explained the situation

to her. She reacted just as quickly. Within moments, she and I were hauling my luggage and computer into the house, and stacking everything on and around the dining room table.

"What about the furniture in there? The rugs?" I asked her.

"Not important." Elliot seemed to come out of nowhere. "Are your things safe?"

I didn't want to get hung up on the concern in his voice, but it was impossible for me to ignore. "Yes."

"Good." He clipped off the word, and like he'd been rebooted, his face went blank. "Mrs. Ria, can I talk to you for a minute?"

She nodded and followed him to a few feet away.

I didn't want to eavesdrop, but it wasn't as though they'd left the room, and I was curious to know what kind of secrets he felt like he had to keep from me. I caught snippets of what he said that sounded like, "Make sure she can replace anything if her things were damaged" and "Put it on my card. That's fine."

Without so much as another glance at me, he turned and walked from the room.

Ria joined me again, and grabbed my garment bag. "Let's get you situated in a real room."

"Thank you." I followed her further into the

house, away from the stairs leading up to Elliot's room.

So much for talking things out with him. I felt both less and more isolated than ever, being inside, but still being so far away from him.

fallyn

Despite the fact that I was staying in Elliot's house, he managed to avoid me the rest of Tuesday night and Wednesday. I didn't know if it was on purpose or if it was because he was busy with work and RinCon prep, but I suspected it was a bit of both.

Ria was wonderful, though. She seemed happy to have breakfast and lunch ready for me, and King didn't mind that I took him out to walk and play several times.

When the first day of RinCon arrived, my stomach was butterflies and acid. The quad shot vanilla latte with extra whip that I had for breakfast, that I washed down with a heavy helping of absolutely nothing else, probably wasn't helping.

But I was going to do this convention thing, the way I'd planned, with or without any support from Puff69 or Archer, and I was going to rock my public persona like no one knew. Elliot could choke on my bald cunt.

I had an outfit for every day. They were all a combination of simple to transport, and cutely revealing. The three of them were laid out on the bed in Elliot's guest room, taunting me. Why did I think I could wear any of these, especially in 30-degree temps?

Because I could. And I would.

I grabbed the red and black *kitty*. It was the only outfit that wasn't based on a popular game character, but it *was* a cat, because I was Demon Kittie. A tiny voice whispered in the back of my mind that I was only picking this one today because I was least likely to run into Elliot or Link today.

That was ridiculous. They could see me in any of these. I didn't care what they thought, or that I might remind them of what we'd shared.

I tugged everything on. Black and red striped leggings, covered by a black and red tutu that only came a quarter of the way down my thighs. The furry bikini top looked loose, but used a swimsuit top as a base, so it would stay in place, even though it covered my boobs and nothing else. I completed the whole look with ears that matched the top, furry boots that came halfway up to my knees, and red lens sunglasses with gold rims.

The only mirror in this place was the one above the bathroom sink, so I had to use my cameras to get a good view of myself. As I spun in front of the webcam on my laptop, and watched the screen, I had to admit I looked pretty adorable. I'd fuck me.

Maybe I wanted Elliot and Link to find me after all. See what they were missing out on.

Nope. Didn't care. If Elliot was going to continue to be a right stubborn arse, I was going to break his heart, and figure out how to be Bad-Ass Bitch Fallyn all the time, not just online.

I yanked my coat over my outfit, requested an Uber, and walked down to the main road to wait. I'd heard Elliot leave early this morning, the same way he did yesterday, and I didn't have any reason to emerge from my room and see him off.

My driver didn't seem in the mood to make small talk, and that was fine with me. I got to the convention center long before the show started because I wanted to ease myself into the crowds, and my media pass let me in early.

There were a lot of industry professionals scurrying around when I walked in the building. Some I recognized from my work. Others, it was clear what they were doing from the hand trucks and pallets they were pushing around. When I saw Link walking toward me, my stomach did a disconcerting little swan dive into my shoes.

He didn't meet my gaze as he approached, and while he didn't strike me as the kind of guy who would ignore me, I wasn't taking that chance. I summoned my next boost of boldness for the day and stepped in his path. "Hey."

"Hey." His smile was thin.

That was disheartening. If he were with any co-workers, I wouldn't dare approach him. Given how Elliot reacted to me, I didn't suspect they'd be any better. "Can we talk?"

"Sure." He didn't sound enthusiastic, but talking was a start. He jerked his head toward one of the rooms across from the exposition hall.

I followed him into a large conference room, the only light coming from under the door. *Please let him still be the sweetheart I know online.* "I know you heard it a few days ago, but—"

"You're sorry. I get it."

I frowned. How was I supposed to explain myself enough to make this right?

"We've worked hard on this game. For more than six years, we've poured our souls into it. Monday was our day." There was an underlying passion in Link's words that his cool demeanor couldn't mask.

"I know. I'm..." *Sorry.* But Elliot was right about one thing—I did it on purpose. What they saw, the video, was my brand. My living. "Did you work with Chloe and Jordan at Rinslet?"

Link's scowl was terrifying. Not because I thought he'd hurt me, but I had a feeling it wasn't an expression he wore often. "I did," he said.

"You know who they were in public." They had faced the internet's love of gossip head-on, and embraced it. They were brash and bold in public, they never shied away from a story, and they kept Rinslet in the spotlight in the best-worst possible way.

"I also know who they are in private." Link didn't look impressed with my statement.

I fucked up taking the bait when Elliot called the other night. Things got out of control when I made the bet. Apparently, Elliot could push buttons I didn't know I had. But even when Link was being guarded, he was listening. I just had to say this right. "That's my point. I'm not her. I'm not the woman in the videos. But I need her to exist for the image I've built up."

"But you want to be her. You bet Elliot that very thing."

"I don't want there to be such a stark difference. Online Fallyn can do and say things I would die before I did in public, and I don't like that fear." Was I telling him too much? This almost stranger? But he wasn't really a stranger, and I couldn't stop. "I'm not a heartless cunt, though. She's a persona, and mean girls get clicks. I promise you I'm not mean. I have limits. There are things about your games I bring to you instead of posting them online. I've been working with Nigel for months…" I wasn't a bad person.

"And Elliot isn't a soulless corporate asshole with a face but no heart."

I cringed. "Are you sure?"

That was a thought I maybe should've kept to myself.

"I know what you do. I wouldn't be this kind of upset, if he hadn't been in the video. You shit on him on our big day. Don't say it wasn't personal, because his name and face were all over that video." As Link talked, passion bled into his words.

He cared, and I was on the wrong side of that. *Fuck.* "I was going to edit him out." That was true. It had just slipped my mind. "I meant to repost without the references to him." Why was it so important that Link wasn't mad at me? "Please. Give me a chance to prove to you who I am. I fucked up. People fuck up. Elliot's never made a mistake?"

Link clenched his jaw.

"Please?"

He shook his head. "I don't forgive you for the video, but I also don't hate you. I could still go either way."

Relief burst inside, and I hugged him. Oh, crap. Did I really just do that? I stepped back, head ducked. "Sorry."

Looking up, I saw a faint smile ghost across his face. "It's okay," he said. "But Fallyn?"

If I spoke, would I lose this concession?

"Don't break Elliot. And don't let him break you. I'll step in if I have to, and no one wants that."

I had no idea what that meant, but I wasn't interested in finding out. "Okay."

Link left, and I stayed in the room a little longer, collecting myself. Would I need to take breaks all day long to psych myself out, for dealing with crowds? I hoped not.

I headed into the convention, and as the number of people around me built, then surged, I was okay. This was what I expected, and the energy in the place was so high, the excitement from everyone wanting to be here, that I couldn't help but feed off it.

I was here. I was part of one of the biggest industry events in existence. *Holy shit.* Right before the doors opened, and the show officially kicked off, I found myself a spot with a great view of the line of people about to come swarming in, and started a livestream.

The instant my camera kicked on, that moment I was *live*, a switch flipped in my head like it always did. My smile brightened, and my anxiety faded behind my mask. "Hey, all. Fallyn here, streaming live from…" I swung the camera around, arm held above my head, to give a shot of everything. "I'm about to spend the next few days getting sneak peeks and first looks at all the hottest upcoming games and tech, so if you want the inside scoop, and maybe a little more, make sure you have your alerts turned on. I don't want to miss anything this weekend, and neither do you."

Clip over. That would be enough to keep people hanging on. Not that I left them there long. The next several hours were a run-together blend of me not knowing where to look first, recording anything I was allowed, and going live every time I saw something I had to share *right now*.

On top of that, people recognized me. They wanted to tell me they liked me. They wanted pictures with me, and hugs, and signatures.

People wanted me to sign things. With my name.

It was all incredible, but by the time the day was half over, I was looking for some quiet. That same room Link had shown me to earlier was empty. The sign on the door said *Staff Only*, but no one stopped me from walking in, and the quiet was blessed.

I stood in the mostly dark, collecting myself again and just breathing. This was so much fun, but it was also way more than I was used to.

"I like the outfit." Elliot's words hit my back, startling me. Before I could whirl, his hands were on my hips. "It shows off some of your best assets."

How was I supposed to react? Nearly anyone else, and I'd jerk away and be looking for the easiest, least confrontational exit. Yet, after two days of him pointedly avoiding me in his own house, all I could think about when he touched me was the last time he'd done the same. That night I arrived. How it felt to be pinned under him in his room. To be controlled by him.

I wanted to yield, but I didn't want to cave. "Are we still on?"

For the bet.

"Damn straight. Rules of sex still the same?"

The ones we'd established the other night. Before everything fell apart. Why would those still be on the table?

Because I still wanted him. "Yes."

"Good." Elliot nipped the edge of my ear with his teeth.

Fuck, that was delicious. It also told me exactly how I needed to act. I would swallow the part of me that wanted this entire clash to vanish, and I would prove to him that I was right—I was better off being bold and brash, and he wasn't as in control of his heart as he pretended.

Fortunately, if my goal was to make him fall in love, I still got to be meek and submissive to a point. As long as I remembered that wasn't my final destination. "So, you see me wearing fewer clothes than normal, and that means I'm here for you to use?"

"No." His answer came without hesitation. "You could be fully clothed or wearing nothing, and I'd feel the same. I think because you want me to help you live your fantasies of being fucked in public, that you're here for me to use."

"Mmm…. You say the most arrogant things." I ground into him. "Tell me more about what an asshole you are."

Elliot pressed a hand to my throat and his chest to my back. My terror returned—the pulse-pounding fear I felt the other night—and it was blended with just as potent a desire.

"No, I don't think I will." Elliot teased a hand up my bare stomach. When he brushed the bottom of my breast, my heart flipped in an entirely new way, and when he slid under the fur bikini top, to lightly brush my nipple, my core clenched in response.

I didn't have the words to argue. *Stop*, that was all I had to say. But I didn't want to. The way he was teasing felt so good. Was that wrong?

"Here's the thing." Elliot's breath was hot on my neck. "I don't think any less of you because you're letting me do this."

I was going to dream specifically about that sensation. And how did his words make this hotter? It wasn't a sexy thing to say. "You could think less of me?"

"Oh, Fallyn." His voice rumbled through my back, and the way my name growled off his tongue was intoxicating. "I could think so much less of you. But the bar is lower than it was a week ago." He slid his hand down my stomach and over my skirt, to lightly brush my pussy through the fabric of my leggings.

This was incredible and wrong and I was already wet enough to soak my panties. I didn't know where that line was between *bad ass bitch* and being compliant enough to seduce Elliot, but I was pretty sure I couldn't do both. I was also pretty sure if he kept this up, I was going to lose this round.

And I wasn't even upset about it. "Your point is?"

Elliot pressed against me harder. Rubbing with enough intensity I felt it *everywhere*. He tightened his grip on my throat. "My point is, I'm not going to make you come because I think you're an object to be used. I'm going to do it because I know you want it. Because you've told me you want it. Because good girls get off, and I like the sounds you make when you do."

The way he stroked my clit… The crass, egotistical words… The precision of his grip and his fingers digging into my clit through layers of fabric, had me close to climax.

"Tell me to stop or tell me you want to come." He didn't ease up, but he didn't dig in harder either.

There were so many voices outside. People right there. Anyone could walk in on us at any minute. It would destroy his career. It would be worse for mine.

My fear was sweet on my tongue the way it mingled with my need.

"Pick one." Elliot lightened his pressure, but not a lot.

Wait. Come back. Please. "I want to come."

Elliot pressed into my clit harder, stroking and letting me grind to get the right angle. This was incredible. Pleasure mounted inside, surging then ebbing, growing stronger the more he worked me over. I couldn't hear anything over the roar of my pulse in my ears, and my heart was about to hammer out of my chest.

I dug my fingers tighter into his arm, needing him to hold me up. Needing—

Fuck. I bit the inside of my cheek when I came, to keep from crying out. A copper taste hit my tongue, and I didn't care. I was consumed by orgasm, and the rest of the world paled in comparison to the rainbow splash that flooded me.

As the sensation faded, Elliot eased up, but he didn't pull away. He held me until my legs stopped shaking. He helped me steady myself against the wall.

And then his touch was gone, its absence followed by another door in the room opening and closing a few seconds later.

I'd never actually seen him.

But *fuck* I was going to remember this for a long time, and not for bad reasons.

When I regained my footing, I pushed away from the wall and headed back into the throngs of the crowd. My face was still hot. Could anyone tell what I'd just done by looking at me? I might soak through my leggings soon, so a stop in the bathroom was in order. Thankfully, there wasn't a line. I grabbed a handful of paper towels, wet a couple, and headed into an open stall to clean myself up,

How was that entire exchange with Elliot supposed to change my mind or help him win? And why was I more conflicted than ever about him? He came across as cold. Removed. Not the kind of guy whose opinions I'd trust for much of anything.

But if I was looking for someone I trusted to get me off, and leave me alone the rest of the time, he was at the top of my list. How weird was that? He and Link were the first men I'd ever been with who didn't make me feel like they'd take it from me even if I told them to stop.

Experience insisted it didn't matter what a man said—sex and love were intertwined. If he was coming back for more, and I was enjoying the results, doing more of the same seemed like the perfect way to make him fall for me. I was going to embrace Bad-ass Bitch Fallyn, who didn't care if she left a casualty at the side of the road.

I finished up, and made my way into the con again. The food was overpriced and I'd never pay so much for it if I weren't here, but for some reason cheap pizza hit the spot. Then it was back to work-plus-fun.

I was heading from the exhibitor hall to one of the developer panels, when I heard someone call my name. Not unusual, it'd been happening all day. I spun to find a man *right there*.

"Fallyn." He grinned. "Hi."

"Hello." So far most people had been friendly, even the awkward ones, so I could return the favor.

He stepped closer, and my back hit a pillar. "I'm a huge fan of your show."

"Thanks." I tried to move to the side, to put more space between us, and he angled his body. Now I was pinned between him, the pillar, and the escalator. "Did you want a picture or something?"

His expression darkened. "No. I just wanted to meet you. Hey, do you want to get lunch? I'm buying."

"I just ate, thanks." Why wasn't anyone interrupting us? We were surrounded by people and no one cared.

He frowned. "Oh. Okay. Maybe coffee then?"

This felt very different than with Elliot. This made bile rise in my throat, and if I dropped to my knees and crawled away, would that help? Should I push him? He was more than a foot taller than me. I didn't know how that would be effective.

I very much did not like this.

After I talked to Fallyn, I stayed at the convention center long enough to make sure the booth was set up, and headed back to the offices. Most of the staff was doing a lot of double duty, rotating between the show and the game. Everyone had a say in where they went, but most of us chose both to keep our minds fresh.

It didn't matter if I was helping move tables into place on the convention center floor, or fixing bugs, the exchange with Fallyn never left my mind.

I didn't want to be mad at her. I wanted to find that same connection I had with her—with Kittie—in the game. But that wasn't an option if I couldn't trust her, and what she'd done…

I was returning to the convention center to take my turn working as *security* for the booth. Which really meant that those of us on duty stood around with looks that said *behave or else*.

A familiar voice reached my ears, though I couldn't quite place it. But the second one was distinctly Fallyn. I followed the sounds to find her literally with her back to the wall, talking to Bryce. I'd worked with Bryce for years, first at Rinslet and then at AcesPlayed. His specialty was digital security, and we'd thought he was one of us.

Judith fired him a few years ago, because he used the excuse of working on a game with sex in it to let his predator side show through. We'd discovered he was using his access to beta applications to stalk some of the female players.

And now he had Fallyn pinned in a corner, and she looked very much like she didn't want to be there.

"Bryce, hey." I made sure my voice carried over the crowds, not just for him to hear, but everyone around us. "I'm surprised they let you in." As I reached them, I maneuvered myself between the two of them.

Bryce took several steps back. His scowl was priceless. "Anyone can buy a ticket."

"Anyone can have their ticket revoked, as well." Out of the corner of my eye, I saw Fallyn move further away, but not out of earshot.

"We were just talking. You know who she is, don't you?" The way Bryce squared his shoulders, stood taller, was probably supposed to intimidate me.

It didn't. "Does it matter who she is if she doesn't want to talk to you?"

"Of course she wants to."

"I don't." Fallyn's voice was tiny.

This fucking asshole. "Problem solved," I said. "You can go about the show, knowing she's done with the conversation, or I can find security and have them keep you from returning."

Where Bryce's fingers dug into his crossed arms, pale indentations appeared. I held his gaze, not blinking.

He flinched first. "I'm good." He turned away.

"Thank you," Fallyn said softly, when Bryce was gone.

I wanted to stay and chat, as much as I shouldn't. She looked even better in her outfit than I remembered from this morning, and she also looked like better company than standing around glaring at con-goers would be.

But I was on the afternoon shift with Elliot, and that was pretty tempting too. Besides… Work. "I have to get to the booth. You okay?"

"Yes." Despite the words, a frown flitted onto her face.

"Good. See you around." That felt weird in a way I didn't like, mostly the walking away part of it, but what else was I supposed to do?

I was halfway to the booth, when I saw Chloe walking in the other direction. She had started at

Cord as a writer, decades ago. Her fan-fiction of their games landed her the job. Now, she was Rinslet's Chief Marketing Officer. This was her show. She'd made it what it was, and continued to outdo herself every year.

I had nothing but respect for Chloe. I waved and gave her a warm smile. "Hey. Loving the event. Of course."

"Thanks." Her grin was bright. Her gaze darted around the room, and she fidgeted even as she stopped. "Loving the game."

"Thanks. I won't keep you, but you should know, Bryce is here."

She was familiar with both the man and our reasons for letting him go. "I assume you mention it because he might be a problem?"

"He already has been. He's not going to stop because I asked him too—He never has before."

She already had her phone out and was jabbing at the screen. "We'll revoke his pass, so he won't be able to get in again once he leaves, and if security finds him before then, we'll escort him out."

Someone called her name, and she was heading in a new direction before I could thank her.

My next task for the day awaited. I headed to our booth. Not that it was hard to find—as headliners, we were front and center in the exhibitor hall. I was surprised to see Xander standing next to Elliot, doing the *I'm imposing* thing.

Xander was a friend of Judith's, and like Elliot, he was an investor. But Xander was more of a silent partner, and he was rarely around.

I greeted him with a smile and a handshake. "Didn't expect to find you here. Well, not *here*."

"Had to see the payoff, you know?" Xander said. Which made sense. Even though he didn't work with us, he'd been here from the start. "And I'm someone who can stand-in if needed, since I don't have to go fix the game if it breaks."

I was grateful for that. I relieved him of his *security* post, and took his place with Elliot. This was a good spot to be right now. Calm. Quiet, despite the roar of the crowds around us. Despite the hectic tone in the booth. There was a pocket of chill around the two of us.

When I was younger, I had a harsher temper, and it got me in trouble. I was happier now, having learned to embrace positivity, but I was also fine with *looking* imposing as long as I didn't have to *be* imposing.

Seeing Bryce tugged me closer to anger, though. He'd cost us one of our best programmers, when he decided if she was okay with writing a game with sex in it, that she should be okay with fucking anyone who wanted her.

She'd been so intimidated by the information he dug up on her, that she hadn't told anyone why she was quitting. It was on us, on me, because I let myself believe that anything he said was as much playful as what the rest of us did. So many of us had been fucking around for so long that I didn't think twice about it when it was happening.

One of our other devs, Alys, had been the one to report him, and we put the pieces together about Cara once she did.

Bryce was out at that point, but I still got furious when I thought about the way he'd treated them, and that he was still doing so to others. I just wanted to make him feel a little of that same fear he'd projected on them—

I needed to stop, or I'd spiral into that mood. "You see Fallyn today?" Maybe not the best topic to bring up with Elliot, but it was the next thing on my mind and it was better than sinking into rage.

"Everyone has." Elliot's tone was flat, but in a forced way. "You?"

"I'm part of everyone."

"Hmm." Elliot did his best Witcher impersonation.

The clock sped toward the top of the hour, and the crowds surged as people got out of panels and headed in to see what was going on in here. The foot traffic in the booth surged to the point where we needed to step in and get people to form a line if they wanted to play the game.

When the bedlam was under control, we returned to our station.

"You talk to her?" Elliot asked.

"Yup. She apologized. Again." And she looked both adorable and fuckable, and by the way, did Elliot really need to go through with this stupid bet?

I already knew the answer—he didn't back down from anything. For some people, for me, any argument like the one he had with Fallyn was a heat of the moment thing. For him, that bet might as well be carved in stone.

"You?" I asked. As in, *you talk to her?*

He shrugged. "She didn't apologize to me. I think she got the point Monday night."

"But you talked to her."

A group of people all cosplaying as X—Rinslet's most popular character—stopped just a few feet away to let several people take their pictures. We watched. They were close enough that conversation didn't seem like a good idea.

Fallyn joined them, and I couldn't stop staring. The only acknowledgement she gave us was a quick glance in our direction.

A murmur rippled through the booth as more of our people recognized her, and died just as quickly as the group of cosplayers moved on and she went with them.

"Talked to her," Elliot said. "Felt her up in a back room. Got her off…"

Fuck me. Wasn't expecting that, but the instant he said it the images flooded my mind, and rented a space. *Hot.* Scorching even. I was saving that idea to beat my meat to later. "She return the favor?" Because that image could be the first one's neighbor.

I was half hard and should probably clear both thoughts from my mind, but I didn't want to.

"Didn't give her a chance." Elliot's reply didn't quell my desire.

I'd simply adjust the fantasy. "Bryce was harassing her."

Elliot's arm where it pressed into mine stiffened, and a glance confirmed he was standing more rigidly. Bryce had threatened Elliot's people, and he didn't stand for that. There was no question he felt at least as strongly about the situation as I did.

"They're working on ejecting him." If they hadn't already.

"Good," Elliot said.

The next few hours passed quickly, with the exhibitor's hall getting busier as people finished work and stopped in, and as panels wrapped up for the day. The last hour before the doors closed, the line to demo the game grew out of control, and Elliot and I spent most of our time handing out 'jump the main line' passes to anyone we had to turn away for the night.

When the hall doors closed, the group breathed a sigh of relief. Everyone from the office who wasn't on call had shown up, because the entire group was attending Opening Ceremonies. We were the star of the show, and Plaid Peanut Butter was playing at the end, to officially kick this event off.

Dustin had arranged for one of the Mexican food vendors to bring dinner by the booth, and for the next hour or so, we all sat wherever we could find—on the stools for people visiting the booth, Luna was perched on a folding table, on the floor—and ate and joked.

Moments like this, like the team conference call the other morning, were the ones I really lived for. The reminder of what a great family I'd found.

I glanced at Elliot, who was trading insults with Nigel and playing the part of Luna's knight in shining armor. Elliot was laughing along with everyone else. Looking incredible. Sounding fantastic.

This was perfect.

Danny and Alys had to break away—they were half of Plaid Peanut Butter. Danny was a founding member along with Reese, and Alys and Maddox had joined a few months ago, adding a new layer of sound to the band.

Dustin left to prep for the presentation that came before, and the group kind of broke up after that. Each of us drifting into our own, smaller cliques.

Two-by-two and three-by-three, we headed to the main hall. The line was still out the door, but security was seating people quickly. We didn't have to wait. A flash of our badges, and we were let in through a side entrance, to find spots near the front of the room.

I tried to avoid looking for Fallyn when we walked in, but when I caught a glimpse of black and red fuzzy ears, I couldn't help but make a mental note of their exact location.

The show started with Rinslet levels of hype. Psyching up the crowd, showing clips of our game, making sure the energy in the room was off the charts. Putting Dustin and Chloe on stage together probably made it possible to power the building off their enthusiasm.

When they introduced Plaid Peanut Butter, and the curtain behind them came up, the noise in the room reached deafening before the music even started.

Most of the band was already up there—Danny on guitar, Alys on drums, and Maddox, our newest artist on bass. But one member was conspicuously absent.

"*RinCon.*" Reese's voice carried above it all as she strolled to front and center stage. "*Are you ready to rock?*"

The response from the crowd probably broke the sound barrier, and the band lit into *Glass Slipper,* the song that had made them a viral internet sensation. Half the room, including me, sang along. I loved their music, and this song especially.

For the next hour or so, we rocked to the music on stage, and I happily lost myself in moving and screaming and singing along. They did a few covers, but most of the songs were their own.

Even Elliot was grinning most of the time.

I tried to avoid glancing into the crowds for Fallyn, but I couldn't help the occasional look. It was probably a good thing she wasn't up here with us, because the glimpses I caught, where she was lost in the music, were enthralling.

As we hit the encore, Elliot leaned close, his mouth on my ear. "Come home with me." His words barely carried over the music, and the offer sent a shiver of desire down my spine.

We rarely spent the night at each other's houses during the week, but this week none of the rules seemed to matter.

Could we reach a point where there were new rules? Where I had more with Elliot?

I shoved the thoughts away before they could become more than whispers of curiosity. No. Elliot and I didn't have that. We weren't meant to have that. We would never have that.

I was pissed when Link told me that Bryce cornered Fallyn.

Because Bryce was an asshole who cost me an incredible developer, and made life miserable for multiple people at AcesPlayed. That was the only reason, regardless of what the low growl in the back of my head, the voice that snapped *mine*, seemed to think. My reaction had nothing to do with Fallyn specifically.

It didn't matter now. The day was over, Link and I were almost to my place, the Chinese food we'd picked up smelled incredible, and we were going to unwind together.

As we were pulling into my driveway, the headlights of my car flashed across a lone figure walking up the path, and highlighted the stark red and black of Fallyn's outfit, and the coat she wore over it. She looked good in that outfit. Incredible even. And I'd be dreaming for a long time about getting her off while she wore it.

I pulled the car up next to her, and she paused, but didn't look at me. "Need a ride?" The teasing question slipped past my lips, sounding a lot more fun than whatever I'd been about to say instead.

"Hardly seems worth your time." Her voice was flat.

If she wanted to see me as an emotionless fuck, I wasn't going to oblige. I was going to let her see I had a heart, even though she'd never have any part of it. "We're hanging out. We have more than enough food. If you want to join us and say *hi* to King in the process."

"We?" She finally turned.

"Hello." Link waved from the passenger seat.

Her faint smile made part of me roar in protest, and I silenced the response.

She waved back. At him. "Hi. Sure. I could join you. But really, I'll walk. It's only a few feet away at this point."

"Suit yourself." I parked the car, and Link and I met her outside at the front door.

I let us in, and the bark that had already become familiar greeted us. King bounded across the room, away from Mrs. Ria. Instead of heading for me though, he yipped at Fallyn and jumped up on her legs.

When she laughed and reached for him, he ran

away, up to me, and barked to be picked up.

I grabbed him from the floor. "You little traitor," I murmured affectionately. His response was to lick my face.

"He really is king of the house already, isn't he?" Link laughed.

It was true.

Link led Fallyn further into the house, and I paused to talk to Mrs. Ria. She assured me King had been an angel, and that nothing had gone wrong today.

She'd gotten the estimate from the contractors, for fixing the pipes and repairing the damage in the guest house, but most of them didn't recommend doing the work in this weather. No one needed the place right now anyway, so I'd wait until spring to have things repaired.

I thanked her profusely for all her work, insisted she let me pay her a bonus, and sent her home for the night.

When I found my guests in the rec room, Link was already setting takeout boxes, chopsticks, and forks on the coffee table, and Fallyn had joined him. Did I have a perfectly good table to eat at? One in the kitchen, one in the dining room.

Was part of me still in my early twenties and loved eating in front of the TV? Absolutely. Didn't matter that we weren't going to turn it on. It felt rebellious.

"I hope you like it hot," Link was saying.

Fallyn had shed her coat and looked even more delectable now that it was just the three of us and we had all night. I liked watching Link fuck her. Definitely something I'd do again.

"There are so many ways I could take that," she said.

There are so many ways I could take you. No need to let that thought out.

Fallyn grabbed a pair of chopsticks, snapped them apart, and snagged a fire chili off the top of the kung pao chicken. She never flinched. "I think I can handle it." Her voice was a dangerous blend of challenging and shy, and her posture matched.

Okay, *that* was hot.

We each dished ourselves out some food, and gravitated to our seats. Link and I had our preferred spots, and Fallyn settled in an empty space distinctly away from both of us.

So much for making me fall in love. Unless she thought playing hard to get was the way to go. Spoiler alert—it wasn't.

"How did you like your very first day ever of RinCon?" Link asked.

Fallyn glanced at me through her eyelashes, and pink spread across her cheeks. "It was good." She shoved the food in her mouth as she spoke.

"Favorite part?" I already knew what mine was,

and suspected she felt the same, given the way her blush deepened.

She took her time chewing and swallowing. "It's hard to pick." Her voice was a squeak.

Link nudged a bottle of soda toward her. "Too hot?"

"Something like that." She busied herself with downing the drink and eating some more.

That told me all I needed to know. I was already winning this battle.

Which meant I could give her a little bit of a reprieve. "What's Fallyn's story?" I asked.

She finally met my gaze, her brows raised. "I don't know how to answer that. What's Elliot's story? What's Link's?"

"You know our stories." Which was total bull-shit. No one but him and me knew the details. "We started at Cord, we moved to Rinslet, then Aces-Played." There were documentaries about the first two companies and their rises and the fall of Cord. "So what about you? Did you love video games as a kid? Did you hate them and breaking and humili-ating them is your vengeance? Did they kill everyone on your home planet, and you barely escaped with your sense of vindictiveness intact?"

Fallyn's mouth twisted and her eyes went blank. "Yes. Video games are my supervillain origin story. If I tell you the truth, is that when you tell me I don't have a right to do what I'm doing?"

I shook my head. "I'll tell you that right now, backstory or not." That should be pretty obvious by now.

"We don't gatekeep," Link said. Always the diplomat. "I genuinely want to know, and as you've just seen, you don't want us filling in the blanks. There's a reason we're developers and not writing the main story."

"Which is something I appreciate about you." Fallyn's reply caught me off-guard. "You know what you're good at, and you embrace it. Your artists are gifted, your story team is brilliant, and your developers..." The rest of her sentence was muffled by her shoving food in her mouth.

I tried to puzzle out the words, but I couldn't quite put the pieces together. "Say that again? Clearly this time."

Fallyn's chewing looked exaggerated as she stared at me.

"I'm willing to wait." At my feet, King sat and whined. I scratched his ears, but wouldn't give him food. He needed to learn not to beg for table scraps.

She finally finished the bite. "Your developers are arrogant fucks who think the world revolves around them." Her reply was meek.

I grinned. "That's because it does. That's why they're *my* developers." I wasn't big on misplaced arrogance, but ours was founded in reality.

"That's something I like about you, ET Howard." Fallyn laughed.

Tension rolled through me at the nickname, but I was willing to let her finish before I said anything.

"You know exactly how good you are, and you don't let anyone take that from you," Fallyn said.

King whined louder. If he kept that up, I was going to cave, but once again I gave him a little attention and went back to dinner and the conversation. "I don't know if I've just been insulted or not."

She licked her lips. "Not. That was all compliment, I promise."

"I mean, you're right, I'm just surprised to hear *you* admit it." I also wasn't about to start having fun. Not with her. Not like this. She could see the mask I wore for the world, and think that I was being friendly, but she didn't get to see the part of me that was boxed safely away.

Fallyn let out an exaggerated sigh that made her chest rise and fall and captivated me.

I tore my gaze away quickly.

King stopped whining at me, and trotted the few feet to Link's chair, before he resumed the begging.

"If I'm going to make you love me, I probably *do* need a tragic backstory," Fallyn said. "It ups the sympathy and draws the player in faster. Gives him something to commit to early on. To feel possessive over."

Excuse me? "I'm not a two-dimension game character. Or gamer."

Link also refused to give King any table scraps.

"I never said you were." She smirked. "Besides, my story isn't the kind of tale a gamer wants to hear. It's full of naughty words like sexism and degradation and me just wanting to be treated like a human being." Bitterness lined her voice when she finished.

Fallyn cleared her throat. "Anyway…" Now she sounded too sunny. "I started in quality assurance when I was younger. I was underpaid because I didn't know how much to ask for and I didn't have a degree. The company I was at loved me until I started asking why we made the same mistakes in our games over and over. I ran into the same most places I went, plus bosses hitting on me, a senior QA guy who insisted I didn't have a job unless I fucked him—and as soon as I stopped he got me fired—and I reached a point where I was too tired to keep going through the same. If people were going to ogle my tits while I broke games, I was going to do it for the world and make a lot more money for it. *That's* Fallyn's story."

Thanks. I hated it. Not hearing it, but that anyone would have to put up with that kind of bullshit. I didn't think she was making any of it up—I'd been in the industry as long as she had, and I didn't doubt for a moment that it happened again and again. "You didn't deserve to be treated that way."

"Thanks." Her smile was tight. She let out a noisy sigh. "Can we talk about anything else?"

King yipped and scrambled across the room to where she sat. As if offering her a solution, he sat back on his haunches and barked.

"Sure, Puppy. I'll bribe you to be my friend." Fallyn's smile didn't quite erase her frustration. She shredded some of her chicken and held a piece out for him.

He reached his nose up, sniffed a few times, and ran back to me.

I didn't know whether to laugh or feel bad that she'd been snubbed. For trying to feed my dog. When I'd made it obvious we weren't doing that. Where was my head tonight?

As a reward, I offered him a piece of beef, and he scarfed it down happily. When he finished, he pawed at my leg and whimpered, and I pulled him into my lap.

"So that's how that works." All the sadness vanished from Fallyn's voice. "I just have to walk up to the pretty man, beg for his meat, and he'll hold me."

If she wanted to move on from the sadness, that was fine with me. "That's how it works for *him*." I nodded at King.

"Hmm." She looked at Link. "Would it work for me?"

Link seemed to consider this. "Depends."

"On what?" Fallyn asked.

"On whether you actually want to be in my lap, or you're just trying to make Elliot jealous."

I hid my smirk. *Busted.*

Fallyn set her plate aside, dropped to her knees, and crawled across the carpet, her tutu-accentuated ass wigging in the air. She nuzzled Link's shin, like a cat. A sexy, fuckable—

Damn it.

"I actually want up." The way she spoke was practically a purr. "You're nice, you're nonjudgmental, and you're cuddly."

Link patted his legs. "I can't say *no* to that."

Fallyn moved to perch on his lap and that damn *mine* voice was back. Worse, I didn't know which of them it was directed at. When she stuck her tongue out at me, it didn't help.

"See, you do that, and I think you're here for his reaction, not mine." Link loosely wrapped his arms around Fallyn's waist, defying his words.

She pouted. "Can it be both? Because yes, I'll admit it, I want to make Elliot scowl. But I do want to be up here." She turned wide eyes on him. "You're cuddly, you're sweet, and you're safe."

Link was only safe if one was on the right side of his sunshine.

"You can be both, if you're honest about it," Link said.

Fallyn leaned her head on his shoulder. "Now

you know all about my trauma. Do I get a snippet of who either of you are in return?" She met my gaze, and I swore she was trying to peer into my soul. "Are you going to tell me your stories?"

Absolutely not. I was aware I'd put up thick walls, and regardless of the abnormal reactions she evoked in me, she hadn't earned a glimpse at what lay behind my defenses. "We already covered this. You know my story."

"Not all of it. Not the tattoos or what they hide."

The ones on my wrists, that covered the scars. And this was the second time she mentioned them. I never should've told Kittie anything.

Not that there was much to guess about why I had jagged, pale lines running down the insides of my arms. The traces of when I tried to take my own life, years ago, were exactly what they looked like before I covered them with ink.

"I wouldn't care if you were the most beautiful creature in existence—which you're not"—I was being cruel again, and her ghost of a frown said she knew it—"no one gets to hear that story."

Link knew it. He'd been there, and it was never an exaggeration when I said he'd saved my life when we were younger.

But Fallyn would never come close to having the kind of place in my world that he did, and she'd never know the details of my past.

12 /
fallyn

Elliot cut the conversation short when he abruptly stood and announced King needed to go out. Link and I both asked if he wanted company, and he insisted he'd be back soon.

"Do I need to move?" I asked Link as Elliot stepped out the back door.

Link loosely interlocked his fingers around my waist. "Not unless you want to."

I really didn't.

It was rapidly becoming clear to me that when it came to this stupid bet with Elliot, I could either focus on my winning or his losing, but I couldn't have both.

And really, why was I focusing so much energy on Elliot anyway? Yes, I wanted to be more like my online persona, the world thought she—I—and he had an eternal feud, and when Bryce had me backed into a corner earlier today, I'd been praying to the gods that I could summon her. *Be* her.

On the other hand, she wasn't actually always bitchy, she was just direct. If I looked like Elliot, people would think Online Fallyn was alpha and hot, instead of bitchy and cold.

He also wasn't the warm, safe, teddy bear of a man who'd come to my rescue earlier, who was at least as kind in person as he had been online, and who was letting me sit in his lap. Just because.

Basically, why was I wasting any time on Elliot, when I could be trying to figure out who I was, and seeing if Link and I could have something? Or at least, enjoying his company while I was here.

And maybe I should stop pushing Elliot to talk about his haunted past. Speaking of, he'd returned, face flushed and neutral expression in place. King barked a few times, ran around in a circle, and laid down by Elliot's feet.

Too. Adorable. Not that it convinced me the bastard had a heart. Or maybe just a teensy one.

"What game did you start on?" Link's question made no sense to me.

"What?"

His chuckle was soft, but shook me in the best way. "You said you started in QA. Who with? What was the first game you tested?"

Oh. That. The topic that brought us down this

awkward road of conversation to begin with. "I don't think I'm legally allowed to say their name. I'm pretty sure their parent company has ears everywhere."

"Wait. Ears?" Link's shock was audible. "You mean... *no*."

Elliot looks just as surprised. "You worked for *them*?"

Them being the gaming arm of the company who made some of the best-known sci-fi movies in the world. That franchise that spanned more than three trilogies across three generations. "I worked for *them*."

"You lucky..." Elliot trailed off with a sigh and a shake of his head.

"Dream job right there," Link said. "I would've given my right arm to work for them back in the day."

While I understood their awe to a point—a very limited point—I also didn't. "Hello? You're Cord babies. OG Rinslet Crew? You can't possibly tell me you would've traded what you have now, for a job *there*."

Elliot clucked. "Not now. Not even close. But back then? Without hesitation."

"What was it like?" Link shifted his weight, but he never pushed me away or disturbed me.

Aside from all the negatives I'd already listed? "We didn't have company-sanctioned orgies."

"They were never company sanctioned," Elliot said.

As if. "You can't tell me the men up top didn't know what you were doing." It was easy to mold my body to Link's. How was this so comfortable? I'd never been much of a touchy person, but I could stay here forever.

"They knew." Link adjusted his arm, and instantly I was that much more cozy. "They looked the other way, and there were murmurs of *don't let this fuck us*."

I couldn't imagine. But I also couldn't imagine loving a nine-to-five so much that I would do it just because I could. Elliot for instance—if he came from the kind of money that owned this house, he didn't need to be working. Especially not for someone else. "I promise, the job isn't one you should envy me for. Though, I did learn a lot about breaking games."

Elliot's scowl said that might not have been the right answer.

But I couldn't worry about what he thought if I was going to learn to be direct. If I was going to figure out how not to be backed up against an escalator by a scary guy, and feeling trapped despite being surrounded by people. "What? You know at least as much about broken games as I do."

His scowl deepened.

"But you still play our games." The dynamic

between Link and Elliot was hard to figure out, but Link didn't seem bothered by my comments.

"I totally still play. I come back to your games over and over." And I likely always would, at least as long as this team was behind them. "I pick on them because nothing is perfect, but I want your games to be as close as it gets. Because they're my favorite. MucasFarts doesn't hold a candle to what you're doing."

Elliot's snort was loud and unexpected. "What did you just call them?"

Heat flooded my face. Why did that happen so often when he was around? Even for simple conversation. "You heard me."

"That's disgusting." The way Link said it sounded as though I was being anything but.

"It wasn't a great company to be at." That was being kind. "They're lucky I don't say worse."

"You have to admit, *ET Howard* is a lot less insulting as a name," Link said.

The way Elliot's jaw dropped was one of the most comical things... Like an old cartoon, but drawn better. "You did *not* just take her side."

"Not *just*. I think letting her in my lap was the point where I caved." There was no malice in Link's retort, and he squeezed my hip when he spoke.

Elliot sighed and shook his head. "I think you caved *way* before that." He didn't sound upset either.

He focused on me. "If you keep corrupting my developers…"

"You'll what?" I pushed the challenge into my retort.

"I'm working on that part. For now, assume it's appropriately threatening." Was he almost smiling?

I laughed in spite of myself. "Yes, sir." Shit. I didn't mean to say that.

Elliot's shock passed in a blink. In fact, it was probably never even there. "Say it again." A hint of command wove into his voice. "I like the way that sounds."

Link's grip tightened on me. It was subtle, but unmistakable. "Don't say it unless you mean it. He already lets being the boss go to his head."

"*Hey*." Elliot's bark lacked bite. "That's absolutely not true. I already had a big head." He leaned back in his seat, spread his arms across the back of the couch, and let his legs fall open.

Seriously?

"Dick joke?" Link didn't sound impressed.

"If it was, it fell a little short." I couldn't help myself. Something vibrated against my butt, and I wiggled. "Is that you? Do you buzz on command?"

Link laughed, but a loud chime came from Elliot before Link could reply.

I hated to abandon my post, but I knew without Link asking that if their phones were going off at the same time, they both needed to answer. I hopped to my feet.

"DDOS." Elliot looked at his screen while Link fished his phone from his pocket.

Someone was hitting their servers with a lot of requests for information, all at the same time. So many hits that the computers couldn't keep up with demand. It was the equivalent of opening a billion browser tables at once, and then trying to let thousands of people play a game on that same computer.

And if it wasn't fixed quickly, it was the kind of thing that could kill a game. Especially a game in its opening week that had most of the gaming world watching it.

"Luna has protocols in place." Link thumbed through his screen.

Deep lines were etched into Elliot's forehead. "They're not working."

This was awkward. I should go. Let them work. My feet were frozen to the floor, as I watched something worse than a horror movie play out in front of me.

"No." The shift in Link's tone made my blood run cold.

Elliot nodded. "It's coming from…" Was that hurt on top of fear?

I knew how much this game meant to them, and the fight with Elliot the other day had driven that home, but this was different, and why were they both looking at me? "What's wrong?"

"The attack is coming through your VPN," Link said softly.

What? "But I'm right here. I'm not— I wouldn't—"

"What is this?" Elliot demanded. "What are you doing to the game? Is this for another video?"

"I'm not doing anything. I'm standing here talking to the two of you. Hand to God, this isn't me." How was I supposed to convince them of that, though? Besides the fact that I'd always gone out of my way to keep their game from crashing, even if they didn't like my methods of doing so.

I grabbed my laptop from my messenger bag and opened it. When I logged into the site I used to give me virtual access, my gut sank. "Someone's in my account." My fingers were already flying across the keyboard. "I don't know..." My mouth couldn't keep up with my brain if I was going to type at the same time. "I'm not the one doing this."

But I was the one who could shut it down. I was only vaguely aware of Elliot and Link watching over my shoulder as I worked. Every time I shut the person out of one spot, they were in another. "I'm not doing this. I swear to you, this isn't me."

I couldn't say anything else. I had to make this stop.

I hated the look of defeat on Fallyn's face when she left us alone to work, and headed upstairs to her room. "This wasn't her fault," I said as her figure disappeared into the shadows on the dark second floor.

"It doesn't matter that she didn't pull the trigger. Someone else did this through accounts she created, and it happened because somewhere along the line, she was careless."

I growled. This wasn't the first time I'd heard this argument—when Brandon's wi-fi was used to steal portions of our game code last year, Elliot blamed him, too. Even though Brandon hadn't been the one to do the stealing.

At least Elliot was being an equal opportunity asshole. *Swell.*

He and I worked until two or three in the morning, with Luna on the other end of the line, to make sure everything was secure and that what happened tonight wouldn't happen again. By the time we dragged ourselves up to Elliot's bed, we were barely conscious enough to strip out of our clothes.

But falling asleep next to him, tangled up with him, was easy. As much as it always had been. Maybe even easier. Why hadn't I ever thought about that before?

The only reason I was thinking about it now was because it was late, and I was getting too old for all-nighters.

In the morning, the faint smell of freshly brewing coffee drifted upstairs. Elliot's groan told me he was waking up next to me.

"I think I love Mrs. Ria." I forced myself out of bed. It was clear she was the one making the go-juice. "Do you think she'd marry me?"

Elliot's laugh was dry. "She's too good for you. And I don't say that lightly. Given that you're too good for the rest of the world, that's a high bar."

Though we hadn't had enough sleep, what we did get seemed to have helped based on his mood. "We should give Fallyn a ride to the convention center. We're heading down there anyway."

Elliot's silence was deafening.

I turned in time to see his scowl vanish behind a blank expression. "As long as she's ready to go when we are."

"I'll go make sure." This was probably when I

was supposed to say *forget it, she can find her own ride,* but I was already tired of this push and pull.

I headed downstairs, King following close on my heels. "Morning, Mrs. Ria." I waved as I passed the kitchen and headed toward the staircase leading up to a different hallway.

"Is Elliot up?" It was sweet that after all these years, she still looked after him.

"He'll be down soon."

Ria stopped me and handed me a travel mug of coffee. "For your guest."

"Thank you. I'm sure she says *thank you* too."

The instant I found the bottom step, King barked and darted past me. I let him run, and ascended at a more leisurely pace. The light spilled under the door of Fallyn's room, so I probably wasn't waking her. I should've texted first. That felt weird though, texting someone who was in the same house, to say *can I come up?*

Why was she staying in a separate wing again? Right, because Elliot. I needed to change that.

I knocked and a moment later, she answered. King seemed to come out of nowhere, running up to her and jumping on her legs.

"Whoa. Hey." Her laugh was almost enough to light up the hallway, and she reached down to pet him. She wore a baggy sweatshirt and mismatched, but just as loose, bottoms, and I couldn't help but stare.

I handed Fallyn the coffee. "Mrs. Ria sends her regards."

"Tell her thank you. Did you come all the way over here just for this?"

"And to see if you want a ride downtown this morning. We're leaving in about half an hour. I know it's short notice, but—"

"I can be ready." She picked up King. "Anything to keep me from another awkward, conversationless Uber ride."

"Great. See you downstairs?"

She nodded, tilted her head, then held out King. "Here. It's dangerous to go alone. Take this."

I couldn't question her logic, I could only laugh. "Come on. Let's go find Elliot," I said to King.

He ran into the kitchen the instant I set him down. I spent the next bit of time getting ready, and by the time I finished, Elliot was waiting with Fallyn next to him.

I had to stop to look her over. Her costume today didn't show off as much skin, but it looked just as good. She wore a blond wig with one red and one blue pigtail, a blue and red satin jacket, and black jeans. Her T-shirt said *Daddy's Li'l Monster*. The only thing missing from her Harley Quinn costume was the trademark baseball bat.

"Our costumes are in the car. You ready?" Elliot's abrupt tone interrupted my staring.

I nodded, using the excuse to drag my gaze from

Fallyn. "Let's go." There was a costume party—masquerade—tonight after the con, and AcesPlayed was hosting. Everyone in the company was supposed to be there, as long as nothing broke, and I was hoping for multiple reasons that we all got to attend.

In the car, Elliot cranked the music, cutting off any chance at conversation.

So much for Fallyn not having to deal with awkward silence.

"At least it's not talk radio," she said as we pulled out of the driveway.

I was really over this tension between them, and I didn't care if they weren't in the mood to talk to each other, I was going to make it happen. "Is that your costume for tonight as well, Fallyn?" I turned in my seat and raised my voice enough to carry over the stereo.

"I have something else planned for the party." She patted the second bag she carried with her. "Are the two of you going as developers?" It sounded like a playful question, but the words were strained.

"Nope." Elliot popped off his response, making it clear he wasn't discussing this further.

"Mine's a secret too," I said. Every time we had these parties, I went as Link, from the Zelda games. I rocked a pair of tights like no one's business, and no one expected the six-foot-six guy to be Link. But this year I was doing something different.

Apparently I needed another topic. We could stay on the party. "I'm looking forward to karaoke."

"Oh, do you sing?" This time Fallyn's response didn't sound as forced.

"I suppose everyone who opens their mouth and lets notes come out sings. But I'm not on the same level as someone like Danny." The drawback to working with actual musicians—it was always clear who was going to shine at karaoke. That didn't stop me from enjoying the entire thing, though.

"Actually"—Elliot turned down the music a few notches—"he's being modest. He's got an incredible voice."

I wasn't bad. I could hold my own through a few songs. "You're going to sing, right?" I was still focused on Fallyn.

She scrunched up her face in hesitation.

"So much for not being shy or timid." Mocking slipped into Elliot's voice.

Not. Cool. I glared at him. "Ease up." The warning in my tone should be enough for him.

"I'm just saying."

"*Now.*" I reinforced the *suggestion* that he stop.

"It's not that." Now Fallyn was barely audible above the radio. "But I was hoping to keep a low profile in that specific room. I'm not exactly a crowd favorite at AcesPlayed."

Elliot's nostrils flared. "Probably smart."

And now the conversation was dead again.

A short while later, we pulled around behind the convention center. It was early enough that only a handful of vendors were here, and no attendees. We dropped her off, and headed on to the office.

At work, the tension was heavy in the developer rooms. Elliot called us all together for a morning huddle. Which mostly meant that most everyone stood up in their cubicles if they couldn't see him from their desks.

"I know the sitting around, fucking off and doing nothing, kind of sucks," he said. "Especially after so many months—years—of pushing hard. Enjoy the calm while it's here, but of course be ready to jump at a moment's notice if something like last night happens again. Go play the game, play something else, wander RinCon... As long as you're close and available for the rest of the week."

There were a few weak cheers, and some grumbles, but mostly people turned back to their computers.

"Shouldn't we be doing more to take care of what happened last night?" Chris's question rang out above the mutters.

Elliot fixed him with a penetrating look. "Link and I took care of it, with Luna's help. The issue is resolved." His tone implied that was the end of the conversation.

"Are you sure?" At Chris's question, several heads popped up above cubes again.

Presumably because no one questioned Elliot. It wasn't that he had a rule against it or anything, it just didn't tend to be needed.

Elliot fixed Chris with a hard stare. "I *am* sure, yes."

"So what was the issue?" Chris asked.

We'd agreed last night, when talking to Luna, that no one needed to know that the attack was related to Fallyn in any way, even if it wasn't her fault. Most everyone here already had enough animosity toward her, though Luna apparently didn't.

"You know what the issue was. There was a DDOS, and we put new security protocols in place to stop it," Elliot said. "Any other questions? No? Good. Back to fucking around." He turned away from the room.

"I thought we'd already accounted for DDOS's," Chris said. "And do we know where it came from?"

Elliot paused, and while I couldn't see his face, I swore I could hear him counting to ten. Instead of walking back into his office, he strolled up to Chris. "You've been doing this for… what? Fifteen years now?"

Chris didn't back down. "About."

Elliot gave him a thin smile. "Have you ever figured out how to make your code completely foolproof?"

"Well, no, but—"

"And have you ever seen me lead the team in the wrong direction?" Elliot's question held a tone of *go ahead, give me the wrong answer.*

Chris clenched his jaw. "You don't want me to answer that."

Elliot's grin was dangerous. "I know what I asked. The issue is resolved to the best of our ability, no one needs to worry about it, and we will deal with the next problem when it arises. In fact, since you're eager to fix something, you and Link can go do a security stint at RinCon."

"Fine." The way Chris spat the word implied it was most certainly not.

On the other hand, I was happy to go. I didn't like the idea of walking away from my desk, of not being here if something broke, but I needed something to do.

Plus, Fallyn might be there. Plus that.

Elliot grabbed my attention after Chris stalked out of the room, and pulled me aside. "I'll let you know if anything goes wrong, and you can get back here ASAP." He addressed my concerns without me saying a word. "But I need you to keep an eye on Chris."

"Because he called you out in front of the room?" I teased.

Elliot scoffed. "Maybe his dick feels extra small today, I don't know. But sort of. If he's doing that to me… Make sure he's not fucking with anyone there?"

"Right." Some of my mood wilted. Chris was starting to say and do things that reminded us of Bryce. Nothing so far that was overt or fireable, but we were extra vigilant now that it had happened once and no one caught it.

I headed back to the convention center, and couldn't help the happy hum inside at the idea that I might run into Fallyn again. Inside, I didn't see her, and I took my place next to Chris at the front of the hall.

Things didn't go too badly. He and I talked about all the announcements for upcoming games, patches, updates, and what we were looking forward to the most. The kind of basic small talk that didn't tend to get anyone in trouble.

"Can you believe someone like that has the nerve to show their face here?" Chris's sneer caught my attention and I knew before I followed his gaze who I'd see.

Sure enough, there Fallyn was, with the perfectly pullable pigtails and the black jeans that made her ass look incredible. "There are hundreds of Harleys here," I was going to play dumb and let Chris dig his own grave. "You a Joker man?"

Chris snorted. "I'm not any man's man. You do know who that is, right? Or did the wig throw you off?"

"I know who it is. She's got as much right to be here as anyone."

"Except Bryce apparently. But does she really?"

I clenched my fist at my side. "She really does."

"Whatever." Chris shrugged. "Just because she's a raging cunt doesn't mean I wouldn't pin her down and let her choke on my cock when she screamed."

"The fuck?" My fury surged and I had his shirt in my fist before my brain caught up. "What the fuck is wrong with you?" My question was a low and threatening growl.

Chris held his hands up in surrender, and his eyes were wide with the fear that radiated off him. "I was kidding. Ha ha, funny joke."

"*Not* funny." I was about to embrace my inner caveman. Intellectually I thought maybe I should back down, but he'd struck a nerve I thought I'd done a better job of deadening, and I was ready to let him choke on my fist while he screamed.

"Chris. Shift's up." Phillip's voice cut through my anger.

I relaxed my grip, and Chris took several steps back. "You need to chill. I don't care that you're fucking the boss, that wasn't cool."

"Rape jokes *aren't cool.*" I snarled, and he left as quickly as was possible without running.

Phillip stepped up next to me. "You okay?"

"I'm good. I probably wouldn't have hit him in front of everyone."

"I don't doubt he deserved it," Phillip said.

As the red cleared from my vision, I realized a small crowd had gathered around us. When they saw there wouldn't be any violence, most of them moved on. That was probably going on a few blogs today, but likely not enough for anyone to care in the midst of the big news.

About fifteen minutes later I had a text from Elliot that said I should call him when I had a break.

The next hour or so was uneventful, then Xander was back to relieve me.

I FaceTimed Elliot as I walked to a quiet corner of the convention center, near the outer walls.

"Chris is bitching about you." Elliot didn't look bothered at all when he answered.

I shrugged. "Because Chris was being a bitch."

"I figured. Good job. Hey, if you want to hang there for an hour or two, take a long lunch, you should."

I didn't know what to make of the offer. Why would I take it easy when everyone else was working? "Because of Chris?"

"In a way. He says I favor you. He's right and he can gag on my big, fat authority. But also because you put in long hours last night."

I didn't miss the slipped in comment, and it filled me with more warm fuzzies. "You worked late too."

"I'm the boss."

Seriously? "That's your counter?"

Elliot huffed a laugh and his smile was worth it. "Because when I crash from pushing myself too hard, I need someone I trust to pick up the slack."

"You've never crashed." I couldn't even picture it.

"I'm getting older," Elliot said.

I shook my head, and out of the corner of my eye, a flash of red and black caught my attention.

"But I know you have my back." The teasing faded from Elliot's voice, and was replaced with a more somber tone. "One of us needs to be rested, even if it's just a long lunch."

There were even more Harley's here than my conversation with Chris implied, but I knew instantly which one this was, and I couldn't help but focus on Fallyn, who sat a short distance away, on the floor, back to the wall.

"I do always have your back." I gave Elliot my attention again. "Fine. You've twisted my arm. I'll take it easy for an hour or two."

"Good. See you in a bit." Elliot disconnected.

I instantly cut a line for Fallyn. When my shadow fell over her, she looked up.

"May I keep you company?" I asked.

She looked surprised, but her smile was invaluable. "I wouldn't tell many people here *yes*."

"Oh?"

"Fortunately, you're on that list."

Good. I took the spot next to her, and mimicked her posture—back to the wall, knees bent, and arms resting on top. I dwarfed her as much like this as I did when we were standing. Hopefully that would keep assholes like Chris from getting too many ideas. Or at least thinking it was a good idea to voice them.

"What do you think of the show so far?" I asked.

Her grin brightened. "It's so much fun. There's so much to do, and the live demos, and I get to go so many places with this." She held up her badge with *MEDIA* stamped down the side. "DM has this game coming—you don't want to hear about that, sorry." She ducked her head.

"Don't stop. I'm enjoying the play-by-play." I meant it. It was unlikely I'd want to hear it from most people, but she said it all with so much genuine enthusiasm that I was willing to listen to her tell me about the whole show, a minute at a time.

She shook her head. "If I tell you everything, you won't have a reason to tune in and watch my recap on my channel later."

"I promise you I will." To watch her. Was I smitten? Possibly. Already? I didn't know what this was or what was going on in my head. I did know it seemed like a bad idea to fight it.

"Are you okay?" Her question came out of nowhere.

I patted myself, and made a show of looking around. "I think so? Why?"

"I saw you in the booth, with that guy you work with." Her laugh was light, but it masked a nervousness I didn't want directed at me. "I didn't think you could look that mad, but you were… a little scary."

"*Never* to you." I didn't mean to say that with so much emphasis, but I wouldn't take it back.

The pink across her cheeks was stark against the makeup of the costume. Stark and pretty. "I'm not worried about that."

Talking about me and my temper wasn't going to work for me. "Are you really going to try to make Elliot fall in love with you?" Not the best topic to shift to, but I hated the idea. The more it sat in my brain, the more I loathed what it would do to both of them.

"No." It was as simple an answer as she could've given, and I'd never wanted to hear a *no* more. "But I am going to try to make me be more bold. Are you and he really…?"

"Really what?"

"Really… not together?"

Ah. That. "We're really not." I'd always struggled with that answer, but it had always been true. Today it felt different though, because Fallyn was a variable that had never been there before. I didn't know what to do with this shift in perspective or even how to define it.

"Would you really have hit the other guy? From your work? Because you looked like it."

I didn't hit anyone these days. That was behind me. "Depended on how far he pushed me. I haven't always been so…"

"Teddy bearish?" she supplied helpfully.

"Close enough."

Fallyn tilted toward me, then straightened again, and the abruptly corrected few inches between us felt like the Grand Canyon. "I didn't mean to pry," she said.

"You shared your past, it only seems fair you know mine." Why was I offering that? She hadn't asked about then, only about today.

She shook her head. "Secrets don't work that way."

"Trust does." I had an out. A reason to stop talking, and I was pushing to tell this story anyway. Why?

Because there was an invisible string tugging me toward her, and it was almost tangible. I wanted to connect with Fallyn, and at the same time I wanted her to walk away and never come back, because she should have better. "You may run for the hills when I tell you."

"I won't. I promise."

This was where I should stop talking and go find

lunch or my co-workers or anything that wasn't this rabbit hole into the past. "I was the bully in high school." And instead, I was doing this. "I could give you all sorts of excuses—it kept me from getting picked on for being fat, it was backlash for what I dealt with at home—but I was relentless. I got in a *lot* of fights, and I don't like that I was ever that person."

"But you're not now." Fallyn hadn't pulled away or so much as flinched.

She would soon enough.

"No, I'm not," I said.

She nudged me with her shoulder, and the spark that ignited was both incredible and unwelcome. "Is there more to the story? Not that there has to be."

There was. "One day my dad pushed hard. Probably not more than he had in the past, but it had already been the kind of day that leaves a person feeling raw. I hit back. I'd never done that before, and I kept swinging until..." I couldn't finish the sentence because I couldn't relive the memory. It wasn't like I'd killed my old man, but it got dark.

Fallyn rested her hand on my upper arm.

Such a simple action, and it cracked a part of my psyche. "I didn't stop until bones were broken and he was unconscious. I spent time in jail for assault. I hated him, but I also hated the fear he had when he looked at me, and that I'd been capable of doing that to another person." I dragged in a sharp breath. "So few things are more important to me than keeping my temper."

"You're not that person anymore," she repeated. She didn't pull away, and the way she studied me was with sympathy, but not pity or disgust.

"He's still there. I just cage him."

Fallyn simply nodded.

Time to climb out of that basement and with a lot of luck never step into it again. "I know it's been a little nuts since you got here, but I'm glad you made the trip, and I'm glad it was you on the other side of the screen." And dig myself a whole new and different kind of pit instead.

"Even though Online Fallyn is a bitch?"

I wouldn't put it that way. I rarely held grudges, and she didn't deserve one. "Even though. Are you still going to be at the masquerade tonight?" After the conversation in Elliot's car, I wasn't sure.

"Until people figure out who I am and I get glared out of the room."

I probably wouldn't go full Link-Hulk on anyone, but if they said something like what Chris had… "I won't let them do that to you."

"You'd risk your reputation with your co-workers to defend me?" Fallyn sounded skeptical.

"Not only that, but I'll tell anyone who asks that you're as much of a friend as they are."

Her grin was worth a million five-star reviews. "I have a panel to get to." She pushed to her feet. "But thank you for the company, and I'll see you tonight."

I watched her walk away, and was more focused on the fact that I'd see her again than how her ass wiggled when she was wearing those heeled boots. Was she really giving me warm fuzzies? It seemed that way.

Was that bad?

I hoped not.

14 /
elliot

When Link got back in the office in the afternoon, his mood was subdued. Normal for most of my developers, myself included, but odd for him.

As we worked our way through a couple of ideas for upcoming projects, I couldn't help but ask, "Do anything interesting for lunch?"

"I spent most of it talking to Fallyn."

Oh. And he came back in this kind of mood? What was I supposed to say in response or do with the unexpected jumble inside? "Cool."

The rest of the workday passed without incident, and then most everyone was heading out to change into their costumes and masks for tonight's party. A few of the developers were staying behind as a first line of support if anything in the game crashed.

I felt guilty leaving them here and going to

have fun, but they had volunteered—they'd rather work than deal with people—and it was as important that I be a public face tonight as it was that they be here. It was tempting to leave Chris here, because I could, but I wasn't sure I trusted him to be on call.

I brought Link's and my costumes from my car up to an empty room. Our offices used to be a satellite branch of the community college, until they took their business classes online. Each department had a classroom or two, but we hadn't filled out the entire place. The way we were growing it wouldn't take long, but for tonight it meant Link and I had a room all to ourselves to change into our party outfits.

He joined me a few minutes later, after he wrapped up what he was working on. The smaller, unoccupied room was set away from all the other offices. There was some storage near the door, which made an artificial wall for us to change behind.

Not that anyone was around to see, and it wasn't as though most of them hadn't seen before.

I couldn't say how many times I'd watched Link in various stages of undress in my life, but it never got old. I had my jacket and shirt off, and my jeans halfway down my thighs, when I had to pause to watch him stripping out of his own clothes.

There was an art in the way his muscles rippled

along his back when he moved. The stretch of defi-nition along his sides. His bare, taut thighs—

"Are you staring?" Link's question cut through my thoughts.

I met his gaze. "Absolutely. It's not every day one gets to watch an Adonis in motion, unobstructed by clothing." Though I wanted it to be. I wanted him there every day. Naked. Clothed. *Mine*.

The sharp thought knocked my brain off-balance.

"Be careful. With pretty words like that, the people in charge will move you to story," Link teased.

I raised my eyebrows. "I *am* the person in charge." Shoving aside thoughts of my own state of undress, I stalked toward him.

Link was taller than I was by a few inches, and definitely bigger, but he still stepped back as I advanced, which made me smirk. My thoughts had shifted, and the need to touch him, to become one with him at least for a little bit, surged forward.

"Don't hurt me?" Link's playful question made me think he wanted exactly the opposite.

It was a shame we didn't have more time, but we could make this work. "Only if you beg." I gripped the back of his neck and pulled his head down to mine, biting his bottom lip hard before sucking it into my mouth in a kiss I felt in my toes.

The sparks that flowed between us at the

connection, at the touch, were delicious and intoxicating. They erased any lingering clouds from the day, and replaced those thoughts with promises of what came tonight. I wanted to drag this out for hours, because a little part of me whispered I may not have another chance. That was a ridiculous thing that I didn't need to worry about, and we didn't have enough time for *hours*.

Kissing Link had me hard, and when I grabbed his cock through the hole in his boxers, I smirked at the confirmation that he was the same. I started with a playful tease, a light touch along his skin that was enough to make his erection jerk against my palm.

It didn't take me long to switch to a more insistent stroking, while I explored Link's mouth with mine and swallowed his groans. When kisses weren't enough, I moved my mouth lower, biting lightly along his chest.

Link's hips worked in time with the beat of my hand on his shaft, and the rhythm built. Faster. Harder. Until he was fucking my fist with abandon, and I was gripping tight. Squeezing pleasure from him. His grunts were familiar and delicious. The sound he made when he was close.

I moved my other hand to his balls, to tease the tight sac.

Link pulled away with a reluctant grunt.

Before I could ask what he was doing, he

lowered himself to kneel at my feet. The way he finished freeing my cock, the agonizing and deliberate glide of his skin on mine, was an exercise in art and patience. Slow. Delicate. When he wrapped his lips around my cock, a groan tore from my throat.

I gripped the short strands of his hair, holding him in place. Slamming into his face while he sucked and stroked. Pleasure built inside me quickly, until I thought I might burst. I tried to hold back, enjoying the contrast of his soft mouth and the hints of five o'clock shadow as they occasionally met my sensitive skin.

Link knew my cock as well as he did his own, and each drag of his tongue over my skin, each pump with his fist, pushed me further past the point of no return.

When I came, it was hard and desperate, and I hammered in his mouth, spilling my load. He didn't pull away or ease up until I was spent. As the last drops of desire drained from me, Link let my cock slip out of his mouth, past his lips, to stand at attention.

Fuck me.

I joined him on the floor, sitting next to him, grabbing his hand and guiding him to grip his own cock. I kept his hand covered and set the pace again, using him, using us, to stroke him.

The way his eyelids fluttered and the guttural

sounds he made were like a fresh wave of life. I pushed him to stroke himself again and again, harder and faster, until he looked lost in desire. And together, my touch overlapping his, we finished him off, cum spilling onto our bare legs and the floor.

After cleaning up the mess, we sat there, backs to the wall, butts on the floor, cool tile and brick biting into our heated skin, while we caught our breath. My laugh slipped out without thought, and it took my brain a heartbeat to catch up. "Good for you?" I asked, breathlessly.

Link chuckled. "Fantastic. You?"

"Yup. Good word." Except the impromptu orgasm didn't deter my wandering brain the way I wanted. "You know I'm always…" *here for you.* The words were so cheesy and out of place, especially after blow jobs in a dusty classroom.

"I do. Me too." It seemed Link didn't need me to finish the thought.

I dragged in a deep breath, collecting myself. "Good. You ready to party?"

Link gestured at both of us, wearing nothing but our boxers, and pointed at our dicks hanging out. "We should at least put these away."

"I guess." I let the exaggeration spill into my teasing retort.

"You ever miss it?"

"Miss what?"

"The old days."

There were a lot of things about *the old days* that I had fond memories of. Link was talking about a specific thing, though. The same one that Fallyn had teased us about—the orgies. Great, now I was thinking about Fallyn and fucking her in front of an audience, and my desire was completely gone.

Regardless of what the twitch in my cock said.

"No," I said. "I wouldn't give up the memory, but I wouldn't go back."

"Good."

What was that about? Did I really want to know?

Nope.

We got dressed—Link as Vincent from the Final Fantasy games, and me as Sephiroth. Not pretty, concept art Sephiroth, though. I was the original 16-bit version, including a half-foam wig that gave me blocky hair, and a trench coat with foam shoulder pads.

Our masks were the finishing touch, though we'd wait to put those on until we got to our destination. Link's was a black mask that covered his eyes, and the high collar of his trench coat covered the lower part of his face. It was impossible to see who he was, if one didn't account for the fact that he would probably be the only six-foot-six wall of muscle in the room.

My mask was more simple, but I felt a little more terrifying—flesh colored and meant to cover my whole face, with holes for eyes and otherwise blank and smooth.

We headed to the hotel across the street from the convention center. Normally I hated stepping foot in this place—the building that bore my family name. But seeing the lobby full of people in costumes, celebrating their fandom, their love of video game media, made me grin. The energy in the air was contagious, and knowing how much my father would hate seeing this in one of his establishments didn't hurt either.

We let ourselves get swept up in the crowds and carried toward the suite where the AcesPlayed party was happening. Several companies were hosting different types of events tonight. It was a kind of mingle-and-wander-and-do-whatever-grabs-your-attention evening.

The AcesPlayed room was packed. We were hosting a masquerade-slash-dance-slash-karaoke. I was pretty sure Brandon had bribed Dustin to tack the *karaoke* part of things onto the end, but Link was looking forward to that as much as the rest of it, and that made it a good idea as far as I was concerned.

By my count, there were a few hundred people packed in here, and at least fifty of those were lined up for their chance to sing. Link got to skip the line and put his name on the list.

A familiar blend of voices came from nearby. It didn't matter that Danny and Reese were wearing masks. Their voices were famous, and their costumes were giveaways too. I wasn't sure what Brandon was wearing. We joined Danny as Ozzy Osbourne, Reese as Joan Jett, and Brandon as... a guy in a powdered wig, and tux that had a long-tailed coat?

Danny was trying to explain to Reese why she couldn't just fill out the karaoke roster with her own name, and kick everyone else off stage.

I was pretty sure he was losing the discussion.

The three of them looked up, and said in unison, "Hey, Link."

Link-as-Victor waved.

Brandon looked at me. "That makes you... Elliot. Nice."

"Thanks." I grinned, though he couldn't see it. "You're going to have to help me out though. Did I miss the part of the eighties where that"—I gestured to his costume—"was a thing?"

Brandon's mask only covered his eyes, so his smirk was visible. "I'm Leopold."

What? "Leopold?"

"Leopold? Leopold. Leopold." Reese and Danny muttered the name again and again, in overlapping whispers of various tones, before dissolving into laughter.

Ah. Fucking creatives.

"Leopold Stokowski," Brandon said.

Of course. Why didn't I guess that? "You did this for a Bugs Bunny joke?"

"And because he was a brilliant composer." Brandon sounded offended.

"Largely for the Bugs Bunny joke," Reese said.

Brandon's scowl was visible behind the mask, but it faded quickly. "Adam's idea."

"Blaming it on your baby brother doesn't make it better." I was kind of jealous I didn't have a joke with a bad pun. Though, 16-bit Sephiroth was still pretty fucking epic.

Someone called the three of them away, and they waved before vanishing into the crowds. It was good to see Brandon more like himself than he had been a year ago. He was a lot happier since he walked away from his job as our full-time sound guy, and switched to more of a consulting role.

More power to him, but I couldn't imagine it for myself. This job was my world and AcesPlayed was my universe. I wouldn't give up this group for anything. Turning the game on Monday was amazing. The energy in the air tonight was even better, laced with the high of a successful release and so many years of hard work to get here.

Still... an obscure reference to a Bugs Bunny cartoon twice as old as we were. Fucking creatives.

Link went one way, to talk to a few people, and I headed to the bar for a drink. I'd stop myself before

I had too many, or by the end of the night I'd be telling everyone how much I loved them.

I had a reputation to uphold.

The longer I spent at the party, talking to fans and other industry professionals, the higher my mood soared. The couple of whisky sours I had didn't hurt, and probably added to the way I scanned the crowd for Fallyn every few minutes.

I caught glimpses of other people—Nigel, who had been my partner in asinine lovelessness until he'd surrendered his heart. He smiled a lot more now that he was with Megan and Landon. Judith, who radiated control, even in a Jessica Rabbit dress. Chloe. Scott.

But I couldn't tell who Fallyn was.

Why did it matter? Did I really want to see her?

Yeah. Maybe drive home the bet and that I was winning, but more just because I wanted to see if she was having fun. I was in too good a mood to pick a fight.

There was a huge array of sexy costumes, and any one of those could be her. None of the body shapes were quite right, though. Yes, I had a crystal clear image in my mind of where all her curves landed.

She could be in a trench coat, or something bigger and bulkier, like Link was. There were big hats hiding faces. Pony heads. Any of those could be her.

But none of the characters reminded me of the conversations I'd had with Kittie online. Not that I thought I knew everything about her. I could stand to learn a little more…

Why?

Because.

Like that, the impulse to know as much as I could about the woman in my guest wing was overwhelming. I didn't care for it, but that didn't stop me from feeling it. I wanted to know her as intimately as I did Link.

As if summoned by my thoughts, his name was announced from the stage as the next singer. I knew before he stepped up to the mic, as soon as the first strains of the song started, what he would be singing.

She's So Mean by Matchbox Twenty. Except the way they sang it, *he* was so mean.

He and Danny were together. It wasn't the same as watching Plaid Peanut Butter, and I was surprised Reese didn't insist on joining them, but Danny and Link could have fun on stage—their performance chemistry was amazing.

I had just enough alcohol spilling through my veins that I started to move to the music.

"I know this song." Fallyn's familiar voice wove into my thoughts and tugged at my senses. That was better than a straight shot of whisky. "But I was pretty sure it was about a woman."

"Supposedly, according to them," I nodded at the stage without looking at her, "the song fits me to a T."

"Lovely friends." Her tone was hard to decipher.

I spun to face her, and my smile grew. I never would've picked her out of the crowd, but she wore the perfect costume—she was Cloud, from the same game Link and I were from. "Best friends in the world. They always have my back," I said.

"Even if they see you talking to me?"

Fair point. Until now, only Link and Nigel knew she was staying with me. But her mask hid her face, and I wasn't sure I cared regardless. "Even if they see me dancing with you." I tugged her out into the throng of gyrating bodies, despite the teensy voice whimpering *bad idea*. Alcohol and my good mood were chanting *dance with her* in much louder voices.

It didn't take much coaxing to get her to follow me, and by the time Link finished his song, we were closer than our bulky costumes should allow. We stayed locked together through several more songs, and I couldn't wipe the smile from my face.

As the music slowed to something sweeter, and Reese finally got her turn, I wrapped an arm around Fallyn's waist. I tilted my head near her ear. "Come home with me," I murmured.

She laughed and mimicked my gesture. "I'm

staying with you. I'd be both hurt and fucked if you wanted otherwise."

"Not like that. Let me make sure you get fucked."

She pulled away, and her gaze met mine. Her eyes were stunning—so dark brown they were almost black, ringed with dark eyeliner, and peering into my soul from behind her mask. "Maybe," she said playfully.

"I wasn't asking."

The corners of her eyes tugged up. "You were begging?"

"I might. But not for anyone else." This was fun.

She moved her mouth near my ear again. "I can't imagine being the person to bring the mighty ET Howard to his knees, but let me pretend for the night, and I'm in."

Something in her words struck a nerve.

I refused to think about that though, because I was having fun, and I wanted to play some more. No reason to let rational thought run the night.

Somewhere between the hotel suite and the parking garage underneath, Elliot lost his mask—the physical one. The metaphorical one seemed to have slipped earlier in the evening.

Not that I was complaining. Or maybe a little. Because this Elliot—drunk, flushed, and with an easy smile and seductive praise—was far more dangerous to me than the stoic asshole. With Jerk-Elliot, I could see myself getting addicted to the sex, which would fade once I was back home with my vibrator collection. With Drunk-Elliot, I could fall for a lot more than the way he used his dick.

Look at me, I'd discovered an all-new kind of red flag covered guy to add to my list. I hadn't been drinking, but that didn't mean my judgment was worthwhile when it came to him.

All of those thoughts raced through my head as he and I and Link approached Elliot's car. What came out of my mouth was, "Are you sure you should be driving?"

"If you want to drive my car, Fallyn, just ask." He held up the keys and the jangle was loud against the concrete around us. The way he said my name, the derision was gone. He almost made it sound flirty or sexy.

Or I was projecting my desires. "It's not that. I—"

"I'm kidding." Elliot gripped my wrist and pressed the keys into my palm. Before I could close my fingers around them, he yanked them back. "Wait. You can drive a stick?"

"Literally, or is this a sex question?" I asked.

Elliot and Link snorted with laughter. "Literally," Elliot said. "Assure me you're not going to grind the gears on my baby."

"Literally, or is that a sex question," I repeated the teasing question.

Both men laughed harder.

Too adorable. "I will drive your car like I have to present it to the president of the world in perfect condition when I reach our destination."

"Why the president of the world?" Link's question was muffled by the high collar on his costume. He growled in frustration, which made me think even more of a teddy bear, and tugged the fabric open. "Better." He let out a loud sigh.

Elliot snorted. "Because the president of the world has the meanest prisons if you fuck up."

Not quite the way I would've phrased it. "Close enough."

We piled into the car, with Link in the front passenger seat and Elliot in back, but leaning forward between the front bucket seats.

Elliot had enough presence of mind to give me directions out of the parking garage—there were multiple exits and he was specific about which one I wanted to take—and get us on the roads toward his house. I was glad he could navigate drunk.

When we were on a main road and heading south, I relaxed a little and tried to appreciate driving such a gorgeous vehicle, with two sexy men sitting next to me, and Elliot's hot breath on my face every few seconds.

"Link told you about his past?" Elliot's question came out of nowhere.

"Yes." And it had been on my mind a lot since. Knowing that he'd learned those kinds of lessons from his past, that he'd grown and changed in the direction he had, and that he'd earned his kind demeanor, made him that much more alluring.

Elliot pointed me down another street. "So he told you how I was his hero?"

Excuse him?

"No," Link said.

"Good." Elliot was the kind of smug reserved

for confidence brought on by liquor. "Then I get to tell my story first." He leaned away from me, bouncing off Link before returning to the center. "Tell her about the hotel we were in tonight."

Tangent, much? Up until now, Elliot struck me as focused and single-minded. He got something in his head and didn't let go. Jumping from topic to topic was an odd shift for him, but I didn't mind. "What about the hotel?"

"It's got his name on it," Link said.

"Did you carve *Elliot* somewhere?"

Elliot pointed out two more turns in quick succession. "It was the JM Howard. That's the hotel chain."

I'd never made the connection before. "Howard is a common last name, Not like *Smith*, but also not like *Zabriskie*."

The men dissolved into laughter. Apparently, the word *Zabriskie* was hilarious. I had an ex-boyfriend who would disagree, which made it really tempting to introduce him to these two while they were drunk.

"No." Link came down hard on the word. "It's *Elliot's* last name."

Pieces were clicking in my head. No. Shit.

"Technically, it's my grandfather's name. There's no way Dad was going to pass that gem along to his son. And really, I'm kind of grateful, because *Johnson* is one hell of a funny name." He fell back in his seat and grabbed his crotch. "Hi, I'm Johnson. It's like naming someone Richard."

"You're one of *those* Howards. The hotel chain Howards."

Elliot was back, his mouth near my ear. "That's right, Kittie."

"I told you he came from money," Link said.

Right. Because he lived in a mansion. But I'd been thinking… I didn't know what I'd thought, but not this. "You're a fucking billionaire."

The way Elliot shook his head was violent and almost scary. He stopped and pressed his hand to his forehead. "Nope. *Dad* is a billionaire. Grandpa Johnson was too. My cousin, when Dad passes the reins to him. I'm technically not part of the family anymore, so I'm still working on reaching that elusive three comma mark.

"But you…" What was I supposed to say? So many thoughts raced through my mind, I struggled to process Elliot's next navigation instructions.

"I what?" he asked.

"You work for a living."

He shrugged. "Debatable."

"Untrue." Link almost sounded offended. "He works *hard*."

I believed that.

"I'm not just a customer, I'm the owner." Elliot slid into a ridiculous infomercial-style voice.

I wasn't going to make the hotel mistake again.

He meant literally. "Trade publications say Judith Walsh is the owner." But I'd also looked into the company before to learn more about its board and investors, and because it was a private company, a lot of that information wasn't available.

We pulled up in front of his house, and I parked where I'd seen him park, in the first spot in the garage. As we climbed from the car, Elliot draped an arm around my shoulder and leaned in closely. "You can't tell anyone. Please. It's a secret. *Shhh*."

How often did he actually ask for something instead of just assuming he'd get it? Me telling other people that he was an owner of AcesPlayed didn't benefit me, and I liked being in on the secret.

"I promise, I won't. Cross my heart. Which key unlocks the door?"

Elliot took the keys from me and proceeded to drop them several times before finally letting us into the house.

Mrs. Ria was sitting in the living room with King, waiting. When she saw the condition Elliot and Link were in, she just rolled her eyes. "You'll take care of my idiots?" she asked me with nothing but affection in her voice.

"I will."

"Good. I'm leaving for the night." With that, she was gone.

Elliot stripped off his wig and set it on the coffee

table, and King growled and jumped on it. "Not a threat." Elliot laughed and picked up the dog.

Link took Elliot's wig and his own, and set them someplace higher. They both shed their trench coats quickly and tossed them over a nearby chair.

"Sit. Both of you." I wasn't sure how drunk they really were, but this seemed like a bad room for them to stumble through.

Link grinned. "Bossy Fallyn. I wanna see you face off with Bossy Elliot."

"Nope." Elliot popped on the *p*. "That is not a challenge I'm willing to take." He fell onto the couch, King still in his arms, and Link dropped next to them.

"I'm going to get us some water." I left the silly boys and their adorable dog and wandered into the kitchen.

Fuck me. Elliot was a billionaire. Or close enough. He didn't act like a snooty rich guy. Well, maybe a little. And how did Link save his life? Did it have something to do with AcesPlayed? Or was that just a tangent I wouldn't get the answer to tonight?

I stripped off my own wig and undid the zipper on the top of my jumpsuit, leaving the tank top underneath on display. Fortunately, the costume was comfortable. Then I downed my fill of water, grabbed two glasses for the guys, and headed back into the living room.

King was on the floor now, sleeping, but Elliot

and Link were still pressed together on the couch. I got close enough to give them their drinks, and Elliot reached for me instead. He wrapped an arm around my waist and pulled me down with them.

I squealed in surprise, and was even more shocked that I didn't get water everywhere. I managed to only splash us a little.

"I got you wet." Elliot snickered.

It wasn't funny, but I couldn't help a laugh. This silly mood of theirs was contagious. "So, did Link convince you to buy into AcesPlayed?" I wanted more of the story. Would I get it?

"No" Elliot took the glasses from me and set them on the coffee table. He maneuvered me so I was half in his lap, half in Link's. "He supported me, but I was in from the start."

"How's he your hero, then?" I asked.

Elliot held out his wrists, insides up. "Do you want to know how I got these scars?"

I wasn't sure which made my gut churn more, his Heath-Ledger-as-the-Joker impersonation being eerily spot-on, or knowing what kind of scars they were. "Only if you're comfortable telling me."

"I went to high school with Scott and Zach." Was this another of Elliot's tangents?

I assumed he meant the owners of Rinslet.

"When they started Cord, I was one of the first developers they brought on," Elliot said.

That was exactly who he meant. I knew he'd

been one of the original programmers. Cord had been publicly traded for a while, which was how Digital Media had acquired them back in the day, and basically canceled them after. It was also where Rinslet came from—rising from the ashes with a lot of the original crew, like a phoenix.

Elliot sighed. "I'd never felt more like I belonged somewhere." The giggles were gone from his voice, replaced with somberness. "Correction—I'd never felt like I belonged. Anywhere. Dad hated that I took the job, especially when I skipped college to do it. According to him, I was wasting my life. I didn't care when he cut me off, because Grandpa didn't, and because I had a new family at Cord."

I couldn't imagine loving a workplace so much that the people around me replaced my family, but that was mostly because I'd never been at a company where I didn't feel both like I had to fuck someone to stay there, and at the same time like I'd be fired the instant anyone thought I had.

Link's expression had gone somber too, and he watched Elliot closely.

"The year after Digital Media bought Cord was rough," Elliot said. "I know, takeovers are always rough, but it hit me hard. The new management and I clashed."

Online Fallyn might say *Imagine that*, but this wasn't the time to be snide or obnoxious.

Elliot stared at the insides of his wrists.

"Everything fell apart at once. Grandpa was diagnosed with pancreatic cancer and moved into hospice quickly. Dad wouldn't let me see him. And then we found out who DM was laying off."

Elliot must have been at the top of that list.

"Elliot was one of the only people they kept." Link dashed my theory in a few short words.

"The offer was simple—take the job, take the money, and don't tell anyone the terms of the contract, or we'd never work in the industry again. And from the quiet asking around that a friend did, it was a serious threat. No one would touch my resume." This was yet another Elliot. Somber. Strained. Haunted.

"DM sucked—they have a horrible culture over there," Elliot said. "The people I thought were my new family, the people from Cord, hated me, and my grandfather passed away without me being able to say goodbye."

"How did you get out of your contract?" There had to be a bright spot in this story, right? I needed to see a hint of it.

Elliot's smile was grim. "Remember years ago, when Jordan and Chloe humiliated DM at E3? That got them to cancel all of our contracts. Very quietly. With some intense non-disclosure agreements attached. So I supposed I didn't tell you that just now, or something."

King growled in his sleep at Elliot's feet, and rolled over, but he never woke up.

Elliot scrubbed his face. "Before that though, and at the risk of sounding like a country song, then my dog, the one I'd had for more than a decade, who was my best friend when I didn't have any friends in school, passed away. And yeah, I get that some people have it worse, but I hit rock bottom. I thought I was completely alone, and I couldn't imagine a worse fate."

His voice faded to so quiet I barely heard it. The silly drunkenness was gone, but so was the asshole. Elliot looked… lost and empty. I wanted to wrap my arms around him and tell him he wasn't alone.

"Elliot called me one night, and told me if anything happened to him, I could have his entire console collection and his gaming rig." Link sounded like it ached to say the words. To relive the memory.

Knowing where things were going, I understood why. I swore ice sped down my spine.

"The conversation felt wrong." Link looked pale and as haunted as Elliot. "When I found him, I didn't think he was still alive. The cuts were so deep. There was so much—" He shuddered.

Elliot made a noise that was part bark, part sigh, and part cough. "Anyway, so that's how Link saved my life, and why I have ink on the insides of my wrists."

Was it also why Elliot put up the heavy stone walls that kept people away from the real him, and was an asshole? Now hardly seemed like the time to ask. "I'm sorry," I said.

Elliot let out a long breath, as if pushing the memories away. "You know what I'm sorry for? That I'm sobering up. How am I supposed to make awkward and overt passes at you that are interpreted as me being a drunken idiot, if I'm not drunk?"

And now we were back to this? "I don't have a response to that."

Elliot wrapped his arms around me in a hug that felt like him clinging on for life. He leaned us both more into Link. "Don't sleep in the other wing tonight. Stay with us."

"Okay." I didn't have the will to argue.

Maybe I didn't want to be bitchy Fallyn full time. Not if Elliot was an example of what that looked like. Regret and sadness masking the real person underneath. If I hadn't already made up my mind already, this would've done it for me.

Did that mean Elliot won?

He squeezed me again.

No. He hadn't won anything. Not like this.

I didn't protest when Elliot pulled Link and I up to his bedroom. He wasn't doing the bossy, *take your clothes off*, thing. He seemed to want to continue the conversation.

I wouldn't have screwed them tonight anyway. I was pretty sure they were near sober, but the way our moods added to the silliness would've made for some impaired judgment.

I did help them out of their costumes, and the three of us fell onto Elliot's bed together in various states of undress. They fell asleep long before I did, with me pinned between them.

Not that I minded the gentle pressure or security of being surrounded by these two, but sleep was a long way off for me. Elliot's story still echoed in my mind. It was clear now why he got so upset about my videos. AcesPlayed really was everything to him. The company. The people.

It was almost endearing. Part of me jerked away from thinking about him like that, but I couldn't help it. At least for an hour or two, I got to see his gooey caramel center. Was it salty? Sure. But it was also sweet. I'd suspected he had a heart, but I hadn't expected to actually see it. Not exposed and vulnerable like this.

So now I had Link, who was default sweet, and Elliot who was one of those sour candies that changed flavor once all the bitterness was sucked off. It was obvious what they were to each other, so it wasn't as if my falling—

Whoa. My doing what?

I wasn't falling for anyone.

Maybe Link. A little. But I wouldn't—couldn't —come between him and Elliot. Not their friendship or their love.

For tonight though, I could be surrounded by it, and that was a pretty comfy spot to rest in.

Sleep finally took me, but I was woken up a short while later, by a weight on half of my body. I forced myself toward consciousness to find that Elliot had a leg draped over one of mine, and his full body was pressed into my side.

The assumption bothered me. "What are you —?" I snapped my abrupt question off. Was he even awake? "Elliot?" I said softly.

He didn't answer, but his erection pressed into my leg. His heat was so freaking tempting.

It wouldn't hurt anyone for me to enjoy the sleep cuddle. And this felt really good for something so simple. As I accepted this new position, Elliot shifted his weight again. He muttered something I couldn't make out, but if I didn't know any better, I'd swear it was my name.

My heart hammered against my ribs, and he continued to snooze through the way he was driving me wild. Link hadn't stirred, and his shape provided a solid wall of muscle on my other side.

Elliot moved one hand, and brushed the bottom of my breast, teasing my nipple. A zing yanked inside me, and doubled in intensity when he muttered, "*Fuck…Fallyn.*"

His hips worked in a grinding motion. Bugger, he was dry humping my leg.

"*Elliot*," I hissed sharply.

No answer.

Should I roll him off me? Or maybe slide my fingers between my legs and get myself off? Because I didn't know if it was wrong or right, but I liked the implications of this. That he was dreaming about me. That he had me half-trapped.

It was cranking my desire up double time, and the throb between my thighs insisted I decide soon.

I shouldn't finger myself to this, regardless of how much I wanted to. "*Elliot*," I hissed again.

"What the…?" Link's sleepy question reached my ear.

I glanced at him with a sheepish grin. Great. What now?

His smile was adorable. "Do you want help?"

"Yes," I whispered. "But I'm not sure with what. Pushing him off or getting me off." Fuck me. Did I really just say that aloud? It was like we were in a different world right now, and I didn't know the rules.

Link bit his bottom lip—apparently that was sexy on a guy. "I've never seen him do that before."

This was as surreal as it was arousing, talking about a sleeping Elliot like he wasn't here, and that Link knew him well enough to feel comfortable making that statement.

Link studied us a little longer, and the pulsing under my skin grew more intense with each passing second. He finally reached an arm out, and my heart leaped into my throat.

"Elliot." Link's voice was deeper, sharper, than before. He gave Elliot a light shake.

Elliot's eyes flew open, his face only inches from mine. Time froze as he held my gaze. "Shit. I must've been dreaming." He didn't move.

I didn't dare do so either. "Seems that way."

He started to pull his hand away, and impulse snaked through me.

I grabbed his wrist, and moved his palm to my breast instead. "I didn't say you had to go."

"Yeah?" His smile went from sleepy to wicked in a heartbeat.

"That is… if you want to see what happens next in your dream." I glanced at Link. "And show the two of us, in the process."

Elliot shifted his weight, this time intentionally, and there was no longer a question of his intent. His weight pinned me down and locked me in place. I was helpless, in the most delicious way.

He looked at Link. "Do you want to watch?"

"No."

At Link's reply, my heart sank.

"I want to help." A growl undercut Link's words, carrying a kind of possessiveness that surprised me and called to the dampness pooling between my legs. He gripped my chin and forced my face toward his. The way he dragged his thumb over my bottom lip sent shivers over me.

I hadn't kissed either of them yet. The realization struck me hard. But, why would I? This was play, not love or romance.

Elliot slid a hand under my shirt, glided up my stomach, and lightly pinched my nipple. That combined with the way he had me locked down made me squirm with need.

Link lowered his head toward mine, and my heart slammed loudly in my chest. The sound was deafening, drowning out my thoughts. When he sealed his lips to mine, my heart nearly burst. The kiss started soft. Tentative.

I was flying. Soaring above the entire world.

And then Link pressed in harder. His mouth demanded more, and he tightened his grip on my chin as he pushed his tongue into my mouth.

I had no choice but to yield, and to kiss back with the intensity of a million fans demanding a sequel. I leaned into him for all I was worth, and everything else fell away except for Elliot's hot touch. That plus Link's kiss…

There was no more incredible way to be captured.

"Maybe I should be the one watching." Elliot's words wove into the moment rather than shattering it.

Link pulled back, and I sighed.

"But I'm not very good at going hands-off," Elliot glided his hand down my stomach, to tease the waistband of my panties. "And I do like to make you come."

I gasped at the spark that filled me when he brushed his fingers over my pussy. His touch made the moment more vivid, and at the same time added to the dream-like shell that made this world ours alone.

Link shoved my tank top up, and brought his mouth to my breast. When he wrapped his lips around a nipple, I arched into the sensation. Where was I supposed to focus? His tongue or Elliot's fingers, teasing along my clit?

Orgasm enveloped me from nowhere, stealing my breath and thoughts, sending me spinning into incredible sensations, and leaving me hoarse from screaming, when Elliot eased up on his attentions.

I was still catching my breath when Link moved his mouth back to mine.

"I want to watch you ride me." It was a command, not a request. He gripped my hips and rolled with both of us.

With me straddling his waist, the size difference was distinct. Suddenly every meme and joke on the internet about size differences in partners was far more personal. He yanked the crotch of my panties aside, leaving a burn of friction in his wake, and teased the head of his cock along my slit.

When he paused with a frown, my disappointment was real.

"Fuck. Condom," he muttered.

"I don't care." I needed him *now*. As I raised myself up, I wrapped my fingers along his shaft. *So big. Birth control don't fail me now.* When I lowered myself onto his cock, the stretch hurt so good. I took my time sliding down, loving the way his groan mingled with mine.

With Link buried inside me, I had to pause. Adjust to the girth. Appreciate how incredible this felt.

Elliot pressed into my back. "Don't mind me. Just enjoying the show." He nipped my neck. Further down, his erection met my skin. The way he slipped against my body was half him jerking off, half-him humping me.

And that made this all hotter.

Link moved his hands to my hips, and matched my rhythm as I rode him. Each time I came down, he struck something deep inside, and it felt amazing.

From behind me, Elliot's grunts grew more intense. Matching our pace. Pulling up my desire.

Link increased the pace until he was slamming inside me. This time, climax lingered just out of reach. Taunting me. Daring me to want one more orgasm.

When Link slid his hands up my stomach to cup my breasts, when he dragged his gaze over me and muttered my name over and over, as if in worship, the dam broke inside me. Pleasure crashed through me. I gripped his wrists, holding his hands in place, clinging to him as if he were my lifeline.

A warm spurt hit my back, and another, as Elliot came. The sensation, hot against my flushed skin, drew out my orgasm, and I clenched around Link until it ached. I never wanted this to stop.

"Fuck. Fallyn." The way Link grunted my name was incredible. He slammed harder and harder, and then stalled. With another long groan, he spilled inside me.

The intensity in the room slowed, but it didn't fade. It continued to wrap us in a bubble, even as we lay there, trying to find our breath, none of us speaking. Even when Elliot left to get a warm washcloth and clean me off, before we crashed into bed again, he was silent.

I had no doubt I'd sleep now. I was safe between these two. Especially Link. He would save me from the world. Even Elliot didn't feel threatening.

At least, not in the way he probably should. I was terrified of slipping further into whatever this was, and letting myself believe the three of us had more than sex. We didn't. Especially not with Elliot. I saw those whispers of what I witnessed in other men, and I had to keep my heart away from him, no matter what secrets we all shared with each other.

A scared little voice inside me asked *what if it's too late*. If I let myself feel more, if I admitted I already did, this could hurt me more than anything ever had.

**17 /
link**

I woke up to Elliot sleeping next to me, but no Fallyn. The house smelled like coffee, and this had the distinct feeling of déjà vu compared to yesterday, except that Mrs. Rita didn't work on Saturdays, especially after a long week. Elliot would never let her.

King wasn't up here either. He seemed to be happy to follow Fallyn around.

Not that I blamed him. *Fuck* last night was incredible. The sex, the talking, the having Fallyn in my arms. What would it take to keep her in my life, because I swore there was something between us.

But Elliot.

Two words that carried so much weight, it might crush me.

I wouldn't think about it. As long as I stayed away from those paths my mind wanted to forge, I'd be fine.

Regardless of the ache in my chest at being pressed close to Elliot, but no longer Fallyn. There was no ignoring how many nights this hadn't meant anything between him and me.

Except, had that ever really been true? Or was it easy to ignore there was more because there weren't external sources making me look closer at my relationship with Elliot?

I should get downstairs. As I climbed from the bed, *what if this is the last time* whispered through my thoughts.

Weird question, because it wouldn't be, but even if it was, Elliot and I would still be friends.

Downstairs, I found Fallyn in the breakfast nook, King at her feet. The little alcove was the perfect place to sit in the mornings in the winter, because the morning sun came in from the side of the bay window, and it wasn't too hot to sit and enjoy it.

She gave me a faint smile, but didn't say anything. Speaking felt like it might shatter this world that only had this house in it.

I sure was contemplative today. Had we really ripped out our insides and exposed ourselves so much yesterday? The memory seemed a million miles away, but also still felt raw.

The smell of coffee drew me into the kitchen, and King followed me, running around my feet as I crossed the room. He slipped and slid on the tile, but didn't leave my side as I made myself a cup of morning worship, then returned to sit across from Fallyn.

What was I supposed to say? Did we keep pretending this was a weird frenemyship? I didn't like that idea, but what else were we supposed to be?

How about straight up friends? I hoped so, since at this point she knew more of Elliot's and my secrets than anyone else.

"Do you want to know the big reason I won't take Nigel's job offers?" Fallyn's question was quiet, but the implications screamed in my head.

"Nigel tried to hire you? Of course he did. He knows talent when he sees it."

She hid her expression behind a giant coffee mug that said *meh* on it. It had been a white elephant gift from Jeremy, years ago, and it was one of Elliot's favorites.

"Pretty sure these days it's just lip service on his part, but yes," she said. "I tell him I make a lot more making my videos."

Which was what I'd expect. "Don't you?" It would also be a massive conflict of interest—her tearing apart other games wouldn't be right if she was QA for ours.

"I do." She continued to hold the mug up, despite not drinking, and stared at the inside as if it held the secrets of the universe. "When I tell you I love your game—this one, the Rinslet ones—I mean it. But my work experience has taught me that the best way to learn to hate something is to draw a paycheck from it. I've left more than one job because I made the mistake of falling for a co-worker who turned out to be…" She huffed. "Dangerously toxic. Verbally abusive. Capable of ruining my reputation. Cruel…"

I'd known guys like that. Bryce, but he certainly wasn't the only one. I wanted to tell her *we're different*, but I couldn't promise that all of us were, as much as I hated to think anyone was capable of what she was describing. "I get it."

"You probably don't completely, but I do believe you're sympathetic. Anyway"—she spit out the last word before I could respond—"how did Elliot save your life?"

Oh, so we were getting intense again. Could I gloss over the question? Did I want to? "He gave me a job when no one else would."

She sipped her coffee.

I took that as a sign to continue, despite the part of me begging me to stop. "I was young, big and scary looking, and a convicted felon. No one would hire me, and believe it or not, my father wouldn't let me come back home after what I'd done." Good. Fuck that asshole.

"I was living out of a car that I only had because I'd paid cash for it before I was arrested. There was a convenience store that let me wash up in their bathrooms in the morning, and looked the other way if I begged for change around the side of their shop." This story hurt to tell once, but now it was my past. I'd dealt with it. I'd moved on.

Fallyn frowned. "God, I'm sorry."

"It is what it is. Really." I meant that. "The place was on the way to work for Elliot, and he stopped there most mornings for Dew re-ups. He'd give me his change. And then it was coffee. And then he was taking me to breakfast." He'd tried to offer me a place to live, but I was too proud for that. This was the part that hurt. Not because of what happened then—I loved these memories— but because no one believed that Elliot now was the same man, and I knew better. "Then he offered me a job. I'd learned a little about computers from a friend in jail, but he was willing to teach me anything I needed to know about programming."

"Wow." Fallyn's tone was impossible to interpret.

I'd make up the meaning I preferred. "Yeah. I'm pretty fucking lucky."

She looked past me. "So you do have a heart in there."

I whirled, to see Elliot in the doorway, lounging against the frame in sweats that hung low off his hips, and no shirt. When did he join us, and why did he have to look so good, even now?

He kicked into an upright position. "I don't. It

shriveled and died eons ago." He didn't sound upset.

"He does have a heart," I said. "Don't believe him."

Elliot shook his head. "I did what anyone would've done."

"You did what almost no one would've done," Fallyn argued. "And now the two of you are intertwined in this bond of honor that will keep you together for eternity."

Was she being serious or sarcastic? "Pretty sure that's not the case," I said.

Elliot strode past us. "Not until we complete the final quest, anyway. We have to defeat the boss monster."

Fallyn laughed lightly. Appropriate response to a ridiculous brush-off, and I liked both.

Elliot grabbed his coffee, then took a seat at the table with us. "Moving on. I was thinking, I know Fallyn's trip is half over, but it's not right that she's sleeping all the way on the other side of the house. You should stay in one of the billions of rooms closer to mine."

Whoa. Did that much change last night?

"Why?" Fallyn looked as surprised as I was.

On other hand, Elliot sipped his drink in the most casual manner possible. "I just told you why."

"But why really?" I needed to know.

He shrugged. "I don't know. Good girls get rewarded?" His tone was almost playful.

Fallyn didn't look impressed. "Wow. So you're *so generous*." Even before she finished talking, her smirk broke through.

"Right?" Elliot grinned.

Wait. Were they teasing each other? In a fun way? Without any alcohol or immediate promise of sex? "No, really." I poked Elliot in the arm. "Pod person? Robot clone?"

"Knock it off." Elliot batted my arm away. "Link likes Fallyn, and I trust his opinion. King does too, and dogs aren't wrong about these things."

The face Fallyn made was exaggerated and almost pained. She sucked in a long breath through her teeth. "I mean... they like you, so it's not a perfect theory."

"Bitch." Elliot was still teasing.

And Fallyn's smile grew. "Asshole."

The banter was light and no malice hid in either of their voices. Their smiles reached their eyes. This was surreal, but I liked it. "If you are robot clones, remember I was already loyal when you enslave the minds of humanity."

"Noted." Elliot pressed a spot on the side of his head, near his eye, and his expression went blank. "Human Link is loyal." His tone went monotone. His face returned to normal and relaxed. "Seriously for just a second. Are you going to the con all day, Fallyn?"

"Not sure yet. There are panels I want to catch this morning, but I really need to get some work in, so I might come back here this afternoon."

"I have to drop Link off at his car and I have first shift at the Aces booth. If you want a ride, we can take you." Elliot offered.

And Fallyn still looked mildly surprised. "Sure."

I didn't know what had shifted in Elliot's head, but I was here for it. Because whether or not it made sense, I wanted more of Fallyn in my life even when this weekend was over. While I wouldn't push her away based on someone else's feedback, it would be a lot less stressful if Elliot liked the idea too.

Whatever weird sense of foreboding I'd had when I got out of bed was gone, replaced with a spark of hope and want that this was about to become something amazing.

elliot

As Fallyn headed toward the other side of the house, I cut a straight line upstairs before Link could stop me. He grabbed one of the guest bathrooms, and the three of us got ready.

I was trying my hardest not to think about how that serious conversation had so quickly turned fun and casual. Avoiding the thoughts wasn't the easiest, especially in the shower. It would be best if my mind was blank and the jumble stayed at bay. Because if I let the thoughts in, I'd wonder what I was doing with Fallyn.

And then I'd wonder why I was feeling jealously possessive of Link. He and I had both been with other people *many* times over the years. We didn't have the kind of relationship where jealousy was appropriate.

Once I pushed those thoughts aside, Fallyn would rush back in, and I'd end up bobbling between her and Link so much, my head might snap off.

Which was why I wasn't giving either of them any brain space.

Nope.

Not a single second of my morning would go to thinking about the two of them. I was getting ready for work and nothing else.

When I got downstairs, Link was already getting King's kennel ready for a couple of hours alone. I wouldn't leave the dog here longer without company. Once I dropped Link and Fallyn off and did a short security stint, I'd come back here for a few hours, and Link would swap with me this afternoon, when it was my turn to go back to the booth.

The ringing of my phone finally blocked my rambling mind. Should I be grateful for the interruption or curse it? I glanced at the screen.

Fuck. "It's the night crew." The developers we had on call in case something went wrong. Which it had if they were calling me now. "Talk to me." As I answered, Link's expression shifted from light to concerned.

"We've had a cascading failure on the servers," Tyler said. "One crashed and then the rest, one after another."

That was what cascading meant, yes. I choked back the sarcasm. "Feed me the symptoms."

As Tyler talked, I whispered to Link, "We need to go. Get my guest?"

He narrowed his eyes, but nodded and headed toward Fallyn's room.

While I talked Tyler through a series of questions, I leashed up King and grabbed some things to take him into the office with me. Some issues could be troubleshot from home, but with the security problems we'd had, a lot of work needed to be done in-office, behind the protections Luna and Danny had put in place.

Speaking of, "Call Danny, give him the rundown. See what he says. Call Luna, tell her to get into the office. Call me back when you're done."

"All right." Tyler disconnected.

I mentally ran through the list of what was happening, examining it from different angles, while King yipped and ran around, excited to be going outside and for a ride. Link and Fallyn met me at the car.

"Is everything all right?" She sounded genuinely concerned.

"It will be." The words came out more clipped than I intended. I wasn't being cruel, but I only had the brain space for this issue right now. There was definitely no time to appreciate how good she looked in what I was pretty sure was an outfit from *My Dress Up Darling.* A blue skirt that barely covered her ass, and a button-down white shirt, tied at the waist, and with a tie hanging loosely around the open collar.

Definitely couldn't give that the mental power I wanted.

I took the return call from Tyler and put him on speaker, asked Link to drive, and we were on our way.

Was it a bad idea to let Fallyn listen in on this call? Maybe. She'd probably figure out most of it anyway, and I needed Link to hear so I could get his input.

As Tyler spoke, the scenario sounded more and more familiar. I put myself on mute, let him continue, and shifted in my seat to look at Fallyn. "Is it just me or…?"

She shook her head. "No. This is something you patched months ago in beta." She'd found the bug and sent it to us through Nigel, so she should know.

Had we missed fixing it somewhere? Were the symptoms just similar?

I unmuted the phone, and talked over Tyler, giving him a list of things to check. "Got it?"

"Yes."

"Good. We're about ten minutes out. Catch me up on everything else when I get there." I disconnected. "Game is completely offline until we get this fixed. On its first Saturday live, during RinCon."

Link nodded grimly. What else was he supposed to say except *obvious news is obvious*?

"If you need my notes, I have them," Fallyn offered.

"Thanks. I'll let you know."

We dropped her off at the convention center, and were at the office just a few minutes later. Inside, no one else had arrived yet, so it was only Link, me, and the two on-call guys.

I pointed at Jesse. "Email to everyone on the team. Copy Dustin so he knows I'm stealing his con security. Every developer needs to be in the office."

As he turned to his computer, I grabbed a marker from the white board tray and began to write. In just a few minutes, I had a list of to-dos, assignments, and additional next steps. I brought King into my office, set him up in a corner, and waited for everyone else to arrive.

When most of the group was at their desks, I moved to the middle of the room. "You know how this works. Tasks are on the board. When you finish something, cross it off, and move on to the next thing. If you need help, I'm here. Ask me. Ask someone. We're working as a team on this."

"Have we checked for database corruption?" Chris's question caught me off-guard. So had the fact that he was one of the first developers to show up after we put out the call.

I stared at him. Why did this feel off? "No. Get on that."

"Sure. Can't believe you didn't think of it though," he muttered.

"Save the asshole arrogance for when we're not in a crunch." I was torn between picking that fight and getting the work done. Fortunately for Chris, my level of *I don't give a fuck* about his personal opinions was as intense as my desire to get the game back online.

I took King out, introduced him to the team—which seemed great for morale considering I'd dragged them into the office on a Saturday morning—then I put him in a makeshift pen and got back to work like everyone else.

As I pored through the code, it was easy to spot some of the issues, because they were things we'd already fixed. Did we really miss this much? That wasn't right. My team had years of experience. Landon was the newest, skill-wise, but he'd already proven himself to be as good as anyone else here.

So what was going on?

I kept my head down and my fingers flying over the keys, tweaking and testing and tweaking some more. I didn't realize how much time had passed until King's whining, accompanied by a horrible smell, caught my attention. Shit, it had been almost four hours.

Shit was right—in his pen. That explained the smell. At least I'd laid down pads. I couldn't give him the attention he needed right now. Even the few minutes I took to clean up the mess, lay down new pads, and take him outside, felt like an eternity while the rest of my crew was working so hard.

He needed to go home, but I didn't want him there alone. I couldn't call Ria because she was spending the day at a church holiday function. My friends were working.

I hated to do it, because she had plans too, but Fallyn was the only person I could think of. Though, oddly enough I did trust her with the request, and I wasn't willing to think about the implications of that.

While King was sniffing trees in front of the office and generally freaking out, in a good way, about being someplace new, I called Fallyn.

She answered on the fifth ring, and the background noise almost drowned out her *hello*. "Hang on," she shouted. "Moving to someplace quiet." The several-decibel chatter continued, then faded. "Sorry about that. Hi." Her voice was bright, and tugged at my cock like an invisible hand.

"Hey. I need to ask a favor."

"What's up? You're not going to ask for a blow job in the broom closet are you? Because I'm not up for that. I mean, I might be, but I'm not."

I let out a short laugh. "What? No." Maybe. But no. Was I really…? With Fallyn? I understood why Link was confused earlier. "I hate to ask this, but…" *Sigh.* "I don't know how long I'm going to be here, and I need someone to take King home who can either stay with him, or check on him and take him out of his crate every few hours. You can use my car. I'll pay for parking."

"Are you sure you trust me with your baby?"

Was this about the conversation last night? "The dog or the car?"

"Both."

I was sure. "Believe it or not, yes. It doesn't need to be now. He just went out, so next hour or so?"

"Sure. I'd be happy to." She sounded light and sincere.

And I was relieved. "When you get here, text me and I'll come downstairs, so you don't have to…" *run into anyone from the office.*

Fuck. It had been easy enough to tell her last night that I was okay being seen with her, but having Fallyn walk into the AcesPlayed offices…

"Yeah, I'd like to avoid that." She sounded as hesitant as I felt.

"I owe you. Big time." I hung up and took King back up to the offices with me. The instant I was back at my keyboard, I was immersed in bug fixing again until Fallyn texted me that she was here.

Once again, I headed outside, and found her across the street at Loading Java, the coffee shop there. She was holding two cups as I approached and she handed me one. "You might need this."

"Thanks." I wasn't used to that. "You might need this?" I handed her King's leash.

Not that I needed to. He was already jumping up on her legs, and she was laughing and crouching down to pet him.

When she straightened up again, I finished giving her instructions, and handed her my car keys as well. "Seriously, I'm eternally grateful for this," I said.

"It's not a big deal. I was going to cut out anyway, and Puppy will be good company." Fallyn shifted her weight from one foot to the other. "So, um, is the issue what you thought?"

I shouldn't have this conversation with anyone not in the team, but especially not her. "Largely. It caused a few other issues as well. Database corruption, things like that, but mostly it's the same issue."

"Can't you just go back to an old save of the code or something?"

What? No. That was dumb.

I swallowed the response. I forgot that just because Fallyn knew how to break our code didn't mean she understood how we created it. Most people didn't. "It's not that easy."

"Why not?"

How to best explain this? "Imagine you're writing a script for your show. You find a section you don't like, you edit maybe half a page, and then you go on to make dozens of other little edits—spelling fixes, etcetera—both in the new and old," I said.

Fallyn nodded. "With you so far."

"Now multiply that by ten thousand, and that's what we're dealing with. Yes, we could roll some sections back, but after we accounted for all the other changes made since then, it's faster to just manually fix things. Hours instead of days, to make sure we don't make the issue worse."

"Oh." She frowned. "That makes sense. But it sucks you have to do all of this twice."

I would've laughed at the simplicity of the statement if the accuracy didn't hurt. "It really does."

"So I'll let you get back to it." She tugged lightly on King's leash.

"Thanks. For everything." A strange impulse snaked through me, to lean in and kiss her. Not a long, drawn-out, tonsil-tag kind of kiss, but a simple *thank you* on the forehead. I ignored it, gave her one final wave, and returned to work.

As I sat down at my computer again, I found myself staring at another piece of code I swore we'd fixed, and the exchange with Fallyn, in the car, rushed back to me. *This is something you patched months ago in beta.* That was what she'd said as she listened to the symptoms.

It made sense she would remember—it was one of the bigger issues she'd pointed out to us. I didn't like the doubt that accompanied my thoughts.

I'd heard most of the conversation she had with Link this morning, and I believed her when she said she loved the game and wanted to see it thrive.

Which made me hate even more that my mind was ticking through how she could've pulled this off. This was a bug she'd originally found. Looking at the code now, what was in here wasn't written by the original developer who'd worked on this module. Code was like handwriting—everyone's was just a little different—and after working with some of these people for as long as two decades, I know how each of them did things.

This code snippet was out of place, but more like it was mimicking what surrounded it.

Fuck if the pieces here didn't fit together the way they should, and the picture they were creating was of *someone* sabotaging the game.

But it wasn't Fallyn. The conversation I'd just had with her told me that regardless of her skillset, she didn't have the knowledge to pull this off.

Someone was working pretty hard to make it look like this was her fault, though. Who?

19 /

fallyn

I didn't want to admit it to Elliot, but being at the con for two and a half days was draining, and I'd been grateful for the excuse to cut out early. Not that I wasn't having fun at RinCon—this was an experience I'd never forget, and I'd definitely do it again. The spectacle, the atmosphere, the collective excitement… It was all amazing.

But I'd also been *accidentally* groped more times than I cared to count, and interacted with more people in the last two and a half days than in the last five years.

As I walked into Elliot's house and let King off his leash, he took off immediately to run around then return to my side. This was the kind of company I needed after the last few days.

Would I be coming back next year? Without question. Now that I knew what to expect, I could schedule in breaks. Besides, Link and Elliot…

I followed King into the living room and settled onto the couch. It was weird being alone in this house, this mansion, that was big enough to make a family of ten comfortable and that Elliot rambled around in by himself most of the time.

Yeah, things got off to a rough start with him and Link, but the longer I spent with them, individually and together, the more I appreciated their company. I hadn't met a lot of people in my life who made me feel like it was okay to just be me, and regardless of what Elliot said about being a Grinch, I saw those hints underneath of what Link saw.

I should do some work. Play a game. Upload a video. Something. Instead, my rambling thoughts kept falling back to Link and Elliot, and I couldn't pull my gaze from an empty corner of the living room a few feet from the fireplace.

The spot that was just begging to have a Christmas tree in it. It was probably a bad idea to remember where Ria said the ornaments were kept, but now that the thought was there, I couldn't shake it.

I whistled and King came running. "Come on," I said. "Let's go explore the basement." Partly so I wasn't leaving him alone, but mostly because basements were creepy places. I couldn't carry him and use my phone as a flashlight, so I put him back on his leash and harness. He tried to run toward the door, and whimpered when I tugged him away.

"We're going someplace else fun." I guided him toward the basement entrance that Ria had pointed out. And by *more fun* I meant *potentially terrifying*, but he didn't need to know that.

When I opened the door, Puppy realized we were heading someplace brand new, and he yipped and tugged against the leash.

I flipped the light switch on at the top of the stairs, and a covered bulb flicked on, illuminating polished wood steps, painted walls, and a lightly textured ceiling. This was the opposite of creepy. So far I liked it.

When I reached the bottom floor, there was carpet. Clean, new, barely walked on. I flipped the next switch and a giant, empty room lit up. This wasn't at all what I expected. The walls were painted a boring white, the carpet was beige, and the room was immaculately finished. The ports on the walls said it was also wired for internet—or at least networking of some sort.

This space was probably bigger than my entire condo, and there was nothing in it except a bicycle and some weights pushed against the far wall.

"Wow." The way my exclamation bounced back at me sounded fantastic. Not too hollow or echoey,

Puppy barked several times, and I got the same experience with the sound, but amplified. If I had a room like this in my place, this vast, open space, it would be where I set up my office and did all my streaming. The large, blank walls made a perfect canvas for a green screen, there was plenty of space for VR, and if Elliot was responsible for the wiring, I bet the internet down here was great.

Not why I was here. I crossed the room to a door, where I found boxes and boxes stacked on the other side. This space wasn't as nicely finished, but it still had a bare bulb for light, and sheet rocked walls.

The Christmas decorations and tree were right where Ria said they would be. It took me a while to go through everything—there was far more here than I needed for a single tree—but I managed to create a separate pile to haul upstairs.

I took breaks to make sure King got to go outside, and in between he *helped* me put up a tree and decorate it. Most of the ornaments were elegant but simple—gold and white. Glass balls, and crystal icicles that looked more like they belonged on a chandelier than on a tree.

It was almost seven when I finished, and the entire thing looked beautiful.

Where was Elliot? Would he be pissed when he saw this? It was a thought I hadn't allowed myself to linger on during setup, but now I couldn't help but focus on it. I was pretty sure Link would love it. Not that this was his house, but I was starting to get the impression it might as well be.

If Elliot was going to yell at me for it, so be it. It

looked lovely and this place needed to feel a little warmth. Something that wouldn't hurt him to experience either.

I grabbed my laptop, settled in on the couch again, and checked the game site. Still down. Poor Elliot and Link.

I busied myself with other activities instead, while I waited for Elliot. As the clock neared and passed eleven at night, my eyelids were growing heavy. I wanted to wait up for him, but I wasn't a night person, and it had been a long few days…

Long nights and weekends came with the territory, and I didn't mind them. But walking into the house at three in the morning, after a day of repairing an issue I didn't know the root cause of, was the kind of draining I couldn't define.

The game was back online. I wouldn't trust it to stay that way until I did some more digging, but I knew my limits and when my brain was this oatmeal-like consistency, I was as likely to make things worse as to fix them. I'd sleep for a few hours, and head into the office tomorrow... Later today.

As Nigel dropped me off in front of my house, a soft glow shone from deeper inside, barely reaching the front windows. I didn't have any lights like that. I gave Nigel a quick *thank you*, for both ride and the fact he didn't feel the need to make random small talk, and I headed inside.

I'd sent Link back to his place because as much as I wanted his company tonight, he needed sleep too.

Inside, it was clear the pale yellow glow of light was coming from the living room, so I went to investigate.

When I reached the doorway, the sight stalled me in my tracks and I swore my heart stopped as well. It hurt to see the tree in the corner. Ached so much a fist squeezed the air from my lungs. Especially since, amid the elegant, clean matching decorations, were a handful I'd made when I was a kid. Ornaments Dad sure as fuck wasn't going to hang, but Grandpa was happy to.

It hurt like hell, but it also made me smile. Seeing Fallyn asleep on the couch, her costume wrinkled and in disarray, and King curled up on her feet, made both the grief and the joy that much more potent.

Except she wasn't asleep anymore. She was watching me with sleepy eyes. "I 'ope it's okay." Her voice was soft, and her accent thicker than normal.

"It is." I didn't trust myself to say more.

She sat up, and patted the couch next to her. "What time is it?"

"Three thirty-ish?"

"In the morning?"

It seemed like a silly question, but it was also

kind of cute. I settled next to her, trying not to disturb King. "Yes. In the morning."

"No Link?" Fallyn asked.

My jealousy spiked, and I didn't like the way it disturbed my bittersweet nostalgia. "No Link. It's just you and me and King."

"I can think of worse fates." She wasn't leaning into me, but she sat close enough her thigh brushed mine.

Her response calmed me. "Same." Maybe… Could I let her in? Not as close as Link, but I could see enjoying her friendship long-term.

We were quiet for a few minutes, and I wondered if she'd drifted off to sleep again when she said, "If I ask you something, give me an honest answer."

"Depends on the question."

"Are you really a Christmas Grinch?"

A short laugh escaped me. "I don't think the qualifier is necessary. I'm just a Grinch."

"Fair point."

I hadn't expected an argument and I was glad I didn't get one. It would've felt forced on her part. "You like Christmas?"

"I loved it back home."

"Not anymore?"

She shrugged and pulled her knees to her chest, making her look even smaller. More vulnerable. "It's not the same here. I call my sister at the start of December and we decorate together. Christmas Day we do something similar—open presents long distance on voice chat. But having her in the room with me was a different experience."

"You never go visit?" I was surprised.

"Sometimes. But it's hard to take time off when you do what I do. I only managed this trip because I knew I could stream while I was here. Flying halfway around the world and vanishing from the internet for a week or more? The world would forget I existed."

I understood, and doubted my *I wouldn't forget* was the kind of reassurance she wanted. "If you're in-game on Christmas, and you want company, come find Link and me."

Fallyn leaned some of her weight into me, and the pressure was both delicious and reassuring. "As Kittie or as Fallyn," she asked.

"Up to you." It didn't matter, as long as she showed up. I wanted to make a different offer—a more encompassing one—but that was an impulse I couldn't indulge even enough to let the details form in my mind.

"Do you remember the Christmas event last year?"

She meant in-game. When there were mini-quests that were just like regular quests, but with

Christmas-themed descriptions and rewards, and there were limited edition outfits and weapons that were more decorative than functional.

The Art and Story teams loved the holiday events, and since players did too, might as well keep doing them.

But last Christmas… That was when I met Kittie in the game. "You mean the event where I saved your ass in the event dungeon?"

"The one where *I* saved *your* ass, by being the healer you needed to get in, and then by healing your barbarian butt every time you charged into the middle of a pack of enemies." Fallyn's words were full of reproach, but her tone was light and missing any accusation.

I shook my head. "Nope. Don't remember anything that happened that way, so you must be thinking of a different barbarian."

Her laugh was delightful. "I must be."

"What I remember," I said, "is that you looked incredible in the event dress." All of the outfits in game were available for any race and gender. Anyone could pick the Santa pants with the matching puppy dog ears, or the short Santa skirt and halter top, with the kitty ears. Even the male orcs could wear the mini. And true to her character's name, Fallyn had chosen the kitty ear outfit.

"My *character* looked incredible. It's amazing how

good a series of pixels can look in an outfit designed specifically for their shape."

I couldn't help but smile at her light sarcasm. "I'll pass your praise along to the artists. But I meant what I said—in my head, you're wearing that outfit, and you look amazing."

"And you're stripping me out of it?" She asked incredulously.

"You said it, not me."

"You were thinking it."

"I am now. Okay, I was before, too." Anything to keep the conversation from getting too serious, right? Except a tiny, insignificant part of me, wished I hadn't gone down this path.

Fallyn rolled her eyes and pursed her lips. "I promise not to tell. I also promise not to tell anyone you ripped off Sadie Sews with the design."

"So first of all, *I* didn't rip anyone off." This was fun. Did I want it to be? Fallyn curled up next to me on the couch, with a Christmas tree sparkling in the corner, and my puppy sleeping on my other side. Link was missing, that sucked, but— "Contrary to what you'd like the world to believe, ET Howard doesn't make every decision for AcesPlayed. And we didn't rip Sadie off, we licensed her designs. She was happy to charge us a fair fee."

"You know Sadie?" Like that, Fallyn was in awe.

One of Sadie's boyfriends had worked with us at Rinslet, and the other was a streamer who did a lot of promo for them. Grayson was almost Fallyn's opposite—he loved most everything he played, and he was happy to hype it all on his channel. "I know Sadie."

"Can you introduce me?"

"What do I get in return?" I was teasing. I'd make the introduction in a heartbeat. Tomorrow even, if I wasn't either in the office or passed out from lack of sleep.

Fallyn scrunched up her face in thought. "The thrill of knowing you made someone's day?"

"Do you really think that motivates me?" Even my sarcasm was playful. Who was I?

She leaned more of her weight against me. "I think you're not the black void of nothingness you pretend to be."

I rested my head on hers. "Damn. My secret's out."

"Just with me, and I promise not to tell anyone."

"Because it's not a bug, it's a feature, so it's not worthy of being on your channel?"

She laughed. *Fuck* I liked that sound. "Clever," she said. "Because I see why Link keeps it to himself. Seeing ET Howard's good side is kind of like being in an exclusive club."

How was I supposed to reply to that? Not with another joke about fantasizing about her getting naked. Nothing that would send her from the room in a huff, and shatter this week and reset life back to what it was before she got here.

"Only for the two of you." Saying that made me feel more exposed than standing in the middle of the convention center and stripping naked, and I didn't like that feeling. But I also couldn't take it back.

21 /
link

I didn't like waking up alone. As I lay in bed Sunday morning, that was the only thought in my head. It had grabbed hold of my mind and my heart and wasn't going to release either without leaving a mark or two.

Correction—I didn't like waking up without Elliot or Fallyn.

I'd lived alone for decades and never minded before. Or maybe I'd always minded and I just never let myself think about it. Either way, going back to a different house than Elliot early this morning left me with a gnawing inside that I couldn't shake.

I wanted to wake up next to Elliot every day. From here until whenever.

The thought hit me hard. What was I supposed to make of that? That kind of commitment and permanence…

I wasn't dim. People could want to spend the rest of their lives around each other and be good friends, nothing else. But I had that with Elliot and it wasn't enough. Did I lo—

No. That wasn't right. Because then where did that leave Fallyn?

Same place as now. In that perfect, let's-see-where-this-goes space that could lead to so much more.

I needed to tell them both. The moment I thought the words, the impulse nearly overwhelmed me. Why *now*? Or maybe a far better question was *why not before*? I didn't have the answer, but I needed Elliot in my life more than he was now. I wanted *more* than just occasional sex and sleepovers.

And I wasn't ready to push Fallyn out either. What lay unexplored between us couldn't stay that way. I was drawn to her, connected by a thread that was stronger than should be possible.

I'd talk to them both today. Probably separately, because as much as it hurt to see, I wasn't sure if the two of them fit with each other. I wanted them to. I knew it was possible.

But Elliot...

Seeing my resolve through meant getting out of bed and getting ready for the day. Nervous excitement thrummed inside. This was going to be amazing.

I grabbed my phone from the nightstand as I got

up and checked for texts or calls from work. Anything else would wait. There was nothing new, so I showered and dressed. The longer the idea rolled in my mind, of telling Elliot I wanted more from our relationship, of asking Fallyn if she was willing to see where things went long term, the more I liked it.

I dialed Elliot, to see if he wanted to grab breakfast or just hang at his place. No answer.

I'd head over anyway, in just a few minutes. As I finished getting ready to leave, I checked my email.

That wasn't right. There were a handful of alerts based on my name. The notifications were a habit I got into at Rinslet—it was company policy to set them up, but I'd never personally needed to worry about them.

I usually only remembered they existed because Elliot got them when Fallyn posted videos mentioning him, and someone shared them.

These had all three of our names attached to them, but they weren't about one of her videos. It was pictures of the three of us leaving the hotel two nights ago. Fallyn still had her mask on, and her bulky Cloud costume kept her shape hidden, so it wasn't clear it was her. But it was obvious that Elliot and I were in the picture.

The suggestion with the few gossip posts was that two AcesPlayed developers were hanging with one of their biggest critics. That there was more going on. That would be a little bit of a conflict of interest, but the photos were tame.

Dustin and Elliot could do damage control in about half an hour. The images were awkward but not damning. The more concerning question was— why did the photos exist and why did someone go out of their way to share them?

Maybe that was why Elliot wasn't answering and hadn't called me back. He was already working on this.

My gut didn't think so. I was worried about my friends. Did I dare think of them as my boyfriend and girlfriend? It didn't matter, because I already was.

I'd head to Elliot's, I'd check on him in person, and things would be fine. Things would be better than fine.

When I got to his place, his car was out front, probably exactly where Fallyn parked it yesterday. There was no answer when I knocked, but that wasn't a big surprise. If he was in his home office working, he may not hear me.

I let myself in—I'd had a key and known the alarm code for years—and was surprised to hear King's whine nearby. I followed the sound to the living room, and what? There was a tree in the corner. Fully decorated. Lights sparkling off the ornaments.

But that wasn't what caught and held my attention. Fallyn and Elliot were asleep together on the couch. Fully clothed. She was still in her cosplay and he was in the clothes he wore yesterday, a blanket covering them.

Curiosity and jealousy surged inside me. That must be one hell of a story.

I took King outside, and once we were in again, I got him water and food. When he was situated, it was time to wake up Elliot and Fallyn.

They both looked more surprised to see me than to wake up with each other. Even as consciousness filled them, Elliot didn't make any moves to get away from Fallyn. He sat up, careful not to jar her. "Time is it?" he asked.

"After ten. I took King out. You probably need to clean his crate."

Elliot wrinkled his nose. "Morning, by the way. Good to see you."

Fallyn gave me a shy smile, and pulled her phone from some unknown place.

"Same," I said. "Though…" I pointed between the two of them and raised my eyebrows. How was I supposed to ask without it sounding like high grade envy?

"We fell asleep talking. The tree was her doing." Elliot made his answer sound so simple.

I doubted it was. Nothing was simple when it came to Fallyn and Elliot. "We need to talk."

Elliot frowned. "Okay?"

"Oh, fuck me in the arse." Fallyn's exclamation came out of nowhere.

"Here? Now?" And Elliot had woken up in a playful mood apparently.

So. Weird. It would be a cute look on him if not for everything. I was reaching for my phone, to show him what Fallyn was most likely looking at, when she handed him hers.

Elliot glanced at the screen, then did a double take and stared a little longer. "Oh, fuck me in the ass."

"I haven't called Dustin yet," I said. "I wanted to talk to you first, but you weren't answering."

Elliot was on his feet and fishing for his own phone. "Looks like he called me."

Grabbing her laptop off the coffee table, Fallyn turned toward the far staircase. "I don't have a marketing team behind me, and I need to get on top of this now from my side."

"Wait." I captured her wrist to keep her from leaving. "We're coordinating our stories."

Elliot was already dialing.

"Hey." Dustin's voice echoed from the speaker on Elliot's phone. "What is this?"

Elliot looked at Fallyn and pressed his finger to his lips. "It's nothing. As innocent as it looks."

"Nope. Give me something better," Dustin said.

"Nothing more to it. Two of us had a bit to drink, everyone at the party saw that, and a fellow industry professional offered to be our designated driver. This was professional all the way. She'll confirm the same story." Elliot made it sound so simple.

"Love it." Dustin's tone was flat. "Except is that really Fallyn? You're going to tell me, tell the world, that out of the hundreds of people at that party, you asked your arch nemesis to give you a ride home?"

At least Elliot had common sense enough to wince.

"It's a persona." I stepped in. "If people don't understand that she's acting as much as any movie star, that's not our fault."

"Uh-huh. Pray to God that her story matches yours, and run with it." Dustin hung up.

Like I thought—not a lot to worry about. There was still the question of why those photos showed up to begin with, though.

"See? Easy peasy lemon squeezy." Did Elliot really just say that? "As long as Fallyn's story matches ours."

She rolled her eyes, but was smiling. "Which it will. Because your story is the truth."

"Great. Sausage and eggs for breakfast?" Elliot asked.

The way Fallyn's nose scrunched up was adorable. Her, "Is that a euphemism?" felt a little off brand when it came to Elliot. Were they flirting?

Elliot laughed. A genuine. Hearty. Chuckle. "It wasn't, but it could be."

"Did I miss something?" This was disconcerting. I should be happy about it, and I was, but it was also nothing like what I expected.

Elliot shook his head. "Not really."

"I'm going to change. Post a few generic comments about those photos." Fallyn turned away. "If the two of you have managed to keep your game online, and are staying home, you can probably convince me to hang out here rather than do one more day of RinCon."

"You can't miss the last day." The offense in Elliot's voice was exaggerated.

"I thought you were moving rooms." Why had I brought that up? Maybe I was relieved that at least she hadn't moved her suitcases into Elliot's bedroom.

Fallyn shrugged. "I haven't had a chance yet. I'll be back."

That felt right, so my world wasn't completely upside down.

When she was gone, Elliot turned to me. "Are you all right?"

We need to talk. The words stuck in my throat. "Just not what I expected to find."

"I know. It's weird, but it turns out she's not that bad."

"Considering she's the same person as Kittie,

who we both really enjoy talking to, of course she's not bad at all." Defensiveness rose inside me and I tempered it.

Elliot leaned against a nearby wall. "Don't tell anyone I said this, but I think I was wrong."

The conflicted feelings inside me—jealousy and adoration—were about to go to war with each other, but I had enough sense to gasp at his words. "No. I didn't hear that."

"You're right, you didn't. Are you sure you're okay?"

I must be radiating actual visible vibes if Elliot was picking up on it. "Of course I am." How was I supposed to bring this topic up? Especially now? *Hey, I think I fell in love with you a long time ago. Also, I'm getting a lot of feels for Fallyn.* Nope. That didn't sound right. I should've rehearsed this before I came over.

"Okay." Elliot kicked away from the wall. "I'm gonna change, and make breakfast."

And I needed to occupy my mind. Maybe stop thinking mopey, lovey thoughts. Cleaning out the dog's kennel should help with that. Gross, but an effective distraction.

I had finished and was scrubbing my hands in a downstairs bathroom, when I heard Elliot shout *fuck*. His footsteps sounded heavily on the stairs. I came out to see what was going on.

He reached me about the same time Fallyn did. They were both dressed in fresh clothes. Hair damp.

Faces pink and eyes narrowed with rage as they glared at each other.

This was more like what I'd expected.

"What did you do?" they both said at the same time.

"It's on your fucking blog," Elliot growled.

Fallyn pursed her lips. "It came from your fucking game."

What? My phone buzzed in my pocket, and I ignored it in favor of getting the answers from them. "What happened?"

Fallyn's nostrils flared.

Elliot clenched his jaw.

I snapped my fingers between them, but couldn't break the staring contest. "Hello? Anyone? What's going on?"

"The chat logs for one D3m0nK1tt13, and her conversations with Puff69 and Archer, were just published on Fallyn's blog. There are excerpts up there. Transcriptions of the recordings. Of the text chat. And links to the core files." The longer Elliot spoke, the more his anger grew.

Fuck me. We were required to keep logs of every single conversion in game, for legal reasons, and that included… How did someone get those? Why did they publish them? "Was anyone else impacted?"

"No. Just us." Elliot radiated fury. "Because they

were pulled using her account. You can tell by the formatting."

He should be grateful that was the answer, but the sick churning in my gut understood why he wasn't.

"I yanked everything as soon as I saw it go up," Fallyn said. "Deleted it. Scrubbed it. It's all off my site."

Elliot shook his head. "It doesn't matter. People have links. They've already cloned the information."

This wasn't real. The strange sensation I had of being disconnected from my body? It was because I was dreaming, and this was some sort of surreal manifestation of my deepest fears.

Because yes, what the three of us did in game was all fun, consensual, and three adults just letting off steam in a game.

But the conflict of interest. The fact that Elliot and I broke non-fraternization rules. That he was my boss. That the person we were with was not only a *rival channel* but an attractive, confident woman?

The internet was going to dogpile on this. The board of directors was going to be furious. I wasn't sure which would be more damaging to our lives and careers.

"Maybe it won't be a big deal." I didn't believe my own words for a nanosecond. This was going to be a big fucking deal.

22 /
fallyn

This was so, so bad.

It was bad for Elliot and Link, but for me…

My channel was based on impartiality. This news destroyed that reputation. Like a right proper Thanos snap.

I could maybe recover. Rebrand myself. Shift my paradigm. Not that I wanted to change who I was online, but I could. It was worse than that, though. I'd known female streamers who had been forced to move. Shut down their channels. Go into hiding. Because the internet discovered the woman they watched for her ample cleavage, while she played games at a level they could never hope to, was actually a real person, who did things like have adult relationships and sex.

I needed to fix this *now* and I didn't want to be at odds with Link and Elliot while I did so. Turning my attention to Link, I said, "You know I didn't do this. Please believe me. It hurts me as much as it does the two of you." More. "And even if it didn't, I wouldn't ever. Not this."

"I know." Such a simple response from Link, but one that meant the world to me.

I turned a pleading gaze on Elliot. Not that playing off his sympathy had ever worked before.

"I know. It wasn't you." Elliot's reply almost made me cry in relief. "We'll figure out who, but we also have to make this right."

"We can't deny it," Link said.

My heart sank at the implication, and that it was his first reaction. I didn't want to deny anything that had happened with him. With them. I didn't want to pretend our relationship wasn't… whatever this was. And I adored that Link felt the same.

I also knew Elliot was thinking the opposite, even if it wasn't for cruel reasons, and that he was right. "I think we have to," I said.

Elliot nodded.

"No." Link was more forceful this time. "How does anyone even know that Kittie in the chats is the same person as Fallyn? We didn't know."

"They don't have to *know* it." I wished this one little thing wasn't true, but it was the way the internet worked. "As long as someone claims it's real, that's enough to make it real."

"It also makes things easier for us to deny."

Elliot was sliding into emotionlessness. Was this where he cut himself off from the world again? I didn't want to see that.

The noise Link made was half growl half sigh and just as much achingly terrifying. "Stop saying *deny*."

The pain in my chest—was that panic? A heart attack? Or maybe my heart cracking and breaking? When did I dig myself in so deep with these two? I wanted to agree with Link, but I had to side with Elliot. And regardless of anything else, "Whatever you do, whatever you say, we all have to agree. I'll stand with you on this. I don't…"

I sighed. This was harder than it should be. "I don't like the idea of hiding anything, and I'm not willing to forget the last week." Had it only been a week? And less than that of getting along.

But nearly a year of online chatting. Of falling for voices and actions rather than appearances or people. And now, that was going to destroy us. "But for the public, I stand by you and your decisions."

Elliot's phone rang.

"Do you need to get that?" I asked.

"It's Dustin. I'll talk to him once we finalize this conversation. Whatever we decide, he'll make it happen. You tell me how much you want him to know about you, Fallyn, and whatever he does, it helps all of us, not just Link and I."

Wow. I actually did have a marketing team

behind me. Weird thing to focus on, but I'd take anything to be grateful for that I could just now. We could not only deny this, but I wouldn't be crushed by the wheels of the AcesPlayed bus in the process.

It wouldn't make a big difference in the overall scheme of things, but a little protection was better than none. I didn't want this to be me versus them. I had nothing but respect for AcesPlayed as a company, and when it came to Link and Elliot specifically—

"So we're going to deny everything," Elliot said. "We all agree."

"Yes." That was harder to say than I wanted it to be.

Link shook his head. Stubborn, lovable jerk. "When the actual truth comes out, that will make things worse."

"Who knows our screen names?" Elliot asked.

"Yours and mine? Everyone in the office." As Link replied, he ticked off on his fingers. "Fallyn. Anyone who plays with people in the office—Reese, Megan, Quentin..."

Elliot winced, presumably at an already long list. "Who knows Fallyn is Kittie?"

This was such a mess.

"You. Me. Nigel. But none of us did this." The conviction in Link's voice was sweet.

But obviously *someone* did it.

"And it's unlikely any of them will contradict us

when we say whatever this looks like, it isn't." Elliot pinched the bridge of his nose. "But if they mentioned to anyone, random person in passing, who Kittie was, or Puff, or Archer…"

"We didn't do anything wrong." I wished that mattered. To a lot of people, we'd done everything wrong. It wasn't just that Link and Elliot worked for AcesPlayed and I dissected their games. Some of the roleplay we'd done in game, the conversations we'd had, wasn't just sexy, it was graphic, it had all sorts of kinks people were going to be offended by from pain to degradation and so much more.

People were going to dogpile on Elliot and Link. They were sexist game developers. They were misogynistic. I could already see the accusations in my mind. And if they'd said those things to a random person, yeah, I'd agree. But everything that happened between us was part of the conversation. Was consensual.

And I was going to be a slut. That would be the nicest thing people said about me.

Fuck.

"Do you trust me?" Elliot asked.

"Yes." That wasn't as terrifying to say as I'd expected, especially given I was about to put at least a portion of my career in his hands.

Elliot had his phone out. "Listen, but don't speak. He doesn't need to know you're here." He dialed.

"What is this?" The Dustin who answered sounded grumpy compared to the man I usually saw representing the company.

Elliot didn't look concerned. Then again, Elliot didn't look like he was feeling much of anything, and that was disconcerting. "Exactly what you think—chat logs from the game."

"Who are you and Link talking to?" Dustin asked.

"Impossible to say at this time." Elliot rattled off the response without hesitation.

Dustin let out a long, noise exhale. "Swell. How did it get out?"

"Impossible to say at this time." When Elliot kept things close to the chest, he really buttoned up. "Players should be assured that no one else's data is at risk, and we're taking all measures possible to ensure that the person responsible for this is confronted and that this situation is dealt with swiftly and without prejudice."

Like he was reading from a freaking cue-card. Both amazing and scary.

"Great." Dustin sounded as though it was anything but. "Do we have anything to say about Fallyn, besides *impossible to say at this time?*"

In any other situation, I would've laughed at his off-the-cuff Elliot impersonation.

"While our company has a friendly rivalry with her channel, we ask that our fans give her the same respect and consideration they give us, while this matter is investigated and after." Elliot met my gaze, and his eyes were soft, rather than the emotionless voids I expected.

There was a silent pause before Dustin said, "off the record, between you and me... Is this real?"

"Impossible to say at this time." Elliot gave away nothing.

Dustin clucked. "You're lucky I'm good at what I do."

"You're the best. And it's not luck, it's planning." Elliot managed sincerity while still remaining an iceberg.

Silence filled the room as the line went dead.

I needed to brace myself for the worst, but this was one less thing I had to worry about.

"We have to get into the office. Make sure whoever got into Fallyn's account isn't in anyone else's," Link said. "Fallyn, what else do you need from us?"

"I don't know yet." I was scared to find out.

Elliot's phone rang again, and he glanced at the scene. His blank mask shattered as a deep scowl rushed in. "It's Judith." Did his voice just crack?

Every muscle in my body tensed, though I wasn't sure why.

"Hello." Elliot's tone when he answered was much warmer and more professional than with Dustin. "It's impossible to tell at—" He clenched his jaw. "It's exactly what it looks like. Exactly what the news online says."

Who was this woman that she cracked him so quickly? I had to meet her.

"He and I are heading in now— No. I— You need me there. I'm not going— *Fuck*. Fine. I understand." Elliot hung up.

I was going to be sick and I didn't even know what he'd heard. I doubted any of the words had anything to do with me.

"Was that as bad as it sounded?" Link asked.

Elliot took a deep breath and straightened up, as if composing himself. "She wants you in the office now."

"Just me?"

Elliot's right eye twitched, and his chest rose and fell again. "She just suspended me, pending an emergency meeting with the board tomorrow."

Yup. I was about to puke all over his expensive rugs.

"She can't." Link sounded both stunned and furious.

Elliot nodded. Slowly. Deliberately. "She can. She did."

The entire world paused.

"*Fuuuuuck*." Elliot's shout echoed off the walls.

I jumped, surprised, and King whimpered.

I didn't blame Puppy or Elliot.

Fallyn went back to the guest wing to make her videos. It made sense that she would—she needed to be taking care of work in a place where I wasn't—but it still sucked. And Link went into the office.

My Sunday passed in agony. I couldn't do anything, and I'd never been good at doing nothing. Asking Link what was going on would risk his career as well if anyone found out. I was dying to know how things were going at work, but I kept my questions to myself.

The only thing I could do was go on my own social media accounts and reinforce the same scripted bullshit that Fallyn and Dustin had posted.

Oh, and watch my corner of the internet devour itself in a violent clash of jeers and cheers.

I didn't care for either side of what I was seeing. People hated me for being a sexist pig. For abusing my position of power. For working on a video game that was basically just porn and no wonder I was such a pig.

People were praising me because *That bitch deserved to be pinned down and fucked and taught her place.*

The only thing I got from the twin blasts of vitriol was the reminder that most people sucked.

I was used to it for me, though not in such concentrated doses, but Fallyn shouldn't have to deal with this. Link shouldn't either.

For me personally, I was more worried about my future at AcesPlayed. One of the reasons I bought into the company, besides believing in it, was so I'd have control over my situation there. So I wouldn't run into another moment like at Cord.

But if the board decided I was a risk to the company, they could force me out. They could buy up my portion of the company with a majority vote, and I was gone. Every single investor contract had a clause like that in it. I just never thought it would apply to me.

That didn't matter. Once I had a chance to meet with the rest of the board, we'd all reach an understanding, and I'd be fine. And the sooner that happened the better, so I could get back to work with my team on my game.

Until that point, I was stuck in a kind of limbo, trying to figure out how our chats with Fallyn were leaked. They came from her account—the way they were formatted, everything about them, said a member of the chat had exported them, and that it was her.

If she didn't do it, who had access to her account who could've? We didn't have the ability to spoof accounts in the office, and we didn't have access to passwords. Which meant no one had that ability. Someone had to have logged in as her.

And they could've picked any of her conversations. Link and I weren't the only people she talked to, so this seemed pretty obviously targeted at all three of us. And there was no doubt it was intentional. Like the DDOS. An attack against her and us at the same time.

Had the other crashes been intentional? Yesterday's? The one from the start of last week?

Had they come from my people?

The thought was foul. Not possible. My developers were the best and they were professionals, or they wouldn't be working for me.

Was it a friend of Fallyn's? It seemed like a bad idea to interrupt what she was doing to ask if she had any friends close enough to do something like this, but underhanded enough to do something like this.

And those photos from this morning, of Link, Fallyn, and me in the hotel parking garage—where did those come from? There had been a lot of people around that night.

Why hadn't we pieced any of these events together before?

Because games crashed, things went wrong on release week, and click bait ruled the internet. But now that I was looking at the entire situation, I couldn't help but wonder how many of our problems were related to each other. Was I letting paranoia get the best of me, or finally opening my eyes?

I organized my thoughts as best I could, and emailed them to Link and Nigel on their personal accounts. The message started with *I know you can't tell me what you find, but if you're not already looking into this...*

Link's quick *thanks* was as much acknowledgement as I needed, but his follow-up text that said *wish you were working on this with us* made me smile.

Me too, I sent back.

This was so much bullshit. I was sitting around doing nothing, while other people did the work, and I hated it.

———

Monday morning, I put on my nicest suit—silk, tailored, and cost me more than any piece of clothing ever should. This kind of dressing up wasn't something I did often, but I was capable when it was required, and today I wanted to show as much respect as possible for my fellow board members.

I got to the offices early, and loathed walking in without being able to work.

Soon enough. As soon as this meeting was over, I'd be back at my desk. The team would get pizza, I'd probably spill something on the Italian silk, and we'd all laugh about it and finish fixing the game.

The instant I walked in the front door, Ivan stopped me. "Judith says I can't let you go anywhere but her office or the small conference room."

"You can pretend you didn't see me. Just for five minutes." I wasn't asking, I was telling.

Ivan's tight-lipped smile said it didn't matter. "No. But she left her calendar open for you."

I should be grateful, but I wasn't feeling it. That didn't mean I'd pass up the opportunity to talk to her. I forced myself to turn away from the hallway leading to the Dev room, and headed to Judith's office instead.

When I sat in the seat across from her desk, she didn't look up. "I shouldn't be seeing you," she said.

"Definitely not. I'm already in trouble for fucking one person in the office." I tried to keep my tone light.

The look she gave me would've cowed the strongest of men. "Do you have that out of your system now?"

I sighed. "Yes." Though she was *The Boss*, I'd

worked with her long enough, and invested as much time in this as she had, that we were equals in private. "Do we really have to do this?"

"You knew this was a rule. You *knew* you couldn't break it. We specifically discussed, and you said you understood." Some days Judith joked. Today wasn't one of them. In fact, she looked more tired, more stressed, than I'd seen her in a long time.

My ego would love to believe it was all because of me, but I suspected there was more going on I wasn't seeing. "You knew I was doing it." Could I not help myself? Apparently not.

She shook her head. "That had better not be your defense in front of everyone else."

"It's not." Time to stop fucking around. Maybe beg a little. "I love this place as much as you do. I can't give it up."

"No one questions that." She tugged on a loose lock of hair. "But what do you expect me to do?"

"I can't lose this." Yup. I was willing to beg. A lot.

She shook her head. "If you stayed, would you stop seeing him?"

Give up Link? The simple question hit me hard, knocking the wind from me. I couldn't. I wouldn't. But an answer refused to be pushed past my lips.

Judith turned away from me. "I'll see you in the meeting."

The window of time that passed between then

and the start of the next conversation was agonizingly long, and ended far too soon. When I walked into the conference room, to find the other four members of the AcesPlayed board, I felt like I was facing my executioners.

Wow, me. Fatalistic, much?

There was no need for introductions. Judith and I spoke almost every day, I'd known Scott for longer than not, Grant Lent, and Oliver Jaggers. And Ivan was here to take notes.

"So there are no misunderstandings, we need to state why we're here, and what we need to accomplish by the end of the meeting." Grant was an older gentleman who had been an investor in Rinslet since its early days, and was happy to fund AcesPlayed when we branched off to do our own thing. He was typically a silent partner, unless he thought his money was at stake.

Judith's nostrils flared as she dragged in a deep breath. "The chat logs from our game that were recently made public involve Elliot Howard, one of our board members and one of the more public faces of the company. While this exposure wasn't his doing, the content contained within puts us at a serious legal risk."

"But does it really? Any more than normal?" I was going to fight this from every angle I could. "Nothing contained in those chat logs violates the rules of the game—a game that exists specifically to allow this kind of interaction, among other things. Anyone who supports the game can't find fault with what I did."

"It's not about what you did, it's about who you did it with," Oliver said. He was with the same investment firm as Xander, the Rafael Group.

Could I play dumb? Like it was going to make things worse for me? "A woman whose face I never saw and whose real name I never asked for or wanted. Not at any point in the game."

Judith clenched her jaw. "Do you want to bring her into this? Because things are already bad for you."

No. Fuck.

"We're talking about a man who works for you," Scott said. "Whose career you hold in your hands. Who you have power over and who you have the ability to fire in a blink or destroy his career."

"But I wouldn't." Not Link. There would never be a reason, but even if there was…

Scott furrowed his brow. "It doesn't matter. You could."

It was true, once upon a time I'd worshiped Scott, but we were equals. "You're going to look me in the eye and tell me you would've done things differently with Kenzie? With—"

"Watch it." The warning leaked into his tone.

I wasn't sharing anything that was a secret, but I

was treading a thin line for other reasons. "Would you have?"

"They don't work for me anymore, and your situation is different."

Bullshit. He'd fucked his PR woman. His VP's assistant. He'd been slapped on the wrist and got to keep the people he loved.

"Link is the best," I said. "You can't—"

"His job isn't on the line." Grant talked over me.

Judith was spending a lot more time studying her hands than was normal for her.

I didn't want anyone in the company gone, but I was grasping to make my case look mild. Tame. Easy to overlook. "What about Adrienne? She works for Phillip still. Jeremy still works for Sonya."

"Both happened before the new rule was put into place," Judith said.

The new rule. The anti-fraternization rule that went into effect a few months ago that said managers couldn't sleep with the people who reported to them. Seemed like an obvious thing to make against the rules, but it hadn't been, and people here tended to hook up.

Which was also why anyone who'd gotten together in a longer-term relationship was grandfathered in under the non-existent rules that weren't there before.

"Besides being more than decades-long fuck buddies, Phillip and Sonya no longer have final say in Adrienne and Jeremy's futures here." Yup. We were in an official meeting, and Scott had just used the phrase fuck-buddies.

I wanted to call bullshit on at least part of his argument. That my relationship with Link was at least as valid, and far older than either of those, but it wasn't. It hadn't been. He and I had always insisted *just friends*.

Whether or not that was a mistake, I wouldn't wield whatever I had with Link like a shield. He deserved better than that.

Which meant I was out of arguments.

"We're all on the same page?" Grant asked.

Scott nodded. "Let's make this official. Do we allow Elliot Howard to stay in this position, or is it time for him to go?"

Time for him to go. Fuck me. The words were a punch to the gut.

The vote was split. Grant and Oliver were in favor of firing me and buying me out. Judith and Scott voted in my favor.

At least that was something.

I would be the tie-breaking vote in any other circumstance, but since I couldn't be, they needed to find a fifth, impartial party to make the decision.

"Take the rest of the week off," Judith said. "I'll tell your team and everyone you're out for a few days. I won't say more until we know more."

I gave her a thin smile, but couldn't manage a *thank you*.

The entire drive home, alone with my thoughts, was agony. This was it. I was about to lose it all again. I felt my entire world slipping through my fingers.

Because why?

Because I was fucking my best friend and refused to call it lo—

Because I might make the company look bad?

Given everything they represented?

Why didn't they understand? I'd do anything for AcesPlayed. I'd give them anything.

By the time I got home, the hole in my heart was gaping and festering. I couldn't give up Link. I couldn't send him away. I couldn't give up this company. This job. These people.

Why had I let myself feel so much again? A decade or two passed and I let the walls crumble. I let the feelings in. The people. The place.

I stepped inside, and found Fallyn in the living room. King was next to her on the couch. The Christmas tree was sparkling in the background. The only thing missing from this scene was Link.

And *fuck* it hurt to look at. It ached so much I couldn't breathe.

"How'd it go?" Fallyn's tentative question was a fist to my sternum.

I couldn't do this again. I couldn't care this

much. I couldn't let those walls down, and I wouldn't go through the kind of pain I'd dealt with before.

Was that selfish of me?

Probably. Right now, it didn't matter, because if I let myself keep feeling, I was going to collapse under the weight of it.

So I shut the flow of emotion off instead. Easy to do. I had a lot of practice. "You can stop."

"I'm sorry?" Fallyn looked confused.

"You heard me. You can stop now."

"Stop what?"

Don't think. Don't feel. Just talk. Instinct will take care of the rest. "The game. The bet. There's no reason to keep playing, you lost."

"I stopped playing days ago." Fallyn rose, holding my gaze.

Of course she had. And I was the assho—

Nope. I was in the right. "Which is why you'll never win. I didn't fall for you, and you figured out that being Online Fallyn full time doesn't serve you. You. Lose."

She stalked toward me, expression blank.

Good. That made two of us.

Take it back. Say you're sorry. Fix this before it's too late.

It was already too late, and I didn't want her in my life. One more person to cling to. One more person to make me vulnerable. Yet another reason to hurt when it ended, so I was going to put a stop to it now. There was nothing else to say, I'd made my point, so I stared back at Fallyn, unblinking.

She flinched first and turned away. "Fuck you."

"Never again."

She stormed from the room, and I couldn't make myself move. My feet were frozen to the floor. For all I knew, I'd stay like this for eternity. Stone Elliot in the middle of a house I was never supposed to have.

I had no idea how much time passed when she returned. Five minutes. Ten. It didn't matter. She was dragging her luggage behind her.

She didn't so much as glance at me as she walked out of the house.

Good. It was better this way.

I knew what time Elliot's meeting started, and I fully expected him to walk in fifteen minutes later as if nothing had happened, shout for an update, and tell us all to get back to work.

When Judith walked into the Dev room instead, I held my breath.

"Eyes on me." Her voice carried through the room, and within seconds she had everyone's attention. "Elliot will be out the rest of the week, at the board of directors' request."

"Shitty time to take a break." Chris's retort was full of derision.

Frustrated anger surged inside, and I clenched my fists.

"I assure you, he would be here if it was possible, and if anyone doesn't know that"—she focused on Chris, and let the thought hang unfinished.

She looked tense. Judith always looked tightly

wound, but this was different. Was it because of Elliot, or was there more? Not that losing Elliot was a small thing.

"But he will be back. Next week." I wanted to hear her say it.

Chris scoffed. "Miss your boyfriend already?"

"Dude." Landon's voice was sharp. "Back the fuck off."

The way Judith clenched her jaw wasn't reassuring. "As Elliot would say, you're the best at your jobs, and that's why you're here. Keep doing what you're doing."

"Who's in charge while Elliot's out?" Chris asked.

I was going to pound his face into the ground in about two-point five seconds.

The glare Judith fixed him with could've peeled the paint off the walls. "Me. I will make room on my calendar. If there's anything you usually get from him, you come to *me*."

Not a huge surprise. She'd started in development, though she hadn't stayed long. Rumor was, she kept at least a little on top of her skills. "Any other questions?" Judith asked.

No one replied and she walked out of the room.

We weren't supposed to discuss any work-related things with Elliot, but I needed to know he was all right. I sent him a quick text. *You okay?*

I shouldn't expect him to reply right away, but I

needed confirmation. I waited about thirty seconds before walking out of the room and dialing his number.

No answer.

Based on the time, and when Judith walked in, he was probably on his way home. I'd give him a bit to get there, get settled, and blow off some steam, and I'd call him again if he hadn't replied.

Judith hadn't said he was coming back, but she also didn't say he wasn't, so all hope was not lost.

When I returned to the Dev room, Chris stood up. "With Elliot gone, we still have a schedule to stick to."

"Sit your ass down." I wasn't in the mood for whatever he was doing.

Instead of listening, Chris moved to the whiteboard in the middle of the room. Elliot's spot.

My anger climbed.

"Team Starburst." He pointed at the board. "Shift your attention to expansion pack content, and helping Team Quail with—"

What the fuck? "Stop." I barked the word and joined Chris. I didn't want to do this in front of the room. Our group didn't do things like workplace drama or infighting. But something had overinflated Chris's balls recently. "Those aren't the team assignments." I scanned the room. Half the people were standing, looking at us. While I couldn't see the other half, no one was typing or talking, and that meant everyone was listening. "We will *not* shift priorities. Nothing has changed."

"We know our jobs, Chris, thank you very much," Landon said.

Alys scoffed. "We also know what your job is, *Chris*." Derision leaked into her tone. She wouldn't mind seeing him escorted from the building.

I didn't blame her at this point.

"I'm just trying to—"

"Well don't." I talked over Chris.

He huffed. "Fine. We'll do a morning check-in tomorrow."

No, really. What the fuck was he doing? Did Chris think he could run this team? He didn't get along with Alys, he bitched about everyone in the office who was in a triad. I frequently wondered why he wanted to work here to begin with.

Today that didn't matter, as long as we kept him in his place. The biggest thing that mattered to me was making sure Elliot was all right. Ensuring he had a functioning team of developers to come back to was second on the list.

fallyn

I refused to let Elliot see me cry, no matter how much his words hurt. I was done putting up with his hot and cold. Done sticking around for the pretty guy who fed me morsels of happiness mixed with scorn. I was so completely done with arseholes.

Regardless of what it cost to change out my ticket, I was flying home today.

I was done here.

The entire ride to the airport, I kept my composure. At the check-in counter, I handed the woman my credit card, and told her to get me on the next plane to Sacramento.

Had I really been starting to fal…

The airline employee gave me back my card, along with a boarding pass and a pleasant smile, and told me to have a nice flight.

I was pretty sure the look I gave her in return was a grimace, but it was the best I had.

The line through security was short this time of day, and I was through within a few minutes. My plane didn't leave for five hours, but where else was I going to go? I headed in the direction of my gate, based on the signs, and turned into the first bathroom I came across.

Inside, I locked myself in the farthest stall from the door, leaned against the wall, and let the tears spill out. I shouldn't be crying over Elliot, but here I was. I couldn't stop.

I sobbed until I was spent, and the only thing that kept me from crying out was sinking my teeth into the side of my fist. When the tears stopped, I washed my face, not successfully scrubbing away my grief, and walked the rest of the way to my gate.

My mind was numb. I'd managed to push the brief but painful exchange with Elliot to the back of it, and other thoughts could flow in. I settled into a plastic seat, suddenly drained. I should tell Link *goodbye*. None of this was on him, and I was going to miss him.

I sent him a text. *I'm heading home. Meeting you was wonderful.*

Please don't mention or ask about him.

I didn't expect a reply right away—he was working—so when my phone buzzed in my hand seconds later, I almost dropped it.

I hoped to say goodbye, he wrote.

Simple words, but they lodged in my throat, and fresh tears stung my eyes. *Me too.*

What happened? Link asked.

I couldn't. If I repeated the conversation, it would be even more real, and I couldn't deal with the reminder that I'd been starting to trust Elliot. Starting to feel more. *Ask him.*

Text me when you land.

It was a polite request, but it hurt in the sweetest way. *Okay.*

I was avoiding my email and all of my online messages. The glimpses I'd caught since yesterday were hatred filled and enough to destroy me with the mood I was in. But I felt like I owed my followers something. I logged on to stream a short message. I faked the smile, and they would know, but it didn't matter.

"Hey, all. RinCon was a blast." I almost choked on the conflicting emotions that came with those words. "But it's time for me to head home. I'll be offline for a day or two. Don't break anything I wouldn't." I cut the stream short, because now I was thinking about broken things. My career. My heart. Elliot.

I wouldn't cry in the middle of the airport. I wouldn't, I wouldn't, I wouldn't.

Waiting for the plane, and the flight home, were agony. I couldn't focus enough to distract myself, and the longer my mind sat idle, the louder the conversation with Elliot played on repeat in my head.

I thought we were...

I thought I might...

I thought he could...

Fuck.

I was going out of my mind by the time I got back to my apartment. It was too late to call my sister, and I couldn't go online. I found myself calling Link, though I wasn't sure why he was so high on my list.

The instant he answered, the instant I heard his, "Hello," and my mind calmed, I knew why.

"Fallyn?" he said when I didn't say anything. "Are you there? Are you all right?"

"No." I couldn't lie to him. "But I'm so glad you answered. I wasn't sure if you would."

"Why wouldn't I?"

"Because Elliot..."

His laugh was rough. "The number of times I've said that in my life. Tell me what happened."

"Get him to tell you."

"He's not answering me. Besides, I'd rather hear from you about what has you so sad."

I sank onto my floor, because even sitting on the couch had bad memories associated with it. "I couldn't stay there anymore, and I won't be talking to him again. He has to tell you why. I'm sorry."

"Don't be. You don't have to apologize for

anything, but I am going to miss you." Link was so sweet. So sincere.

"This was always going to end with me going home."

"That doesn't mean I have to like it."

Now I wanted to cry again, for completely different reasons. There was a knot in my chest that I couldn't breathe past. "I have to go."

"Wait. Can I call you later tonight? When I'm done with work?"

No. He couldn't. It would hurt too much. But I couldn't refuse him. "I'd like that."

Hanging up ached. Everything ached. It shouldn't. None of this should impact me the way it was. But that didn't change the way I felt.

It hurt to have Fallyn leave, though she was right—the week was always going to end with her going home.

When Elliot finally answered me, his reply was short, but at least it was a reply. *I'm fine. I need time.*

What happened with Fallyn? Possibly not the way for me to make sure he stayed *fine*, but I needed answers.

Nothing.

Fury snaked inside me at Elliot's brush-off, and if he was here, even if he was on the phone, I'd demand an answer. My, *tell me*, wouldn't carry much weight via text, but I sent it anyway.

Those three little irritating dots appeared and vanished, over and over, for several minutes. His reply was *Did they tell you they suspended me? For fucking you. Don't let the same thing happen to you.*

Not what I asked. I glared at my screen and waited for his response.

There wasn't one. *Fuck.*

I doubted this would be a repeat of all those years ago, but the parallels between then and now, the threat of Elliot losing what he loved, were too similar. Since he wasn't being forthcoming with me, I needed outside help. I called Mrs. Ria and tried to be as non-alarmist as I could, while also reinforcing it was important, when I asked her to keep a closer eye on Elliot than normal.

She muttered something about how she'd murder him if he hurt himself, and assured me she would watch over him.

When I got home from work that night, it was late and my brain might as well have been the consistency of oatmeal.

I needed to step away from my world in a way I hadn't needed in a long time, and the only thing I could think was *Fallyn*. I wanted to hear her. See her. Pretend our lives weren't falling apart.

She answered on video when I called her, and I couldn't help but smile at the sight of her face. Her smile was subdued, but her greeting was warm.

"I have a favor to ask," she said when the *hellos* were out of the way. "I don't care what we talk about, as long as it's not the game, work, or co-workers. Yours or mine."

"I need to know one thing first." My question

wasn't pressing, but it had been sitting in the back of my mind. If I was going to ruin the moment, might as well do it up front.

She frowned. "Please don't ask me about him again."

Elliot. "Not unless you tell me it's okay." That felt like a dangerous promise, but an important one. "And I won't, but this is work related. Did you ever figure out who logged into your accounts, or anything more about that?"

"It was me." Her voice grew soft, and her words filled me with disbelief. "Not me who did it," she added quickly. "But whoever logged in, was there as me. They tethered to my phone." She sounded upset. "But it wasn't me who did it, I swear to you. Even if it looked like me."

I'd never doubted. "I know it wasn't you. I'm going to make this right. Somehow."

She nodded, and the low frames per second gave the motion a jittery, almost surreal appearance. Somehow that felt appropriate to the situation.

What now? "How's the weather in Sacramento?" I asked.

"Are you serious right now?"

Now what? "Yes?"

"You want to talk about the weather."

It was a safe topic. "Yes?"

"I have never, even in game, even when things were awkward or stilted, heard you bring up weather as a conversation topic before," Fallyn said.

It wasn't my favorite, but it was better than ending the call. "I don't know where we stand—you and me. I want it to be somewhere and I don't want to scare you off. I want this to be more, but I don't know how to get you there."

Wow, I didn't mean to say all of that. *How's the weather* wasn't as safe a question as I thought.

"I want more too. So what next?" Her reply was the sweetest thing I'd heard in days, without question. One of the best I'd heard in my life.

Asking about things like favorite colors and songs rarely led to deeper conversation, plus we'd covered all of that online before she got here. I didn't know where to start. "Tell me something you've never told me before. It doesn't have to be earth shattering, or some deep dark secret, or any type of secret at all. Maybe you didn't want to give away too much about yourself when we talked, or maybe it's something that just never came up."

"Ooh. Tough one." The way she scrunched up her face was adorable, and it didn't take any imagination at all for me to picture her being directly across from me, rather than two states away. "*Oh, okay. How about this?*" Her face lit up. "When I was little, I used to watch beauty pageants. Don't judge—I didn't know the word *objectification*, let alone how to use it in a sentence."

I started to hold up my hands in surrender. Didn't work too well when I was holding the phone. "I would never judge."

"No. I suppose that's not you. Anyway, I loved the dresses in the evening wear category. I would redesign them in my head. I wanted to make them one day. And I *loved* the talent show. The way some of those women kicked and danced… When I grew up I was going to design dresses and model my own creations and do the splits on stage while using a yo-yo."

That last bit didn't sound possible, but what did I know about the splits? "That sounds amazing. Did the dream change or…?" *What happened?*

"Everyone convinced me I was too short to do things like model. Too short. Too clumsy. Too timid."

Suddenly I wanted to smack every person who'd ever told her that. "I think you're the perfect height," I said.

"For you to squish me." Her laugh was forced.

"For you to be you." It wasn't that I had a short girl fetish, but I was pretty sure I had a Fallyn fetish.

Her blush was as pretty over video as it was in person. "What about you?" she asked. "Tell me something I don't know."

"I collect dragons."

Her smile grew. "Real ones, I assume."

"That would be amazing." Talk about childhood

dreams coming to life. "But just these for now." I turned the phone toward the wall in my home office that was covered with shelves, and each of those shelves was filled with little dragons, big dragons, cute, and serious dragons, and every kind in between.

"*Flove,*" she said with awe.

Her genuine reply, her enthusiasm, made me smile and soothed my soul.

We talked until my eyelids were tugging shut, and I desperately wanted her here with me as much as I did Elliot.

She made me hang up, so I could work tomorrow, and promised to call me back in the afternoon,

The next couple of days passed in a manic blur of working during the day, texting Elliot after I got home, just a quick *hey*, and then talking to Fallyn the rest of the night.

Thursday morning, I was feeling the strain of the highs and lows. I skipped arm day at the gym, and headed straight for Loading Java for coffee and carbs instead.

As I was walking out, I brushed past Bryce, who was heading in.

"Link. Hey." He surprised me by stopping and spinning to face me. In the three years since we'd fired him, I'd never heard of anyone running into him near the offices.

No reason to get into anything with him here, he

had as much a right to Lyn's chocolate croissants as anyone. "Hey, Bryce."

"How are things?" His tone was almost genuine but something more sinister cut underneath.

Unfortunately, I was too polite to just brush him off. "Good. You?"

"Yeah? Good? I saw the game crashed a few times. Is the guy you got running security any good at his job?"

Bryce was friends with Chris. It was likely he knew exactly who we had working on game security. "She's the best. Can't stop all the assholes all the time."

"I guess you can't." He smirked. "Anyway. I'll let you get back to it."

I was happy to walk away, but the brief encounter lingered in my thoughts as I headed across the street to the office.

fallyn

The conversations at night with Link kept me sane. Every night I fell for him a little harder. I couldn't ignore that he was connected to Elliot, but at least ET Howard never came up in conversation.

The rest of life wasn't so great. Thursday morning I was staring at my streaming rig, trying to convince myself that *today* would be the day I made a video. That after so much time away, I'd get back to work today.

I needed to. My revenue was rapidly falling off. If I wasn't putting out new content, the algorithms stopped showing *any* of my content to people, and I was losing the financial subscribers as well, thanks to the gossip about what had happened with Elliot and Link.

The denials we all put out didn't do much of anything. Go figure.

It was about that time when something else should happen on the internet, crisis-wise and move people on to a new topic, right?

But apparently not.

I'd always prided myself on running a one-woman operation, but I'd let the admin slide off too. I couldn't look at my inbox, or the comments on posts. I couldn't face the number of people calling me names. I'd tried Tuesday night, and I had to shut everything down.

Apparently it didn't take me long to reach my limit being called a slut, people telling me I was an embarrassment to empowered women everywhere, hearing that I was disgusting and pathetic, oh, and that I deserved to be raped until I was dead.

Even thinking about facing that again made my stomach churn.

I got a text from the place where my PO Box was located, letting me know the box was full and I needed to empty it.

That was something I could do. Getting out, getting some air, reminding myself that the entire world wasn't insane, would be good for me.

Driving my Rav4 was nothing compared to Elliot's Bentley, but it was mine, it was comfortable, and it was the perfect shade of red.

I took my time sifting through my mailbox, separating out junk to throw away, letters, and the little slips that said I had packages. Usually I looked forward to fan mail, but today I was dreading it. It hadn't been long enough for people to be sending me physical hate, though. I needed to calm down. Living in fear forever wouldn't serve me.

"Hey, Fallyn." The sneering tone came from behind me as I walked in line to grab my packages.

I glanced in that direction before I could think that might not be a good idea.

A man was standing near one of the copiers, watching me with a kind of seething hatred that should only be reserved for serial killers and child molesters.

"Can I help you?" Just responding to him set off a billion warning bells in my head.

He sneered. "Don't you think you've done enough? You fucking bitch. It wasn't enough to ruin an incredible game, but you had to flash your cunt around and destroy the career of a great man, too? You streamer sluts think all you have to do is flash your tits—"

"*Enough.* I'm calling the police. You are trespassing," the employee working the counter said.

"I'm done anyway. Stupid ho isn't worth my time." The man's scowl deepened—which should have made his face concave by now—and he spat at me before turning and walking out.

What the actual fuck? Now I was going to have to change my mailing address. Wonderful.

"Police are on their way. Do you want to wait in

back for them?" The clerk gestured toward the back room of the store.

I did. I wanted to hide away from the world and never emerge. But with the adrenaline racing through my veins, I didn't want to be anywhere that wasn't public—witnesses were good—until I got home.

The police weren't much help. They took statements. They told me to be careful. They left.

That was great. Not.

As I drove home, I couldn't stop checking my mirrors. Would I know if anyone was following me? How long had those cars been behind me? I took the most convoluted route home that I could, and every time a car behind me took the same turn I did, my paranoia spiked.

By the time I got home, I was shaking. I needed to get out of town for a few days. Someplace safer than a strange city where strange men waited for me. I couldn't stay here anymore.

I called my sister.

She answered and we made some light small talk. Exactly the kind of thing I didn't want from Link, about the weather, and how her kids were. At this moment, it was more soothing than most things.

"What's up?" She asked. "Not that you can't call to just chat, but you're usually working right now."

Would I ever work again? That was melodramatic, of course I would. "I just wanted to say *hi*."

"Uh-huh. Nearly forty years, Fall. I know you. You didn't call just to chat. What's up?"

"I was thinking I might come visit for Christmas. See you. See the kids. Spend a few weeks back home." As the words rushed out, they sounded like the perfect idea. Exactly what I needed.

The way she sucked in a short breath crashed my hopes before she said anything. "I'm so sorry. Al's aunt got us a trip to visit them in Milan for the holidays. We won't be home, and we'll be spending most of our time there with them. You're still welcome to come stay in the house. It's all yours while we're gone."

All of the will drained from me, and I let my body sink into the couch. "No, I don't need to do that. It's totally fine. Have fun in Italy and we'll do this another time."

Totally fine. I'd be fine. Everything would be fine.

I didn't believe it for a second, but I needed to start or the weight of reality would crush me.

elliot

I didn't know how to sit and do nothing. Not being able to work when I knew how much I could be doing, made me twitchy.

It didn't help that King spent a lot of time sitting at the door whining, and sleeping in the chair Fallyn had claimed during the start of her time here. On top of that, Mrs. Ria asked me multiple times on Tuesday day if I was all right and when that darling woman, the one with the purple in her hair, was coming back.

I wanted to have an answer for her, for King, that was more than *she won't be back*, and I didn't just want that for them. I also missed Link. Desperately. And the people from work, though not with the same kind of intensity.

And yeah, I missed Fallyn, too. Admitting it to myself didn't make it hurt any less. This was exactly what I hadn't wanted to happen, but now that she was gone, I could work on going back to life as normal. The ache wouldn't be there for long. That empty hole in my chest that carried two names. That would fill in soon enough.

The text from Link at the end of the day was simple, but enough to make me smile. *Just checking in.*

Still good. I hit *Send. And thanks.*

That was that. There were no follow-up texts—not that there should've been. But Wednesday morning I decided to shove my phone aside and set it on silent, to keep me from checking it obsessively.

I tried to drown out the lonely and impotent feelings by putting on my headphones, picking up a controller, and playing classic video games. Like Final Fantasy.

That definitely didn't help my state of mind, when the memories of the masquerade party rushed back. Both the incredible night and the fallout after.

I was right. What has gaming gotten you besides a spot on the couch and no future?

Wonderful. My father's voice was back. I hadn't been haunted by that in years.

I managed to shove the taunting words aside, but the roller coaster of emotion wasn't any less nauseating than yesterday.

When someone rang the bell that afternoon, King was on his feet in a heartbeat, running toward the noise, and yipping with excitement. My mind raced ahead to possibilities. This wasn't the kind of place where I got a lot of visitors, or any really. I rarely even ordered delivery because drivers couldn't find the house.

Link was working, and tended to knock, so it wouldn't be him. It wasn't as though Fallyn was going to walk back into my life. Ever.

I scooped up the puppy. "Calm down. It's no one exciting," I muttered as I opened the door.

"There are a number of people who would disagree with you." Brandon was on the other side.

Though any reason for why escaped me. He hadn't been here since… It had been many years. Back when this was *the* place to party. "I think that's a given." I eyed him suspiciously. "Some might even say it's my schtick. I'm not an agreeable person."

"I meant that I was exciting." Brandon held out a pizza box.

That had King's attention, and if I was being honest, mine as well. It smelled like sauce and meat and the fact that I hadn't eaten much over the last few days. But it wasn't like I had any free hands to take the food from Brandon. Besides, the offering made me suspicious, so I held up King in response.

Brandon shrugged. "I heard you had a new friend. He's adorable."

"Thanks." No. Really. This was weird. King

strained against my arms, trying to get closer to the food, so I let him sniff Brandon. "He likes people a bit too much for my taste, but he's not bad otherwise."

"Hey, little guy." Like that, Brandon's voice shifted up an octave, and he scratched and petted King. "You're adorable, aren't you? How'd you land yourself such a grumpy old man?"

I rolled my eyes and tried to fight a smile I didn't understand. "Did you stop by just to meet the dog?"

"Nope. I heard you get to take the rest of the year off." Brandon focused on me again.

Any of my creeping good mood vanished in a blink. "Just the rest of the week," I said. Brandon had been suspended last year because he was fucking up and picking fights. Not the same as what I was dealing with. He'd been burned out and dreading working at all. I actually wanted to be at work. "Why are you here?"

"I'm paying it forward." He nodded at the pizza.

"I can buy my own food." I was being abrupt on purpose, because it was easier than admitting his presence made the ache inside worse. It was both nice to see someone else from work, and wrong that it was Brandon. He was all but a traitor, since he'd mostly quit after last year.

His smile was a kind of patient I didn't want to

see. "I know how hard the Cord thing hit you, back when. Most of us know," he said.

Hurray. Pity for something that wasn't relevant. For something I never talked about. In fact, Fallyn was the only person I'd told the story to. Anyone I worked with may have drawn conclusions, but they'd never heard everything. "You don't know."

"We're not blind. We do know." Was his glance at my wrists intentional, or just a subconscious reaction? "I'm here because last year, someone else did this for me and I hated them for it."

"Wow. *Awesome.*" Was that sarcastic enough? I was torn. It was nice to know Brandon cared, but he wasn't the person I wanted to have this conversation with. I didn't want anyone digging around in my psyche or heart this much.

Maybe Link.

Maybe.

And Fallyn.

Nope. Definitely not.

"But I needed it," Brandon said.

Still no clue what we were talking about. "Needed what?"

A heavy pause hung between us, punctuated by his sigh. "I know you're already thinking about worst case scenarios." *Ouch.* "But even if this unfolds in the worst way possible, nothing changes."

"Everything changes." Fucking idiot. Him and me.

"No." This time there was no hesitation from Brandon. "You'll still have your knowledge, your experiences, all of us..." He pulled down the shoulder of his jacket as much as was possible, to reveal the tip of a tattoo that matched one I had. Most of us from AcesPlayed had. "That spade tattoo on your chest means more than just being a piece of ink. I don't care if you think it's corny, it connects us all. But don't worry, you'll also still be an intolerable asshole."

Rah. "Is this where we share our feelings and hug and have a slumber party? Is the pizza part of this?"

"*Yes* to the pizza, I assume *no* to the rest. I think this is where you tell me to leave, you sulk a lot more, but you can't stop thinking about what I said."

I shrugged. No point in denying what he said if he wasn't going to believe me. "I don't care if you go or not, but the conversation *is* over."

"I meant everything I said. I swear it on Danny's good nature." Brandon shoved the box at me again.

I shifted King into one arm and took the box. No reason to let it go to waste. "Yeah. Okay."

Brandon turned away.

"Thank you." The words forced their way past my lips without permission.

He waved over his shoulder, and walked to his car.

Thank fuck that was over. I kicked the door shut behind him so I could set King down without him getting out.

The pizza didn't patch the aches inside, but it made me less angry about them. When I finally retrieved my phone later in the evening, the message from Link made me smile. I was surprised to see texts from other people too. All of them asking if I was okay. If I needed anything. Phillip. Chloe. Nigel.

Damn it, I didn't want to feel better.

One thing was guaranteed to piss me off. I headed to Fallyn's channel.

No new videos since Monday, and that one was a short livestream of her in the Salt Lake airport. She'd almost hidden the red-rimmed eyes, but her voice cracked before she abruptly ended the stream.

What was I doing? What was I supposed to do? Where was I going to find answers… to anything?

Brandon's visit stuck in my head far longer than I wanted it to. Thinking about what he said, about the other messages from friends, came with a consequence I didn't want—it turned on the emotion. Mostly good ones, but some really shitty ones as well.

The last thing I wanted to be doing was thinking about what I could lose at AcesPlayed. What I may have already lost by pushing Fallyn away. By pulling back from Link.

If I thought about those things, my heart would ache, and I'd question a whole lot about my recent life choices.

I definitely didn't want that.

Thursday in the office, I struggled to focus. Elliot wasn't here. Bryce was. Not *here* here, but across the street, and that was close enough it put me on edge. When the game crashed again, it was a relief in a sick and twisted kind of way. Not that I wanted it down, but at least now I knew what I'd been dreading. Judith wasn't available, we weren't allowed to call Elliot, no matter how badly we needed him, and a looming bubble of *we're fucked* hung over my head.

"All right everyone, listen up." Chris strode to the middle of the room, to Elliot's spot, the same way he had a few days ago. He barked out a few commands, telling different developers where to look for issues in the code.

What the fuck was he doing?

When he said, "Dev Girl, tell Ivan to make sure

we have coffee and snacks," something inside me snapped. Alys deserved better than that.

"Sit down, and shut the fuck up." I stood and stalked toward him.

Chris stared back. "We still have to do work, even though your boyfriend's not here."

Was he really…? I wouldn't get into a dick measuring contest with him, because he'd lose and then he'd be butthurt and then we'd have to hear about it all day. "We also have processes that don't involve guessing where the issue might be, but discovering where the problem actually lies. Every person in this room knows that, and they don't need to hear your random assumptions. Sit. Down."

I'd learned a long time ago that all I needed in order to look imposing was to stand my ground. I looked at Chris, not saying anything else, until he walked back to his desk.

Great. "Show's over. Each team knows where to focus. Check in with the group when you find something. We're on a timer. Don't let that freak you out, but find this issue."

I returned to my own computer, and dove into work. The conversation with Chris wasn't right. It wasn't just that he got bossy and aggressive, it was how he'd approached this issue.

Like he wanted us to look in very specific places.

What bothered me even more was that when

Team Beta checked in, they'd found the problem exactly where Chris told everyone to look. Stranger still, while the crash was hard enough to take the game down, the fix would only take a few hours to put in place and test. The crisis would be averted before most of the world even knew the game was down.

I wanted to call Elliot. I was desperate to talk to him. Not just because of this, though that certainly added to the urge. There was simply a longing to connect again. Over game crashes. Over anything. The only reason I didn't dial him was because if it got out that I'd consulted with him, it could make his situation worse.

He needed to be back here next week. I wasn't going to jeopardize that.

I could bounce some of my thoughts about Chris off the other developers. Alys was great because her experience gave her a lot of insight. Landon was great because his inexperience kept him from thinking things weren't possible.

Both were horrible ideas because this conversation was going to drift toward Fallyn, which would mean bringing up that I was still talking to her, that I was unlikely to stop… Why was I keeping my relationship with her a secret again?

Because she asked me to, and that was the only reason.

The longer we worked, the more the tampering became evident. If I hadn't been looking for it, I wouldn't have seen it, but now it was like shining a blacklight over an adult movie theater.

Gross.

Infuriating.

Covered in Chris's filth.

We brought everything back online within a few hours. Amazing how much faster things went when we had an idea of the cause and exactly where to focus our efforts. The job well done wasn't enough to cool my simmering rage, though.

I needed to walk away for a couple of hours, and blow off steam in a way that required more than just thinking my way through it. A short scroll through my contacts landed me on *Luther*, and I dialed the instant I saw his name.

The phone call was long enough to say *hi* and agree I'd meet him at a boxing gym a few miles away for a late lunch punch session. I told the other developers to call me if things went south while I was out, and I took off.

I'd met Luther in jail. He came from a family with money, parents who didn't care for his hobbies, and a quiet but intense desire to find a place he fit. Apparently, I liked my men rich and broken with daddy issues. Biggest difference was that Luther was actually just a friend, and Elliot had never been anything so simple.

Luther had wanted to be CIA, digital ops. Even twenty years ago, he'd been a brilliant hacker. He'd found himself involved with an older man who promised to show him the ropes and hold the door open for him at the agency. Instead, the asshole had used Luther to take the fall for a botched operation.

When Luther and I met, I taught him how to defend himself and he taught me the basics of programming. His criminal record meant no one was hiring him for any position that required security clearance, so he'd gone into private security. The wealthy needed their digital lives protected at least as intently as their physical ones.

Luther was waiting outside when I pulled up at the boxing place. He was tall, wearing a suit that was a stark contrast to the white, cold weather, and looked like the single pillar of him was worth more than the rundown building he stood in front of. It was still weird to see him without glasses, even though he'd gotten rid of them years ago in favor of laser surgery.

He gave me a tight smile and an abbreviated nod when I approached, and we headed inside.

In the locker room, we changed into more appropriate clothes for beating each other up, then grabbed an empty ring at the edge of the main room.

We knocked gloves, then circled each other, each of us looking for that first opening.

"So what's up?" Luther's tone was casual and friendly, which was immediately a red flag.

I never heard him do *casual and friendly*. "I can't just call to say *hi*?" I threw a testing jab before he could.

He ducked and swung. "We're not that kind of friends."

"Fair point." So far, this was easy. It wouldn't be for long, and I was already enjoying the distraction. "I'm trying to figure out an issue, and I feel like I'm missing pieces to the puzzle. I need an outside perspective."

"What've you got?" Luther struck again, harder this time. I took the hits in favor of returning a cross of my own. I landed a solid punch and he danced out of reach.

"I've got a lot of game crashes that may or may not be related, a DDOS, and some leaked information. The second two came from the same person's accounts." I traded a few more low-impact hits with Luther. Each strike pushed me further toward a clear head.

Luther wasn't weathering the strikes as well as I did, which wasn't surprising. He was more about speed and maneuverability than taking punches. "I assume this person isn't a suspect?"

"No." Not for an instant. I had no doubt Fallyn wasn't part of this.

"Are they hot?"

"Sexy. Smart. Sassy. She's the full package."

"Does Elliot know?"

At the reminder of Elliot, my mind froze, and my limbs locked. It was only for a second, but it was enough time for Luther to sweep his foot under my legs.

I stumbled, but didn't fall. No surprise—we weren't playing by standard rules. "Doesn't matter what Elliot thinks of her." It should. It bothered me that he and Fallyn—

It wasn't relevant to this. One of the best and worst things about sparring with Luther was he had a knack for getting under people's skin, and using it to get his hits in. He would force me to approach this issue rationally and without emotion, or get my ass kicked.

"Is how you feel about her relevant?" Luther asked.

"Yes."

"Which is…?"

She was one of the best things to happen to me. Top of the list. And I was terrified I was losing her before I had her. "She didn't do this, regardless of what it looks like."

"Ah." Luther ducked under my swing, came up behind me, and hit me in the side before dancing away.

Fuck that one hurt. "No. Don't give me an *ah*. Help me figure out how someone framed her."

"Need more info. What makes it look like it was

her? How do you know it's not? Is her pussy really worth this kind of effort?"

There was the rage. I came in with a cross, but swung too wide, and Luther side-stepped. I corrected, but it didn't help, and his foot to the back of my knee landed me on my back.

"So, two and three"— He offered me his hand —"You just know, and yes."

The only answer I had was a low growl.

"What makes it look like she did it? Give me more than *it came from her accounts*." Luther tugged.

I flexed my fingers as I hopped to my feet. "They tethered to her phone. Or it looks like they did."

"Did they clone it? Her phone? What are the odds she stood next to someone long enough for them to do that?"

His question was a needle popping the bubble of my fury, and realization rushed in, pushing the anger out. After spending several days packed into a convention center with a hundred thousand other people. "Fuck."

I needed to talk to Elliot, and I didn't care what the rules said. I had to see him in person, make sure he was all right, and figure out what was going on.

Mostly though, I needed to see him. Period.

Before I could, I needed to take care of Chris. With my fists would be preferable, but Elliot would be mad if I landed myself in jail again. I headed back to the offices, and called Judith while I was driving.

When I told her what I suspected, what I'd seen so far, she said, "Are you certain? I have to be positive, one-hundred percent, before I make this kind of call, because there are legal repercussions for being wrong."

I wasn't used to being the final say in matters like this, but I was right. "I'm certain. And I want his execution to be public."

"I should tell you *no*." Judith's laugh was dry. "But to find out he's been doing this? That he could've cost us everything? Find me in my office when you get back. I'll start on the paperwork now, and you can escort him out for me."

"Shame Elliot can't be here for it." I couldn't help myself.

She let out a strangled sigh. "He made his choices, and he'll be grateful *you're* here."

When I walked into Judith's office, she was waiting for me. I hadn't visually confirmed my suspicions, but it didn't take long to find our proof, and show her. Less than thirty minutes later, we'd had Luna kick him off the network, and we were walking toward the Dev room.

When we walked in, he was asking if anyone else was having trouble logging in. Was the network down?

"Chris," I barked his name as we walked in the room. "Shut off your computer. You're done."

He stood, his head popping above the cubicles like a little gopher. When he saw me with Judith, he paled.

"Done with what?" He had balls though, arguing even now.

"Work. Your employment here is terminated, effective immediately." It didn't matter that Judith was a foot shorter than me. She did intimidating at least as well. "Link will see you to your car."

Whispers ran through the room. Fingers clacked on keys. I assumed everyone was either talking or chatting about this.

Chris joined us. "I will sue you."

"And the best fucking contract lawyer in the country owes me a favor," Judith said. "You will *not* win. We'll mail you your things."

I pointed toward the elevators, and tuned out a string of curse words and threats from Chris as he and I rode down. I'd been called a lot worse than a chubby, small-dicked, muscle-head in my life. As we strode toward the parking garage he said, "I didn't do this alone."

"Did you just rat out your partner?" I stared at him in disbelief. "Really?"

"No. I just wanted you to know he's still out there." Chris's gaze drifted toward Loading Java.

Where Bryce had been this morning. Very possibly still was. Fucking idiots. "That's nice. Leave the premises. If you come back, we will call the police."

I watched Chris drive away.

As satisfying as that was, apparently I wasn't finished. I headed upstairs again, and directly to Luna's office. I closed the door behind me as I walked in. "We have a leak, and I need your help shutting it down."

"Of course." Like a switch had been flipped, pixie-Luna was gone, and professional-Luna was in her place.

I had my phone out as well, and sent Fallyn a text. *We need to make some changes to your phone.* "We—I —think someone cloned Fallyn's phone." As I explained the thought to Luna, I sent a similar message to Fallyn. "I need you to revoke all of her current access, and at the same time, help her make sure she can get in through new means."

I finished a similar message to Fallyn, ending with *We're going to call you..*

"Does Elliot know you're letting her stay?" Luna asked.

I wanted to both bless and curse her for her loyalty. "Elliot's not here." Saying the words ached.

"Is it true the two of you, and her…" Luna shook her head. "Sorry. None of my business."

It wasn't hard to guess what she was asking. "All three of us together, yes. The chat logs are real, and

Fallyn's, and she was here partly to visit us." It felt good to not hide that, even if Luna was only one person. I dialed Fallyn, and put my phone on speaker between me and Luna, while I made brief introductions.

"O.M.Geee," Pixie-Luna peeked through. "I can't believe I finally get to talk to you," she said to Fallyn. "I love your videos. I wanted to meet you while you were here, and I'm sad I couldn't. Your kitty costume day one? *Envy*. Plus, you're so sexy."

"Thanks?" Fallyn's reply was shy.

This was sweet, but we did have work to do. "Luna?" I said.

"Yes?"

"Help Fallyn fix her phone and accounts?"

"Halfway done already." Luna's fingers flew across her keyboard. "And seriously, Fallyn, are we allowed to talk to you now? Because I'm so tired of talking to you through Nigel."

Did Elliot know about that? Would thinking about him hurt this much forever?

"I'll send you my personal email," Fallyn said. "Don't share it with *anyone*. You can talk to me whenever you want."

"*Yay*." Luna clapped. "Okay, you're set on this side. I'm sending you instructions for the rest. Let me know when you get them."

Luna and Fallyn spend the next little while making sure Fallyn was set to get back into the game, and that her phone no longer matched the clone, so it could be blocked. When Fallyn hung up, I was pretty sure they were BFF's.

We couldn't escort Bryce off the Loading Java property, but Luna made a call to Violet, who made sure Bryce was asked to leave, and that he wouldn't be allowed back in.

The adrenaline of the find, of the fix, of the entire day, still pumped through my veins.

Now I had to see Elliot. Fuck the consequences.

I knew when the game went down. The alerts still came to my phone, and I could see as well as any other player in the world that the servers were offline.

The only thing that kept me from driving into the office right then was the concern that if I did, it would be the last time they let me set foot on the property. And even then, I only thought that because Judith texted me to tell me as much.

If the game hadn't come back online by noon, I was fully prepared to call her bluff. But it did, and that left me wondering if I was prepared to drive in anyway. I wanted to know everything was okay. I wanted to see people. I wanted to see Link.

Maybe the visit would be the thing that stopped the conversation with Brandon from playing on repeat in my head. His words shouldn't have hit me so hard or made me feel *so much*. It was the *feeling* that I hated the most. At least, when it was this raw and empty.

If I had to have feelings, I wanted the good ones back. The ones caused by waking up next to Link. By collaborating with people I trusted and appreciated. By having Fallyn here.

The last thought smacked into me hard, and I didn't like it. If I thought about her, I'd have to face the emptiness her name summoned, and I wouldn't have the time I needed to numb those spots in my heart and move on. As if summoned by the repeated flashing of her name and face in my mind, my phone chimed with an alert that she was about to do a livestream.

Oops. My thumb must've slipped last time I was on her channel, and I accidentally signed up for notifications or something.

I couldn't stop myself from clicking the link, any more than I could look away from the *Stream Starting Soon* flashcard that included the graphic that wasn't supposed to look like a broken penis, but totally did, with *Fallyn's Phallusies* scrawled across it.

The woman who appeared on screen didn't match the *fuck you* tone of her title graphic, and she barely looked like the Fallyn who had left here just a few days ago. Her hair was pulled back into a tight ponytail, dark shadows lingered under her eyes, and she wasn't looking at the camera.

I wanted to tell her it was going to be all right.

That everything was. I didn't have that right, she didn't want to hear it from me, and it wasn't a promise I could keep.

"Hey, all." There was no brightness to her voice. "I'm sorry there hasn't been any new content in a while. I always wondered if I'd ever be making one of these videos and here we are. Achievement Unlocked, am I right?" Her laugh was flat. "Anyway, I'm dealing with some burnout, and I need to take some time away to re-evaluate… everything. Not sure when I'll be back or if the channel will look the same as it does now. But while I figure it out, thank you to everyone who's supported me, fuck you to everyone who hasn't, and go out there and break something I would."

That was it. The screen went black. The stream was over.

"You can't." My own voice startled me. Was I talking to a blank square? Was I arguing for Fallyn to not quit?

Yes. I wasn't going to survive denying myself or how much I missed her.

I heard the front door swing open and shut, and footsteps. King ran toward the sound with happy barks, which didn't reassure me as to the safety of the situation. I stepped into the hallway to find Link stalking toward me. His scowl said I probably shouldn't smile, but I couldn't help it.

"What are you doing?" His question didn't have any point of reference.

The correct answer might be *pondering my own mortality*, but I wasn't willing to risk it. I showed him my phone, and hit *Replay* on the video I'd just watched.

Hearing Fallyn say it a second time didn't make the news any easier to process, and watching Link's expression shift to angry definitely made the situation worse. He fixed a glare on me. "No more bullshit. What did you say to her that made her leave?"

Nothing. I did what needed to be done. There was my reply. Easy. Direct. No emotion. "I fucked up." *Fuck*, it hurt to say so, but the confession was also a relief. "I fucked up and I don't think I can make it right."

"Seems that way." Link's voice was tight.

I swallowed a lump of frustration and it lodged in my throat. "Not pulling any punches, huh?"

"No. I'm done with that. Tell me what happened between you two."

Nothing complicated, but everything was wrong about it. "I told her she could stop pretending to like me. That the bet was done, she lost, and no one needed to play anymore games."

Link dragged his hand down his face and let out a silent exhale. "You're such fucking idiot. No wonder she won't talk about you."

"*You're* still talking to her?" The relief and jealousy were bitter together, like mixing the wrong kinds of liquor. *Why didn't you stop her from doing this?* The question wouldn't do me any good—I already knew he would've if he could.

"I talk to her every night, and I'd be talking to you too, if you weren't being so fucking emo."

I opened my mouth.

"You're such a jackass." Link talked over me. "I don't spend time with you because one of us saved the other or because the sex is good—it is, but that's not enough. I'm here, always, because I love you. Even though you're an idiot, and there are days when you don't deserve it, I love you anyway and I have for a long time."

The confession stole my breath and my thoughts, and hurt in an entirely new way. I wasn't sure I liked it, but I also loved it. What was I supposed to say in return? "I don't—"

"In case there's any question, you're currently in the *don't deserve* it box. Just because I love you doesn't mean I'll put up with your shit, but when you pull your head out of your ass and stop trying to fight the world, those are the moments when I know you're worth it."

I'd fucked up so badly. With Link. With everything. I didn't see any path out, even if I said it back, nothing would be fixed. "I love you too, but I don't know how to make any of this right. I don't think there's a way."

The way Link gripped the back of my neck sent a

shock through me, and I wrapped my hand around his forearm in response, digging my fingers in. He crushed his mouth to mine. This was power and strength and the rock I'd let go of, that I needed to grab again.

I kissed back hard, searing this moment and this stability into my mind, and pushing away the doubt.

"You know you don't have to do this alone, right?" Link's voice was gravel when we broke apart.

"I do now."

"Idiot."

I couldn't help but smile. "Sometimes. But never tell anyone I admitted that." Nothing was resolved, except I felt better than I had in days. "And I know I have to earn my way back in."

"Not with me." Link pressed his forehead to mine. "With Fallyn… I can't say. If that's what you did? I wouldn't forgive you. And by the way, I'm not going to stop talking to her. I'd prefer if the two of you got along, but you can't take her from me anymore than she can push me from you."

"I think that's fair." I had no idea how I was going to make things right with Fallyn. Not after what I'd done. She was facing the same thing I was —losing everything she'd worked for—but I had no idea if she had a recovery plan.

I needed to think hard about how to approach her. How to…

Beg.

I was willing to do that to get her to hear me out.

That was how far I'd fallen.

Until I had those answers though, "Tell me what happened at work this morning. Tell me how we're putting a stop to these crashes for good."

"I have such a story for you," Link said.

My anger was back, far more potent and with a better direction this time, as Link explained his theory that Chris was sabotaging our game. "Plus" —Link pulled out his phone, made a few jabs, and zoomed in on something—"I got Luther to look up Fallyn, to see if she was showing as nearby." He showed me a map, zoomed in to the address level, and the image was of Loading Java. "Bryce has been over there most of the morning."

"Is Chris still working?" This was something I could act on. I'd see those assholes burn for this.

Link shook his head. "No. We escorted him out. Had Violet kick Bryce out."

Good. Just because I had to wait to be told I could have my job back didn't mean I was going to let someone burn the place to the ground while I was gone.

I looked up to find Link watching me with an expression I couldn't define.

Not that it mattered. The only thing I cared about as far as that went was that he was here. I hadn't lost him. And I was going to do everything in my power to make sure things stayed that way.

I hadn't been in game since I was suspended. Staying away had hurt, but being back was its own kind of ache. Link had refused to give me the information I wanted, so I went around him and asked Danny. He only helped me under the explicit condition that no one find out, especially Luna.

It was tempting to tease him about being afraid of a little pixie, but I liked Luna, and I was obsessed enough with Fallyn to do this, so I didn't have any room to talk.

I found B1tchKw33n—bitch queen—farming resources on an isolated part of the game map.

The instant I moved closer to her character, she stopped her harvesting.

"Stay." I'd hijacked her audio, too. I doubted she was going to be happy with that.

Fallyn's familiar sigh echoed through my headset. "Puff96? Did you even try to hide who you were?"

"Nope. Not even for a second. Do you think they won't shut you down for skirting the profanity filters?" I winced at the harsh words. This was the opposite of how I wanted this conversation to go.

Another sigh from her. "Breaking the game.

Cheating. That's what I do, right? Whoring around. Falling for the wrong guys. Is this what I have to look forward to every time I log into the game? Are you harassing me?"

"No. I knew you wouldn't take my calls or emails, though."

"That should've been a sign." Her voice was tight.

Fuck. I'd screwed this up so hard. "If you don't want to talk to me, I'll go. You can even block me. I'll take the hint and won't make new accounts to get to you."

"No offense, *Puff*, but you're not the most believable person right now. It's your game. You can find me whenever you want."

Of course she'd think that of me. What had I done to make her feel differently? Her mistrust hurt as much as what I was about to say, and that wasn't right. "It's probably not my game anymore."

Her silence should've been gratifying. "What do you want?"

"Not to fight. Not to throw shade or exchange insults or do anything like that. I want to apologize. I'll tell you I'm sorry as many times as it takes. I'm so sorry."

"Nope. Blocked." She vanished from my screen.

Hiding from Elliot felt like giving up, and I hated myself for not being strong enough to stare him down until he was the one who backed off. Even in digital form. I also hated myself for not hearing him out. And then I hated myself for giving this so much brain power.

Elliot was right, he had won. In so many ways.

But did he? He sounded sincere just now. His apology. *It's probably not my game anymore.*

Why did I care? Why was I still thinking about him? Because part of me thought every cruel narcissist who stuck their dick in me could be healed?

Elliot's not like the others.

Great. Now my own brain was taking his side.

When Link called me a few hours later, I was still chasing my tail about whether or not I was right to block Elliot and walk away. It was going to be obvious I was upset, but I answered anyway. I needed that comfort.

"Tell me what's wrong." He didn't even bother with *are you all right?* Link had a way of seeing through the bullshit. Of understanding me. It was one of the things I adored about him. One of the reasons I was falling for him.

I wasn't sure how to frame this, so I grabbed the simple answer and tried to keep the emotion from my reply. "I was in game today. I decided to try it again, under a new name." *Because I missed it. Because it's not fair I should have to give up what I love because of this.* "And Elliot managed to find me."

"*Fuck*." Link's response carried a startling punch. "I told him not to do that."

Wait. That meant… "The two of you were talking about me?" This might be a drawback to my *please don't talk about Elliot* request.

"Yes."

"Give me some context for the conversation?" That was something I shouldn't ask. It wouldn't help me feel any better.

"Are you sure?"

That *definitely* didn't help me feel better, but now I needed to know even more. "Yes."

Link made a series of soft clucks that sounded more like line noise than a person. "You know I love him, right?"

"I do." That didn't stop the words from slamming into me like a fist to the gut. I'd known pretty much from the start that the two of them were in love, and had no idea how they hadn't figured it out.

"I told him. I finally said the words." Link's voice was quiet. Contemplative.

Was that ache in my chest what a breaking heart felt like? I was pretty sure it was.

"I'm sorry." Link sounded like he meant the apology, and I didn't have any reason to doubt him. "I don't know how to put that differently, and you wanted context. But I also told him, the same way I'm telling you now, that doesn't change the way I feel about you."

I couldn't handle this roller coaster of emotion. "Which is?"

"I hate that you're gone. Talking to you every night isn't the same as having you here, and I miss you desperately. Not that I would give these conversations up for anything. Never. I can love him and you at the same time."

Did he just… Did I hear him… "Say that again. Not all of it. The important part."

Link's chuckle, his smile, threatened to engulf the jumble of emotions inside me. "I'm falling for you," he said. "Some days it feels like I've known you forever and at the same time I don't know if I can ever spend enough time with you. Maybe it's too soon for *I love you*, but… I don't think it is."

The combination of emotions, the highs and

lows, the muddy mess in my heart and mind, choked a giggle from me.

"What's funny?" Link asked.

"Falling for Fallyn. From far away. It's not really funny." But I was laughing anyway.

"I love that sound, too."

Damn it, I needed to ask him to stop. This was too easy. Too comforting. Too exactly what I needed. "What sound?"

"Your laugh. Since the first time I heard it."

Unlike Elliot, Link was perfect. Which was its own kind of scary, but... He was warm, he was empathic, he was adoring, he was sweet. "What do you see in Elliot?" That was a perfect way to ruin this conversation, but I had to know. "Why didn't you ever give up on him?"

"Because..." Link sighed. "Because I know who he is. I've watched him build the walls he hides behind and he's still himself in that fort. That doesn't mean I forgive him when he's an ass, and it doesn't mean what he said to you was okay."

"He told you." Did I dare believe it had been the truth? No self-important narcissist would take the blame for a conversation like that one. "Did he say something like I overreacted, or he didn't know why I was so upset?"

Link frowned. "No. He told me he was wrong and he wished he could take it back. But I'm not the one he has to apologize to."

"I don't want to talk about Elliot anymore. Not that he's off-limits." Not now. "But I want to talk to you." And try to ignore that nagging question inside. That little voice asking if I should've heard Elliot out in the game. I was talking to the perfect guy right at this moment, and I still wanted another, broken one on top of that?

Selfish, selfish Fallyn.

Instead, I'd enjoy my evening with Link.

"Is asking about why you're taking a break off-limits too?" Link asked.

Right. That. "No, but there's not much to say about it. I just can't right now." My voice cracked.

"Okay." Link sounded kind. "Do you want to hear a secret?"

I wasn't sure I could handle anything else emotional. "Depends? Is it the kind of thing you have to kill me if you tell me?"

"No. But you do have to swear not to tell anyone."

Now I was intrigued. "Cross my heart."

"We signed off on Art's spring festival costume designs," Link said conspiratorially, and he moved his phone away from his face, to point at his computer screen.

"I'm pretty sure you're not supposed to show me those."

"You promised to keep it between us, and I trust you."

Simple words. The kind of thing people tossed around without care. Considering the man he loved might lose his job for breaking company rules, and that I was on his company's *most hated* list, because of the kind of information I'd shared in the past… My heart soared as I put the pieces together.

And my awe rose with it when he showed me the designs. One sexy, one tough, both in pastels and with the kind of details even real clothes didn't have. "They're gorgeous."

"Next time you're here, I'll introduce you to Adrienne. I think you'd like her." Link was back on screen,

Next time you're here. We were making plans to meet again. "I'd love that."

"I wish you were here now." Like that, Link's tone shifted to something deeper. Huskier.

"Me too." So very desperately. I wanted to talk to him face to face, and cuddle with him, and feel his touch, and so much more. Though I couldn't have any of that, I did have an idea. "What else would you do if I was there?"

Link seemed to consider my question. "I'd take you to see the lights downtown. We didn't get to do that."

"The glimpses I saw from the convention center *were* gorgeous. I wouldn't mind spending some more time there. What else?"

His chuckle was like skilled fingers gliding over

me. "I can think of a lot of things I'd do to and with you, and only half of them involve clothes. What do you want to do next time you're here?"

I wanted to feel closer to him, but I didn't want to wait. Right now I'd give a hell of a lot to be wrapped up in him. Even if I couldn't have it, maybe we could pretend. I fiddled with the bottom of my oversized sweatshirt, and embraced my boldness. "I like the sound of that *no clothes* thing. I'd spend at least a day in bed with you, learning what you mean by that."

"I'm not super creative as a rule." Link grinned. "I can strip you down, devour your body, and fuck you until you're sore, but I'll need your help with the details."

"If I help you with those kinds of details now, it's going to turn me on, and without you here…" I let the playful suggestion blossom on its own. "I might have to take care of whatever resulting *urges* I have on my own."

"That sounds like a decent compromise, as long as I get to watch," Link said.

I set my phone down a short distance away, propped up, and stripped off my top, leaving me in just my bra. "How's that for a starting point?"

"I like where you're going so far with this." Link watched me attentively.

"What next?"

"This is your story. I'm along for the ride."

I liked this so much. It was easy. Fun. Not the same as having him here, but pretty freaking good. "What do I get to see in return?"

"Hmm…" The camera shifted away from Link's face and traveled down his body, to land on his crotch and the noticeable bulge he was stroking with one hand. "I'll show you the same. You get to see what your voice and mind and sexy words do to me."

"Show me." Did I really say that? *Yes.*

He dragged his zipper down and freed his cock. I'd never been turned on by a dick pic in my life, but tonight, seeing him stroke his massive length, remembering how good he felt buried inside me as he stretched me out until it hurt…

Yup. I was completely turned on. "I'd love to have a taste, if I were there. Draw you into my mouth. Lick you like a lollipop."

"I like that." His voice was gravel. "One thing I wished I'd done more of with you was suck on your nipples. They remind me of bubblegum. I like bubblegum."

I liked that visual. I stripped off my bra, leaving me topless and on display for his eyes only. Cupping my own breasts wasn't the same as having him do it, but I knew now what his touch felt like, so I could imagine. I rolled my nipples between my fingers until they were red and puffy, and the ache between my legs pulsed so hard I'd have to give it attention soon.

"You know what else makes me think of cherries." I winced as soon as the words were past my lips.

"What's wrong?" Link was still stroking himself. Still letting me watch.

"That was a horrible line. Sounded a lot better in my head. I'll edit it in post and replace it with something more seductive."

He laugh-groaned. "You're letting me watch you pleasure yourself on camera. It doesn't get much more seductive. And if you were going for a pussy joke, be assured I'm already fantasizing about burying my face in yours."

One-hundred points to Hufflepuff Link.

"This is making me so wet." I had to redeem myself with something simple, despite his assurances.

"Show me," He commanded. "Take the rest of your clothes off, spread your pussy, and show me how wet it is. Show me how you get yourself off."

I was happy to comply. I squirmed out of the rest of my clothes. This was a whole new experience compared to the sexy chat we'd done in game. That was voice. Text. Digital avatars doing naughty things. But this… I was stripped bare for Link, both emotionally and physically.

I loved it. It took a little adjusting to get the

phone to stay up between my legs, and then I was stroking myself. Personal porn for the man on the other end of the line. Teasing my fingers over my slick core, while Link watched, felt wicked and incredible and the best bits of right and wrong.

Link's grunts made me want to come as much as the way I teased my clit. How did people in actual porn keep from getting off too fast? I couldn't draw this out much longer. I wanted to touch myself harder, faster, and in all the right ways.

Fuck holding back. I gave myself into the sensations of my fingers drawing along my own skin, and Link's reactions. I pushed myself until my body clenched with need, and gave into orgasm when it overcame me.

The sounds Link made told me he was close too. I kept teasing myself, letting out soft sighs and shudders, while I watched him shudder, and come hard, coating his hand and pants.

We apparently had forgotten how to speak, but it didn't seem to matter. I moved the phone back up to my face, and he did the same. We lay there for a few minutes, our giggles mingling together as we caught our breath.

"I'd do that again," I finally managed.

"I don't think I'd survive that again," Link said. "Not unless I knew I could have you again, at some point."

How did he manage to push so much sweetness and longing and desperation all into one statement?

"You will. We will." There was no way I could think of the alternative.

We kept talking until I couldn't think or speak straight, and I was pretty sure I fell asleep with him on the phone, but I couldn't let him go. Not tonight.

In the morning, there was a text waiting for me from Link. It simply said *Morning, pretty kittie.*

I'd absolutely hate that from anyone else, but from him it was sincere. I sent him back a reply. *Morning, to my favorite teddy.*

Favorite? Who's your least favorite? His reply came quickly.

My smile grew, and giddiness flitted inside. *No one. You have zero competition.*

Damn right. Talk to you tonight? Link asked.

Damn right.

I let him get back to work.

If Elliot was part of that conversation, what would he be? Belligerent Badger? Why was I wasting my time wondering such a thing?

Because I was still thinking about calling him.

Idiotic thought. Not the dumbest thing I'd done, but *giving Elliot a chance to apologize and hearing him out* also wouldn't make any sort of *top ten smart things Fallyn's done* list.

My taste in men was just the worst.

But Link wasn't a mistake. I knew that without

question. Was I willing to play the odds twice in a row and give Elliot another chance?

I had to, or I'd spend the rest of my life asking *what if..?* And I already had enough regrets in my life.

F riday morning, I strolled into Judith's office at five minutes before nine in the morning. If they weren't going to give me answers, I was going to camp out here until they had them.

The look she gave me was pure *unimpressed*. "I have a nine o'clock."

"That's me." I gave her a tight grin, closed the door behind me, and took a seat. I hadn't had to persuade Ivan as much as I thought, to get me on her calendar. "I have your time until ten."

"To do what? I can't make a decision without the board."

Bullshit. There were some things she could do, and she had more influence than she was claiming. "That's not like you. Standing aside. Not fighting," I said.

She raised her brows. "I don't want to do this. I

don't want you gone and neither does anyone else. Everyone would prefer you stay."

"Then let me stay." I didn't like her implication that I was closer to out than in.

"We're not those kids anymore. Our world has rules and consequences."

The old *world* did too. I rubbed the inside of my wrists. This time, it was just more obvious to more people. "I guess that makes you happy."

She'd always been more of a *by the book* kind of person than the rest of us. "It should, but firing you had to go and be one of the consequences and fuck that all up."

"Defying the status quo. Kind of my thing." I wasn't trying to apologize to her or convince her I was a good man. Judith knew exactly who I was. "Come to think of it, why didn't you and I ever hook up?" Not a serious question, and I didn't think for a second she would take it that way.

Judith stared back. If possible, more of her humor had faded. "Do you want to do things this way?"

"I want to do something. Go back to work. Get an answer. I have your time for another fifty minutes, so this is what I'm going to do."

She rolled her eyes and shook her head. "Because you're not ambitious enough for me."

"Fair point." I had a lot of drive, but when she

set her sights on something, she was a truck with no brakes barreling down a six-percent grade.

"Besides," apparently Judith wasn't done, "you've always been in love with Link."

I could deny it, make some sort of big protest, but I was tired of hiding how I felt from myself. Apparently it had never been hidden from some other people. "Which brings me to my next point."

"You actually have a point?" Judith scoffed.

Perfect time for a dick joke. Or, worst time ever, given the circumstances. "I do. You're right. I've loved Link for a long time. Which means we were together before this stupid rule went into effect, which means we didn't break any rules."

"I hope you brought a better argument than that." She almost sounded disappointed. "Nope. Doesn't work."

Why not? "Why not? Phillip. Sonya. You've already set a precedent."

"And they surrendered final say over whether or not Adrienne or Jeremy stays with the company. Phillip and Sonya can't fire them," Judith said.

That was easy. "Why would I fire Link? Ever."

"I don't know. Things change. I have to be realistic about that," Judith said.

Fuck, fuck, fuck. "Okay. I give that up too. I'll sign something promising I won't fire Link."

Judith pulled her hair loose from its bun, rewrapped her hair, and pinned it up again. "Let me cut off all your excuses now, even though I think you know all of this. You're not in the same position they are. You own part of the company. You sit on the board. You have a say in how things go here."

I opened my mouth.

"Sonya is an investor. She's got money in the pool, not a voice," Judith said.

Damn. I was rapidly running out of arguments.

"Give up your seat on the board, give up the management position, and you can stay without the board's vote."

I stared at Judith in disbelief. "No."

"Then give up Link."

I let out a barking laugh. "Fuck no. Give me another option."

"There are no other options." She sounded tired. Stressed. "You pick or we'll pick for you. Don't make me do that." Was she pleading?

Was this about more than me? "I can't pick either of those things. Or rather, I can't give them up. AcesPlayed is my baby as much as it is yours. This game… It's everything."

"But it's not, or you wouldn't have a problem giving up Link. Not that I'm saying you should. We're getting older, and we've given up a lot. If you have the perfect guy, that's longer term than a game. Let me ask you—why did you sign on for this?"

For the game? For AcesPlayed? "To build something incredible. To be a part of it. To shape this thing the world had never seen, that no one else could make the way we did."

"You're right, no one else could've pulled this off. And we did do it. Past tense. Not that the game is going away, but it exists now. We breathed life into it." The passion that tinged Judith's voice was familiar. Personal. Relatable. "How much will its shape change as we move forward?"

"As much as it needs to."

She nodded. "But it's unlikely we'll ever completely reshape *this* again. Any changes will be built on what exists."

"Yes." I wasn't sure where she was going with this. "It's still in its infancy though. And I'm not interested in going to another company to do this again. I like it here. I love what we all have here." That was hard to say, but it felt good.

Judith was silent for a moment. She tapped the tip of her pen against her bottom lip and furrowed her brow. "What if…"

"Yes?" Anything that kept me from having to give up something I loved.

"I don't know."

Fuck. One of us was supposed to have the answer. Always. It was one reason we made a great team. She had her strengths, I had mine. There had to be something. "What if I moved into a consulting position? More like a part time contractor? Put someone else in charge, but let me have a say. Let me keep my stake." As the words rushed out, they seemed so obvious.

Judith almost smiled—not something she did often. "Would you do that? *Could* you do that?"

"I don't know. I'd be willing to try. But only if you replaced me with someone who could do my old job." More inspiration, of the most brilliant sort. "Link."

And now her frown was back. At least that was predictable. "If I promote Link, it looks like I'm rewarding him for breaking the rules."

"But it doesn't." I'd talked to him at length yesterday, and I knew what he'd been doing while I was gone. "He's stepping into a position that needs filling, after taking those reins and doing the job without being asked. Tell me he hasn't owned this crisis. No one here sees him as anything but amazing and competent." The longer I thought about this, the more acceptable it was.

Not that I liked the overall idea of stepping down, but if there was one person I trusted to take my place... And it wasn't as if I was leaving my family behind.

Judith grabbed the phone and dialed.

"Hello?" Link's voice over the speaker made my pulse race.

Yes, even with such a simple response.

"We need to talk to you," Judith said. "Can you come to my office?"

"We?" Link asked.

Judith shot me a *keep your mouth shut* look. "Yes."

Not the solution I wanted, but the solution that would work. I needed this to not be a mistake, and maybe if I could work this out, I could make things right with Fallyn, too.

Talk about wanting the world.

But if I wasn't pushing for that, was I even trying?

**33 /
link**

I didn't know what to make of the call from Judith. *Can we see you in my office* was as ominous as things got around here. When I walked through her door and saw Elliot though, my heart flipped. It stumbled and crashed when I saw his flat expression.

"Close the door please. Have a seat." Judith gestured.

Elliot smirked the moment I found my chair. "Missed you."

I had no idea what was going on, but that look was one of the biggest reliefs ever. Still, he didn't get to mess with me like that, when the situation was what it was. Especially in front of other people. Like one of the people who could still fire him. "It's been a day."

"Half a day," Elliot said. "But it was a week before that, and *God* that sucked."

He was speaking, acting, like the bad was over. I looked between him and Judith. "Does that mean he's back?" Did I dare hope?

"Yes and no." Judith's answer wasn't crushing, but it was close. She gave Elliot her attention. "Do you want to…?"

"Hardly my place anymore."

Fuck fuckity fuck fuck.

Judith pursed her lips. She had an entire arsenal of stern and disappointed expressions, and if she rolled even a fraction of them out today, that was bad. "You haven't technically signed any paperwork."

"But it was done before the conversation started." Elliot on the other hand was more casual than I'd seen him in a while.

"It's your show," Judith said.

Elliot shrugged. "You're the boss."

"Enough." Whatever they were doing, they either needed to let me in on the gag, or drop it. "Answers. Now." Was I demanding information from the boss? "Please?"

Elliot chuckled. Judith rolled her eyes. Neither of them was carrying the weight they had been on Monday, but she was still masking something.

"Elliot is going to be moving into a consulting position. He'll be available for questions, coding, and anything and everything development related, but he will no longer be in charge." When she relented, Judith's answer was both better than I'd feared and worse than I'd hoped.

"Are you looking for someone new?" We brought in outside people on a regular basis—Adrienne and Landon were only a few—but we never had for management. It was bound to happen eventually. It wasn't right that the first time would be to replace Elliot.

"We hope not. I'd like to offer you the position."

I glanced at Elliot. What was I missing? "You just took it away from him, though. Now you're giving it back?"

Elliot laughed.

Super weird. Nice, but creepy.

"Not him." Judith looked amused too. "You, Lincoln. I'd like to offer you the position of Director of Development. Effective immediately. There's no one else in the world who knows this job as well as Elliot, and you've shown in the last week that you're capable of stepping into the role."

Uh... What? "I don't... I can't..." What? I could never fill Elliot's shoes. This wasn't right. If I were replacing anyone else, I'd say *yes*, not to get rid of them, but because of the opportunity. But not Elliot.

"Don't turn it down because of me." As if he'd read my mind, Elliot spoke directly to my hesitation. "My fate is the same regardless of what you say, and

I'm lucky it's not worse. Don't make it a wasted gesture on my part."

When he put it that way… I still felt odd stepping into his position, but, "In that case, I'd love to. Yes. I accept."

We talked a little more about an offer, about timing, and about the fact that she wanted me starting now in case things broke this weekend. Which was possible, but seemed far less likely since we'd escorted Chris out the door and blocked Bryce's way in.

Judith, Elliot, and I went to tell the rest of the development team. The cheers and flurries of *congratulations* were overwhelming, but reassuring. As the bedlam faded, another reality sank in.

"Does this mean we can stop pretending we're not together," I whispered to Elliot.

"Not like anyone bought it anyway. Apparently. But yes."

Good. I brushed my lips over his, to see how it felt in public.

The whistle from somewhere in the room made my cheeks heat, but the kiss itself was as incredible as it was simple.

The three of us left the crew—my crew? That would take getting used to—to work, and stepped back into the hallway.

"Tell me when you need me in the office and I'll

be here, boss." Elliot saying that didn't make it any more real.

Judith held up a hand. "You can't ask more than ten to twenty hours a week of him. I have to hold you to that."

I snorted. "Sorry, but do you really think that's going to happen?"

"If it's more, just don't tell me." She sighed, resigned to the truth.

I looked at Elliot. "I trust you to set your own hours."

"Great. Congrats everyone. Problems are all solved. If the two of you are doing something else, take it outside, the rest of us have work to do." Judith shooed us away.

I walked Elliot down to his car. When we reached it, he gripped my shirt with both fists, leaned his back against the side of the SUV, and pulled me with him. I had to press my hands on the vehicle on either side of my head to keep my balance.

"I can't believe we're losing you." It wasn't true, but in a lot of ways it felt like it.

He shook his head. "I don't think I could've gotten better, and I'm happy with what I did get." He leaned in and pressed his mouth to mine. Kissing Elliot wasn't new, but I couldn't imagine it ever getting old. The heat that sped through me. The security.

"I'm happy it worked out," he said when we broke apart. "And you earned this."

I was about to dive in for another kiss when my phone chimed. As the new boss, I should probably make sure that wasn't something critical. When I read the message, I frowned with curiosity. "It's from Fallyn. *Tell Elliot to check his messages. Tell him I mean it.*"

"It's on silent because of meetings." Elliot grabbed his phone. He scrolled. "The only thing I have from her says *call me.*"

"You probably should, if she means it."

"*As soon as I'm home,*" Elliot talked as he typed. He looked up at me when he was finished. "In case it hurts."

Please, God, Don't let it hurt. "I'm tired of it hurting."

"Me too. Come by tonight?"

I grinned. "Wouldn't miss it for the world."

I hated that he had to leave, but it helped that I knew he'd be back. It was probably selfish of me to hope that Elliot and Fallyn made things right too, but I was going to anyway.

fallyn

This was a mistake. I shouldn't be doing this. I needed to let Elliot go and be happy with what I had.

But Link's voice was in my head. *I know who he is behind the walls.* And I'd seen glimpses of that too. On top of that, what I saw even when Elliot's defenses were up wasn't cruelty, but…

A man who was scared to open himself up.

Not that I'd tell him that. Or maybe I would. I didn't know. What was I doing?

When my phone rang, I jumped. His name on the screen didn't calm my racing pulse, but I answered anyway. "This is Fallyn."

"I got your messages." Elliot's voice still had the power to send pleasant chills down my spine. It was disappointing to not have him on video, because I wanted to look him in the eye while we did this.

But at the same time, I didn't want him seeing

my face go through the myriad of emotions I expected. "Yeah. Hi."

"I'm sorry to keep you waiting, I was in a meeting. What's up?" Was his tone casual? Cool?

I couldn't tell. Why was I doing this? Was he in a meeting with Link? A meeting for work? Too many questions that would have to wait for answers. "You wanted to apologize, so I'm listening. Make it good." When in doubt, embrace Online Fallyn. Not that she had served me well recently, but she was still my shield.

His laugh was definitely strained and nervous. "I'm sorry."

"That's a good start." I wanted to say a lot more, but I'd let him finish.

Elliot sighed loudly. "Stick with me on this, because I promise it has a point."

Interesting.

"I've been thinking a lot lately about..." The abrupt silence was deafening, until another sigh interrupted it. "About when I tried to take my life. Because, well, for a lot of reasons. But one of the big ones is, after that I built some pretty powerful walls to keep everyone out. I swore the world wasn't going to tear me down like that ever again."

This wasn't what I'd expected, and I had no idea what to think. It didn't feel like a sympathy play, but bringing up one's own suicide attempt didn't typically bode well for a conversation. I didn't dare interrupt, for fear I'd either stop him from talking, or fuel whatever he was doing.

"I think you found the weakness in my defenses," Elliot said.

Oh. "Me?"

"Yes, you. I don't know if you crashed through or dug your way underneath or climbed over, but you've landed on the other side."

I didn't… That was good news, right? I'd never had someone tell me something like that before. "What about Link?"

"He was already inside. Fort for two. But you're here now too, and I don't want to kick you out again. You win."

My creeping hope slipped a notch. "I don't want to win anything. I already told you, it was never about winning. I just wanted you to look at me and see *me*. Not whatever villain you made me out to be because of my videos. Not your little sex kitten. That's the only thing I've ever wanted from anyone" —including myself. *Oh, fuck*—"is to see *me*…" I trailed off as realization sank in. I was pushing for him to recognize something I couldn't even define for myself.

"Okay. I want that too. Who are you?" Elliot asked.

"I… I don't know."

"May I give it a shot?"

I wasn't sure I wanted that. From Link it would

probably be okay, but it seemed like asking for trouble to let Elliot speak his mind as I was in the middle of this revelation. For so much of my life, men like Elliot had defined me, and I was done.

Which must've been why I said, "Sure. Go for it."

"There's the obvious." The way Elliot started wasn't encouraging. "You're smart. Not like a little smart, but the ways I've seen you break my code blow my mind. You're sexy as fuck."

And here we went. It was all downhill from here. I clenched my jaw.

"Don't take that wrong. I don't just mean you look smokin' in absolutely anything, but the way you think. The places your mind goes. Your creativity, your thoughts, your heart… You're kind. You're a little shy and a lot terrified and I don't blame you. The world sucks sometimes, and I have no doubt it's been at least as cruel to you as to me."

Elliot went quiet again.

Was he done? Because that was a pretty good list so far. He saw more in me than I expected, and really it wasn't the easiest thing to make a list of someone's good traits on demand.

"I've never met anyone like you." Elliot's quiet words yanked my attention. "Not even close. No one in the universe compares to you, Fallyn. Yes, I love Link, but he's not you. I'd never want him to be you, or you to be him. I was an idiot to say the things I did. To push you away. To treat you like anything other than the one-of-a-kind that you are. I'm sorry, and I'll spend as long as it takes to show you that, if you let me."

Oh. Oh, wow. "What if I tell you *no*? Apology not accepted. What if I tell you to fuck off?"

"Then it hurts, but I respect that."

No *then you're a stupid cunt* or *you'll be sorry* or *I'll make you forgive me.* "I'm not telling you that, by the way. I'd be sad if you fucked off."

"Would you?"

"Yes. I'd miss you." And I did. I missed him as much as Link, but in a different way. "You can still grovel a little more if you'd like, though."

Was that a snort? "Oh great and generous Fallyn. I'd worship at your feet if you were here."

"Not really a foot person." Were we using play-fulness to lighten the mood? Sure, but that was okay, wasn't it?

"Hmm." Elliot managed to put a lot of depth into a single grunt. "Higher, then? I'd still kneel at your feet and grovel with my tongue."

Heat flooded me. "Then I guess it's too bad I'm not there."

"It really is." His serious tone was back, squeezing my heart until I gasped.

We talked a while longer, about what happened to him at work—I made a note to congratulate Link later today—about my plans for Christmas—none

—and about how King was doing—he tried to lick the screen when Elliot turned on his camera to show me.

It was all wonderful and bittersweet at the same time. Talking to Elliot… I'd never enjoyed that more.

But when I hung up, all I could think about was how much I hated that it took putting the distance between us to figure this out. Hated that our lives were in shambles. Hated that some of the problems didn't seem to have solutions.

Link called me that night, from Elliot's. I wanted to talk to both of them all night, but it also hurt too much. I put them off on Saturday and Sunday, too. I wouldn't avoid them forever, but I needed to figure out what I was doing. With Elliot. With Link. With my heart.

When I woke up Monday morning, there was a plane ticket to Salt Lake waiting for me in my email. It had a short message in the notes. *Sorry for the short notice. Come visit for Christmas. Link.*

My heart soared. I got to see him again—them, I hoped. Even for just a little bit was something. And it wasn't as though anything was pressing here. Sure, I'd need to figure out work soon, but my plane left in less than three hours, and I still needed to pack, get to the airport, and go through security.

I tried to call Link a few times, but his voicemail

said he was in the middle of a work crisis, and Elliot's said the same.

So I sent Link a *thank you* text, and I was on my way back to Salt Lake.

It wasn't until I was in the air that it caught up to me how insane this was. I was flying across two states because a random guy sent me a plane ticket.

No, not a random guy. Two and a half weeks ago, it had been a little crazy. Insane and exciting and terrifying. But I knew who I was meeting now. I wasn't worried about how things would go with Link. Few things had ever felt more right in my life.

When I landed, I was more nervous than the last time I'd made this journey. It felt like so much more was at stake. Wait, was I supposed to go to Link's? I didn't have his address. I'd call him again once I had my bags. He hadn't replied to my text yet.

He should have a breather soon, and I'd be able to talk to him. Tell him I was here.

I was waiting for my familiar red suitcase to come around on the luggage carrousel when a hand rested at the small of my back. My heart leaped into my throat then plummeted into my shoes. Link? A stranger?

"Give you a ride?" *Elliot.*

Why hadn't I put those pieces together, and why was my mind a traitorous bitch who was remembering the last time he pressed into my back in public? I spun to face him. "The tickets aren't from Link."

"No."

"Does he even know I'm coming?"

Elliot grinned. "Nope. Christmas surprise. Also, I wasn't sure you'd take them if you knew they were from me."

"I would've thought about it a little longer." But I still would've come. I was hooked on both men. "Did you fly me all the way out here so you could apologize in person?"

His smirk was almost enough to melt my panties off, and when he dropped to his knees in front of me, in the middle of the airport, I almost died.

"Get up," I hissed, and tugged him to his feet. Heads were already turning in our direction. "You're going to give people the wrong idea."

"They'll understand when I start pawing at your crotch."

Oh. My. God. I probably matched my suitcase at this point. "How does Link take you out in public?"

"He avoids it when possible." Elliot stepped around me.

I spun to ask him where he was going, until I saw him grab my suitcase, and drop it to its wheels.

"I can apologize in the car, if you prefer," Elliot said when he joined me again.

Did he mean… In the airport parking lot? Why did that make me hot? "I don't. Not today, anyway."

"My loss." He shrugged, and gestured toward the exits. "Regardless, your chariot awaits."

This was right and not at the same time. I walked with Elliot toward the garage, and heading to his familiar SUV was a new kind of anticipation. I was really here. And I had no idea what to do or say. He stuck my luggage in the back and closed the hatch.

When he faced me, he managed to box me against the side of the Bentley. Not that I minded.

"I'm going to be serious for a minute." Elliot trailed his fingers lightly up my arm.

Even through my coat, the playful touch lit up my senses. I could tease him about *are you sure you can handle that*, but I needed to hear what he had to say.

He loosely cupped my neck, and held my gaze with his. "I really am sorry about what I said." Sincerity bled from his words. "I'm glad you're here, and I'll do whatever it takes to not lose you again." He dragged a thumb along my bottom lip.

Sparks flooded me. Whispers and shouts of need.

When he pressed his mouth to the corner of mine—our first kiss—the rest of the world vanished. He moved in with tiny nips along my lips, until he'd claimed them completely, and then he tightened his fingers in my hair. Somehow he managed to tug back and push me into him at the same time.

I could melt into this kind of security and control for eons. Nothing existed except Elliot's hard body pressing into mine. His demanding tongue. His grip and taste and hypnotic grunts.

A horn echoed over concrete, and I jumped at the abrupt reminder of where we were. I was giggling as he pulled away. "Sorry." I couldn't stop.

"Not the way I thought that would end, but far better than I imagined it beginning." He kissed me again, lightly this time. "And I've imagined doing that a lot."

"Kissing me?"

"Of course."

My face was probably hot enough to melt all the snow in the valley at this point. "I'm glad I'm here too." So very happy. Maybe I didn't quite know who I was, but it was going to be easier to figure it out with these two men in my life.

In fact, my future looked far less terrifying with Link and Elliot in it. I might even say enticing. Alluring. Incredible.

Maybe my taste in men wasn't so bad after all.

link

I thought it was odd that Elliot was such a stickler about only working a few hours on his first day back, but I also understood that he was trying to follow the rules at least a little. What surprised me more was finding out my phone hadn't buzzed all day, because someone had set it to silent. The text from Fallyn that said *Thank you* was a little perplexing as well.

When I got back to my condo, Elliot's SUV was in visitor parking. My day was full of surprises apparently, and that was one I didn't mind. As I headed inside, I was looking forward to seeing him, and hoping Fallyn would take our call tonight.

The front door was already unlocked, no big surprise. "I didn't know you were coming over," I said as I pushed inside. My brain stalled when I saw Fallyn sitting on the couch, next to Elliot. "What are you…?"

Her answer didn't matter. I was already crossing the room, pulling her to her feet, and lifting her up. She wrapped her legs around my waist and her arms around my neck, and I held her tightly as I crushed my mouth to hers. She tasted so good it ached, and she felt incredible wrapped around me. I didn't ever want to let her go.

"I thought you bought me a ticket to come visit," she murmured against my kiss. "Turns out it wasn't you."

Gee, I wonder who it could've been. I set her on her feet, gave her another kiss, this time on the forehead, and looked at Elliot.

"Thank you," I said to him.

"It wasn't completely altruistic."

I wasn't surprised. "No kidding. Not that I'm complaining. How long do we get to keep you for?"

Fallyn caught her bottom lip between her teeth. "That's an open-ended question."

"The return ticket is for the day after New Year's. I can switch it if you want," Elliot said.

The way Fallyn puffed out her cheeks and pushed out a noisy breath as they deflated was adorable. "I didn't bring enough clothes for that."

"Pft. Who needs clothes?" This felt incredible. The easy banter. Having her here. I had one of those *we can do anything, even conquer the world* feelings.

Fallyn scoffed. "*I* do. It's twenty freaking degrees outside."

As much as I loved the idea of spending a week and a half mostly naked, possibly in bed a lot of the time, she had a point. "I have a washing machine. I even know how to use it."

"*I* can take you shopping," Elliot said. "New clothes."

I narrowed my eyes and exaggerated my glare. "Did you really just try to one-up me? With your credit card?"

"Are you really intimidated by three inches of plastic?" Elliot countered, teasing in his voice.

"*No.*" This was fun. I'd missed fun

Elliot stepped up behind Fallyn and rested his hands on her hips. "I could go shopping and surprise you."

"You don't want that." Watching them together made my blood race. The two people I loved, wrapped around each other... Comfortable together... Smiling and joking.... Fucking sexy. "You let Elliot shop for you and you'll end up with a closet full of blazers and band T-shirts."

The way Fallyn scrunched up her face in thought turned her nose into a cute little button. "That doesn't sound so bad, to be honest."

"Excellent. Then we need measurements." Elliot tugged up the bottom of her sweatshirt.

"You're not holding a measuring tape. Unless it's hidden in your pocket." Rather than pull away from

Elliot, Fallyn hooked a finger in the waistband of my jeans, and tugged me closer to them.

I tilted her chin up and searched her face. So incredible. So real.. "We'll use our hands."

"To measure me?"

Elliot drew his mouth along the back of her neck. "To do an entire evaluation of your body."

I wanted to worship Fallyn and Elliot. I wanted to have them both, and to watch them both together. "We have so much catching up to do." Instead of letting Elliot strip Fallyn down in the living room, I scooped her into my arms and carried her into the bedroom. We needed more laying down room for this.

Elliot followed us, and had his hands on Fallyn the instant I set her on her feet.

He and I took our time stripping her out of her clothes, and I couldn't help but lay kisses along her neck, her chest, her stomach, and nearly everywhere over her entire body. Every few seconds, between relishing having Fallyn back, I had to pause to crush my mouth to Elliot's. There was a frantic need in the air that wouldn't be quenched by something so simple, but these kisses, these touches, were the start.

With Fallyn naked between us, Elliot pressed into her back and nipped her ear. "Protection?"

"No."

I had no idea what I was doing next, but that

was music to my ears. I set her on the bed. "We'll be right with you," I said.

Elliot and I undressed each other in a flurry of limbs that was more about feeling each other, biting and teasing and stroking each other's cocks, than it was about taking off our clothes. I was hard and hungry for both of them when he and I finally reached naked.

Did I want to fall to my knees and taste him, or spend hours consuming her?

"Am I participating or just watching?" Fallyn's question was playful. "Either way is fine with me, but a girl likes to know."

I knew exactly what I wanted. I turned to her. "You're not just participating, you're the main course."

The flush that flowed over her was alluring. Captivating.

I knelt over her, caging her body with mine. It didn't matter where I started, as long as I reached my destination. I resumed what I'd started earlier, pressing my mouth to every hollow that made her groan, and nipping at every peak that made her squirm and gasp.

Elliot sucked on her nipples and kneaded her breasts, while I covered her body in kisses. Along her stomach. Down her thighs and calves. Up her arms.

Until I reached her pussy, and couldn't hold

back anymore. When I dragged my tongue up her slit, she let out the most delicious, shuddering gasp. I buried my face between her legs, and devoured her. Licking up her juices. Diving my fingers inside her, while I wrapped my mouth around her clit.

The way she gripped the short strands of my hair and ground into my face told me I'd hit the right spot, and I doubled down with my attentions. Licking and sucking, as she gasped and then screamed in pleasure.

When her body spasmed around my fingers, and she moaned, "Oh, Link. Oh *God*," over and over, that sent a new rush of desire over me.

I continued to bath her pussy with attention until her entire frame shuddered, and she jerked away from my touch. Then I crawled up her frame to kiss her. To let her taste what I had, and share the experience with both her and Elliot.

Fallyn pressed a hand to my chest, and I thought she was stopping me. Instead, she nudged me onto my back. "I want to taste *you*," she said. Her face was pink, and she was smiling and gorgeous.

I had to prop myself up on my elbows to watch her crawl between my legs. Most. Stunning. Sight. Ever.

When she dragged her tongue up my shaft, a shudder of need raced through me. When she took me in her mouth, I let myself get lost in the sensation. I gripped her braids in my fist, and fucked her face while she lavished my cock with attention.

Young Link never could've imagined this kind of acceptance. This kind of peace. The job was great, but the people were incredible. Especially these two people. *My* people. I couldn't imagine a world without Elliot and Fallyn, and I didn't have to.

This was perfection. Right here with me.

Watching Link and Fallyn together was my new favorite porn.

But I'd missed them both so much, watching wasn't enough. I needed to be a deeper part of this connection. Fallyn's ass was in the air, and her legs spread just enough to give me a teasing glimpse of her gorgeous pussy. I knelt behind her, and slid my cock inside her, while she sucked Link off.

She felt so incredible wrapped around me. Tight. Slick. I wanted to grip her neck, tease her clit, and make her come hard while I spilled inside her.

I also wanted this to last longer than thirty seconds. So I built to a slow, even pace. Sliding almost all the way out of her before plunging back in, and feeling how she tightened around me at each new penetration.

Link's grunts as she lavished him with attention added to the atmosphere. The entire bubble around us was an addictive shell of desire.

I knew from the sounds Link made, from the energy in the air, when he came. His grunts and the jerks of his body were familiar, but still incredible to witness.

When Fallyn pulled away, and Link's dick slipped from her lips as he shuddered, my restraint snapped. I needed to experience more. I pressed my fingers to her clit, stroking and teasing orgasm from her. And when her cries hit that peak, when she clenched around my cock the tightest, I plunged inside her as deep as I could.

Link sat up, pushing Fallyn into me, trapping her between us, as I fucked her hard. He crushed his mouth to mine.

I wanted to capture him, too. To hold him here. But I couldn't let go of her. I gripped her hips tight and slammed harder. Faster. Losing myself in the rhythm and letting pleasure overtake me.

Need tightened in my balls and coiled through my entire being, until I couldn't hold back. I came hard, spilling inside Fallyn, biting Link's lower lip, and feeling the passion that consumed all of us.

We collapsed together, all three of us, in a pile of breathless satisfaction.

I was so lucky to have this, to have Link and

Fallyn. I'd almost given them up, and I never would've forgiven myself for that.

It sucked that I had to dial back my participation at AcesPlayed, but I was still a part of it. I got to be involved, see things grow with both the game and the company.

But life without Fallyn and Link…

Fortunately, I didn't have to face that consequence.

We did have to deal with something else, though. "I should've brought King with me. He misses you," I said.

Fallyn looking flushed and content was one of my favorite sights. "I missed him too. I probably would've come back just to see him."

"I'll remember that next time I need to surprise you with a plane ticket," I said dryly.

Link chuckled. "I think you've used that trick up."

"I'm just lucky I have you as bait, too." I nudged him playfully.

"Damn right you are." With a reluctant groan, Link pushed himself into a sitting position. "But I think that's Elliot's way of saying we need to go back to his place."

"It is." I forced myself to climb from the bed, and tugged Fallyn to the edge. "But once we're there, we can lose the clothes again, and not leave the house for days."

Fallyn seemed to consider this. "Sounds like a fair deal."

It took us a lot longer to get dressed than it should have, since we kept stopping to kiss and grope and tease each other. We finally finished, and I agreed to meet the two of them back at my place, and that I'd pick up food on the way.

When I reached my house, Link's car was already out front. I'd missed that sight. Inside, Fallyn and Link had already made themselves comfortable on the couch, and I wasn't surprised to see King had claimed Fallyn's lap.

The puppy barked when he saw me, but he didn't get up until he realized I had food. Over the last week, I'd already lost the fight when it came to not letting him beg for table scraps. It was just easier to make him his own plate, so he'd be occupied while we ate.

This felt right—the three of us sitting next to each other, in a single spot, doing something as simple as enjoying fajitas. The arrangement also forced me to face some realities. Fallyn was only visiting, she may not be able go back to her job, and mine would never be the same again.

"I hate to ruin the mood, but what does the future hold for Fallyn's Phallusies?" I asked.

She picked at loose vegetables on her plate. "I don't know. I can't go back to what I was doing, but I don't want to stop."

"You could do what Grayson does." Link wouldn't have suggested it if he didn't mean it, but I saw the flaw in the idea.

"Grayson is a shill," Fallyn said.

About the response I expected, but not in those words. I didn't try to hide my mild surprise.

"Sorry." She shrugged. "I have a lot of respect for what he does, but he gets paid to love games."

"No. He loves games, and he's figured out a way for that to pay," Link corrected her.

I understood where they were both coming from. "One implies the money changes his opinion, and the other means that he enjoys the games regardless of the paycheck. Similar to you. But I get it."

It took Fallyn a moment to finish chewing her food. "The world already thinks I'm a fraud. If I go on to review games, I'm like everyone else, but I've turned my back on my brand. I wish that weren't the case, but tell me I'm wrong."

"You're not wrong." A week ago, I would've jumped at the chance to say the opposite, even if she was right, but it was the last thing I wanted now.

Fallyn set her mostly empty plate aside. "Do you have a better solution for yourself, Elliot? To go from conquering the world to part time… Are you going to dedicate your time to raising Puppy?" There was no derision in her question.

I'd been asking myself the same thing over and over, and kept coming up blank. King was fun, but I needed to get back into coding. Creating. "I don't know."

"What do you love most about the job? Besides the people," Link teased.

Despite rolling my eyes, I did love the people I worked with. "I love being there from the start. From the point of conception, if you will."

"Okay, so… we'll hire you out as a breeding stud, and you can fuck a few servers and see if they have game babies," Link said.

I had to admit, it was both an amusing and disturbing visual.

Fallyn snorted with laughter. "All right boys, I knew this day would come. That's not how baby video games are made."

"Oh yeah, smart lady? How does it happen, then?" I pushed the teasing challenge into my voice.

"Oh. *Oh*, that's good." The way Fallyn responded was both sensual and nothing like what I expected.

I shifted my position to get a better look. "Is Link fingering you and I can't see? Are you ready to go again already?"

"You're such an ass." There was no malice in Link's reply.

"An incubator," Fallyn said.

Was she having a different conversation than I was? Or multiple different conversations? "That's how baby chickens are made."

"That's also how some baby apps are made." Now Fallyn was sliding into a lecturer voice. "Think about it—you have this massive house that you ramble around in. What if you turned it into a game incubator?"

I could make a joke, but her idea was too tempting to let slip away. "That is good." An incubator, in this case, was where ideas went to become more. Frequently, someone with money and extra room—me—provided a place for developers to stay, so they could develop their ideas into salable products, and not have to worry about things like rent in the process.

"Ooh, oh, oh!" Link waved his hand.

It was ridiculous. The whole mood in here was light and fun, and thank God.

"If you do that, what if…" Link paused and screwed up his face. "Fallyn said she was tired of seeing developers make the same mistakes over and over again."

"I did, and I am."

"And your videos, where you make the super powerful characters—Jarlett Scohansson—are some of your most popular," Link said.

Where was he going with this?

"So what if Fallyn was part of the process early on, and instead of breaking those games, she showed the developers what to avoid, and then streamed the final product, including the ultimate character build-outs."

Look at us, being all smart and idea-filled and stuff.

"That might be fun." The way Fallyn said the words, it sounded like she believed anything but. "But even if Elliot opens the doors tomorrow, the first game is years off from being able to stream, and I doubt he wants me doing that."

"Are you kidding?" Wow, I'd been such an ass. "You're not just good at what you do, you're incredible at it. Besides, you can do it for other games. Avoid AcesPlayed for a while, if it helps. Don't demolish who you are, shift your focus. Instead of finding the cock-ups in games…"

Fallyn grinned. "I'm showing people how to get a bigger cock."

"That sounds so wrong." Link laughed. "I love it."

The way Fallyn studied me made me nervous. "I could even tell my haters *fuck you* by having ET Howard on the show occasionally." It sounded like more of a question than a suggestion. "I mean, that would probably lead to telling people we were dating. Would you do that? Either and both?"

A sliver of hurt formed inside that she'd think otherwise, but I didn't blame her. I still needed to prove myself. "I would. I don't plan on keeping us a secret, and where am I going to get my *being in the public eye* fix, if not from your show? Unless you need to keep all of us being together a secret."

"No. Fuck no." Fallyn looked relieved. "I'm tired of secrets."

"It's about time." Link tilted up her chin and kissed her hard.

I knew what both halves of that kiss felt like, tasted like, and I loved watching it. But I wanted one of my own, too. I tugged Fallyn's hair, and stole her away for a kiss of my own. Even brushing my lips over hers was an experiment in the electric. "I tried to fight this, tried so hard to ignore it, but that was stupid of me. I love you Fallyn. Kittie. Mistress of all that's unholy. Whatever you want me to call you. I love you intensely and deeply and completely."

She giggled against my mouth, and kissed me back. "I love you too, ET Howard, first of your name, and saver of puppies and lost kitties."

"You're not lost." Link kissed her on the top of the head.

She leaned into him, taking me with her. "Not anymore, I'm not," she said.

And I wasn't either. I'd spent so long keeping people out by building walls, all in the name of trying to protect myself. In doing so, I almost lost two of the best things that ever happened to me.

I was grateful I'd figured the truth out before it was too late. Grateful…

For all of it. I couldn't imagine a better life than one with Fallyn and Link in it. This was perfection.

epilogue

sixteen months later

elliot

I sat at the table in the breakfast nook, across from the latest applicant to my incubator. The April sun was on the other side of the house, leaving us with a shaded view of the spring trees here.

This was my third time talking to Harper, and today was basically a formality. She'd already earned the spot that opened up when the first of my developers reached the point where their game was successful enough for them to move on.

Her ideas were fantastic, and I was excited to give her a chance. We were to the *do you have any questions for me* part of the interview.

"Is it true?" she asked.

I searched my brain for a point of reference in the recent conversation. "Is what true?"

"You and Fallyn…" Harper flushed and trailed off.

I hoped that wouldn't be a problem. Fallyn, Link, and I didn't hide our relationship, and while we weren't fucking around the house, not when I had several other people living here, the fact that we were together was pretty in-your-face. "Is it true that we faced each other in mortal combat and fought to the death?"

"That's what mortal combat is, yes. But no, that's not what I heard."

"It's true." As if summoned, Fallyn walked past the doorway. "Do you want to meet her?" I called Fallyn's name.

She joined us, a tiny smile on her face. "What's up?"

"This is Harper. She's deciding if she wants to live in the guest house," I said.

Fallyn grinned and extended her hand. "I've heard a lot about you. I hope you say *yes*. The place is recently remodeled, and it's actually really comfy."

"So you two are actually together? It's not just for show?" Harper asked as she shook Fallyn's hand.

"We actually are," Fallyn said.

I grabbed her wrist, tugged her into my lap, and rewarded myself with a long kiss.

Fallyn pressed her palm to my chest and pushed me away, but she didn't stand up. "You're going to give your guest the wrong idea."

"No. This is the very right idea."

Fallyn rolled her eyes and turned back to Harper. "I'm sorry about him. He really does know better."

"I really don't." I shook my head.

Harper didn't look bothered by any of it. "It's wonderful to meet you. I mean, you're *the* Fallyn."

***

fallyn

Once upon a time those words would've made me ill. It took me months to be okay with even streaming again, and a lot of that was thanks to the support I got from Elliot and Link. They told me repeatedly that I was amazing, and while I thought that was a bit much, they also stepped in with anyone who was an asshole.

I gave Harper a short bow as I moved into my own chair. "At your service."

"No, I'm at yours." Harper watched me with wide eyes. "Seriously, you're the reason I got into this. I used to watch your Phallusies videos and think *I could do better* on all the games you broke." She looked at Elliot. "I can't believe you get to… I would totally…"

What? Elliot had told me he was really liking this developer, but he hadn't mentioned anything about this. "Get to what?" I asked.

"Fuck you." Leave it to Elliot to be direct. "She can't believe I get to fuck you, and she totally would too if you weren't taken."

Harper ducked her head. "Not how I was going to phrase it."

"Be nice." I smacked Elliot playfully in the arm.

He gave me a withering look that didn't hide the affection underneath. "You forgot who you were talking to."

No. I never did. I knew exactly how lucky I was to have Elliot and Link, and I never forgot it.

Elliot slid Harper a house key. "You're welcome to move your things in whenever you want. As a reminder, I require progress reports, but I'm not worried that you'll produce great work. Everyone here is available to ask for help. That includes me. And Fallyn."

Harper blushed and took the key. "Thank you." She shook both our hands again. "I'll be back this weekend to move my stuff in."

"I'll show you out." I walked her to the door, wished her good luck, and told her it was nice to meet another fan of quality games.

After I closed the door behind her, I spun away, and when Link was standing *right there* my heart lodged in my throat.

He cupped my face and backed me into the wall as he kissed me. His mouth on mine still stole my breath after all this time.

"I have a present for you," he murmured without letting me go.

I teased his half-hard cock, where it pressed into my belly. "Is it in your pocket?"

He grabbed my wrist with a rough laugh. "Not unless you decided not to stream this afternoon. Or you're changing your content."

"I should probably stick to the schedule." My sigh was exaggerated.

One of the changes I'd made to my channel was that Elliot and I had taken our rivalry live, as much as our relationship. We gamed together, and we drew in lovers, haters, and everyone who either wanted to see us together or was waiting for us to crash and burn.

"I was hoping you'd say that." Link handed me a post-it note with a code scribbled on it. "That's our first expansion area in the game. Doesn't go live for a week, but that will get you onto the test server."

No shit. Exclusive access? Live? "Are you sure?"

"I have it on good authority that their development manager signed off on it," Link said.

I threw my arms around his neck, tugged his head down to mine, and kissed him hard. "Thank you." I kissed him again and again.

"Hey. Save some of that for me." Elliot's voice came from behind Link.

Link smirked against my mouth. "Nope."

"He bribed me," I said.

"With kisses? I can do kisses." Elliot joined us.

I held up the post-it note.

"You got the sign-off." Was that awe in Elliot's voice?

Link nodded.

Elliot kissed him too. "I'd say you're the best, but I think you're trying to one-up my surprise."

"No. I would never." Link shook his head. "The two really go hand-in-hand, though. Don't you think?"

"Boys? What are we talking about?" I should be happy with just the test server code. And I was. But if there were more surprises, I wanted to see them, and Elliot tended to have good surprises.

Elliot pointed to the coat closet a few feet away. "In there. But before you look, you should know that accepting this gift makes you a shill. Everyone will know you're in bed with the people who write the game."

I stared at him in disbelief. "Pretty sure everyone already knows. Can I look now?"

His deep bow was ridiculous, but fun.

I opened the closet to find a dry-cleaning bag hanging among the jackets. As I pulled it out, Elliot said, "Sadie Sews original. She mocked up the real thing, and Adrienne built a one-of-a-kind skin based on it."

No way. I was looking at a recreation of a costume I'd designed for my in-game character. I made a version myself, last year for RinCon, but I'd never been happy with the results.

But this... This was stunning. Better than I'd pictured.

"We were thinking, it would be fun if you wore that while you streamed a character in the same outfit," Link said.

This was incredible. Not just the gifts, and the attention from Link and Elliot, though that was all great.

But the fact that they knew. That there was no doubt for them that this would make me happy. That they cared. And I'd do similar things for either of them in a heartbeat.

Because the three of us fit together so perfectly. I didn't question if the relationship was out of balance, or fear the next big catastrophe or spend nights wondering what I was going to do wrong next and how it would cost me my career.

There was none of that, because this was actual, healthy love. They were the best thing to ever happen to me, and I knew it was the same for all three of us.

"You're going to help me put this on, right?" I teased.

---

link

Elliot and I helped Fallyn change into her custom made healer costume. I wanted to spend hours playing—the sexy, no-clothes kind of play—but she and Elliot had work to do.

Elliot didn't have a custom costume, but his outfit was part of this as well. Same clothes as always—jeans, T-shirt, blazer. Except he wore a monocle when he streamed with Fallyn. He was ET Howard on camera.

The get-up made her smile and pissed off his father, because Elliot had stopped hiding who his family was.

And I was here for all of it.

We made our way downstairs, to the large room we'd configured specifically for streaming. When I was here, I did camera work, but they really didn't need me for that. It was mostly an excuse to watch them together. It didn't matter what they were doing —fucking or flirting or playing games—I loved to watch how much they lit up around each other and me.

They logged onto their accounts, and I was watching Elliot closely. His brows rose, and then a grin spread across his face when he got into his character screen. "What is this?"

"It's exactly what it looks like," I said. I'd had a custom character skin made for him too, and his also matched his outfit. He was in-game himself.

"*Flove*." Fallyn clapped.

There was one more surprise for both of them, and it was the reason I had my laptop logged into the game as well. But they'd have to find me, and they wouldn't know until they got there.

It had been hard to hide this from Elliot, even with him only working part time on the game, but I'd managed to keep this a secret, and I was so excited for them to both see it.

I watched as they worked their way through one of the new side quests, while tens of thousands of people watched. They had so much chemistry on camera, it was a shock they didn't light the feed on fire.

They were working their way through the quest that unlocked in-game marriage, one of several highly anticipated features being released with this update.

When they reached the end, when they realized

what they'd found and that my avatar was waiting for them, Fallyn squealed with joy.

Elliot grunted, but that meant just as much as the sounds Fallyn made.

The in-game ceremony was simple. A series of rendered game clips that featured all three of us. But it was the symbolism that meant so much to me. We were the first players to do this. And I got to experience it with the most incredible people in the world. The two people I loved more than anything.

My perfect future.

At the end of the ceremony, Elliot and Fallyn kissed on camera, on the live stream. And they convinced me to join them for a rare appearance on my part.

This was so perfect. No end of quest loot could ever be better. No real life achievement could ever come close to how I felt right now, with the two of them, knowing that our entire future stretched out in front of us.

***

Thank you for falling in and out and in love again with Link, Fallyn, and Elliot.

If you've been waiting for Judith's book, if you'd like to see what she was up to while this book was taking place, make sure you check out BOSS LEVEL.

It's lonely at the top.

Judith knew it would be when she clawed my way up, trading away favors and any personal life to get to where she is today—the head of the hottest new video game company in the industry.

When an old friend calls in one of those favors, she's happy to help Xander out. His partner, Dominic, needs to impress some conservative clients, and showing up to get-to-know-you dinners with a heavily tattooed man on his arm isn't the way to do it.

And there are far worse things Judith could be doing than pretending to be Dom's fiancée.

When the fake kisses with Dominic start to feel real, she realizes there's something missing in her life. Worse, she's starting to realize she never should've let Xander get away.

But the three of them together will bring everything they've worked for toppling down around them. There's no way love is worth that kind of sacrifice.

www.ingramcontent.com/pod-product-compliance
Lightning Source LLC
Chambersburg PA
CBHW011157190726
48286CB00009B/2820